BOB HUERTER

The Seanachie

Jim,
To a fellow mick!
Bob Huerter

Outskirts Press, Inc.
Denver, Colorado

Outskirts Press
http://www.outskirtspress.com

ISBN-10: 1-59800-554-5
ISBN-13: 978-1-59800-554-7

Printed in the United States of America

ACKNOWLEDGEMENTS

I'd like to acknowledge the following people: First and foremost, my wife, Maureen, and my five children - Erin, Molly, Clare, Mick, and Frank – for putting up with me and my writing. Marty McCaslin, my editor and friend, who never gave up on me and my passion for writing this book. Mike Sterba, author and friend, who taught me patience and loved nothing more than to find that misplaced comma. Professor Nancy Houston for translating a poem I wrote for the book from English to Irish. It was a selfless act from someone I have yet to meet in person. Thank you so much. Colin Huerter, Irish poet warrior. Thanks for the poetry lesson. Meg Brudney, whose support and encouragement can't be calculated. Thank you Charmin. My siblings Jane, Tom, Tim, Jim, Kevin, Chris, Judy, John, and Meg. Thanks for putting up with me all these years and for being there when I really needed you. John Berigan for helping me get my life back. Cheryl Sacco, Carl Finocchiaro, Nancy Micek, Chris Doocy, Andy Walsh, Pat and Lily Coyle, Sam Dodson, Rick Dooling, Vince and Margaret, Mary and Vic...Thank you all for everything. Lastly to my dad, Jim, whose enthusiasm and encouragement never let up, even though I never did develop that outline. Darn it.. Thanks dad, you're the best!

DEDICATION

This book is dedicated to Therese Ann Quinlan Huerter for passing on to me her love of all things Irish and her love of literature. May God hold you in the palm of His hand.

CHAPTER 1
THE DECISION

Frank McGrath quickened his pace yet again. Cars raced by on the busy street whipping cold drizzle at him and forcing him to tuck his chin further into the flimsy jacket he wore.

"What was I thinking," he said aloud as if he weren't walking alone, "leaving the house this morning in just a damn jean jacket. Nice move, Melvin."

The high top Chuck Taylor's that covered his tattered sweat socks did nothing to keep the winter cold out and he hadn't felt his toes in the last mile or so. The tips of his fingers were turning blue and he cussed again as his runny nose was getting sorer with each swipe of his rough jean jacket sleeve.

With a sudden thought, warmth temporarily shot through his body like a jolt of electricity along a copper wire and he smiled. Thinking, for a brief moment, about the way he showed up General Richardson in class brought a smile to his face, but the stinging winter's wind replaced the grin with pain and reminded him of why he was walking. Shivering, hands deep in his pants pockets, he thought, "Screw it. It was worth dogging The General like that."

Mr. Alexander Richardson was tough, pompous, and smart. He ran his class like a boot camp, calling himself the "Lord God Richardson." He didn't entertain even casual familiarity with his students at the all-boys prep school. So when he asked Frank McGrath to spell five "i before e" words aloud, the last one being "relief", and when Frank, to everyone's surprise including himself, got the first four correct he simply could not resist reaching for the low hanging fruit in front of him.

"Relief. F-A-R-T. Relief."

At first there was disbelief and disquiet among his classmates as they looked from Frank to Richardson and back again. Then a brief pause. Finally they exploded with loud, spontaneous, and sustained laughter. McGrath, however harmless, did the unthinkable. He showed up the Lord God Richardson in his own box-shaped temple.

"McGrath," said a flushed, but controlled Richardson, "I'll take your card. I hope you enjoyed the levity as much as you'll enjoy the detention, because that nonsense just cost you five demerits."

Continuing his trek, inexorable darkness gaining support from the heavy cloud cover, Frank replayed the scene in his head. In his mind, he got the job done. His classmates looked to him for these sorts of shenanigans, and he had delivered. But he lost his ride because of that detention and hoped his dad wouldn't find out.

He reached into the breast pocket of his jean jacket and pulled out a joint. His darker tendencies getting the better part of his good judgment, he decided to celebrate his victory over The General.

He fired up as he walked and cupped the joint in his hand so as not to draw any unwanted attention to himself. As he rounded the corner a police officer was just setting upright some garbage cans that had blown into the street and were blocking traffic. In his surprise Frank stopped momentarily, smoke billowing out of his nose and mouth. He dropped the joint and stepped on it thinking, "Shit, this is just my luck."

The cop smelled the weed in the breeze and said, "Hey, hold up a minute."

Frank's stomach dropped as the police officer walked toward him.

He said, "What's that I smell?"

Frank said, "Somebody must be burning leaves."

The officer walked back a few paces and picked up the smoldering joint that Frank had just stepped on and said, "Is this the type of dried leaves you're talking about?"

Frank said, "I wouldn't know anything about that."

"Is that right?"

Frank looked down and the fear spread through him like slivered shards of fear and anxiety

The officer held up the smoldering joint and said, "Is this it?"

"Is what it?"

"Is this all there is?"

"It's not mine so I wouldn't know if there's more or not."

"Why don't I believe that? Do me a favor and put your hands on the car and take a step back and spread your legs."

Too naïve to even think of being frisked, Frank's first inclination was to bolt. Then he thought better of it, did what he was told and sighed, bile rising in his throat.

The cop frisked him up and down and said, "Interesting," as he pulled a dime bag out of Frank's sock.

The officer held the bag in front of Frank's face and said, "You in some trouble, boy. You got some ID?"

"Yeah, my wallet's in my back pocket."

"Let's have it and don't be stupid, I've got a gun."

The policeman put Frank's ID in his top shirt pocket, pulled the cuffs out and slapped them on him as he read him his rights and then gently helped him into the back seat.

Frank became distraught, convinced that he had just spent his last day at the private Catholic high school that his parents couldn't afford in the first place. And depending on how many beers he'd had, his dad would beat him within an inch of his life and ground him for a year or so.

When the cop got into the driver's seat Frank said, "Am I going to jail?"

Not paying any attention to the question, the officer pulled the license out of his shirt pocket and looked at it. Then looking at Frank through the rearview mirror, he said, "You one of Emmett McGrath's boys?"

"Yeah."

"Liam O'Conlan's your granddad then?"

Frank starting to see a small fissure of daylight at the end of a long dark tunnel said, "Yeah, do you know him?"

"Yeah, I played ball with your old man when we were kids and your granddad did me a big favor years ago."

There was a pause as if the cop were replaying something he had forgotten and yet now savored.

He said, "You're a lucky kid."

"Yeah?"

"Yeah, if it weren't for your granddad I'd be running you downtown, instead I'm giving you a ride home."

Frank sighed with relief thanking God he wasn't going to jail and for the granddad he hardly knew. Then he went pale and got sick to his stomach. He just remembered it was his Granddad O'Conlan's birthday and the whole family would be there when they got home.

Francis Xavier McGrath was the eighth child of ten in a South Omaha Irish Catholic family. His dad was a foreman for a local construction company and money was scarce. Survival and self-reliance were skills developed at an early age in the McGrath household.

Frank's nine brothers and sisters, his parents and his grandfather, Liam O'Conlan, eighty- three-years old today, had just finished up dinner.

His father Emmett, said, "Where in the hell is Francis?"

Elizabeth McGrath said quietly to her husband, "I'm sure he's got a good excuse. Let's not ruin dinner."

Emmett stood, let out a loud belch and went to the refrigerator to get another beer and said, "Ruin dinner? I'm not the one ruining anything. That goddamn kid knew it was Liam's birthday."

Elizabeth got up to put the candles on the cake, more worried about the boy's safety than punishing him. She came back carrying the cake, complete with candles and they all sang Happy Birthday. Liam hated the attention and hated his blushing even more.

When they had finished eating cake, Mary, the oldest daughter stood and started clearing plates. Emmett said, "Wait a minute, there's something we need to discuss."

All movement stopped as they all sat back down.

Emmett took a long gulp of beer and said, "Your granddad needs some help. He wants to go back to Delmar this weekend and needs a ride. Your mother and I would be glad to take him but we've got the union dinner Saturday night."

Liam sat, hands involuntarily shaking, staring off out the window at the hard cold mist spitting defiantly outside, hating the attention and irritated that his eighty-three-year-old body was forcing his dependence on others.

There was a lull and when no one said anything Liam spoke up, "Listen kids, I know you're all busy with your own lives and I really don't want to be a bother. I'll get a ticket on the bus."

Frank's mother Elizabeth said, "Nonsense, Dad. We have seven able-bodied drivers sitting right here and we can get this figured out."

Emmett said, "Yes and it would be eight, if that no good son of yours were here."

The oldest son Bill said, "Come on gramps, you've never been a bother. I'd do it in a minute but I've got to work."

Mary said, "Granddad, I'd loved to but I'm signed up for the career seminar at Creighton."

Emmett looked around the table and everyone's eyes moved away. He said, "Sean, you and Mick?"

Sean said, "No can do, Dad. Baseball tryouts this weekend."

Teresa said, "Dad, I'll do it."

Elizabeth said, "How about that?"

Emmett said, "Honey, the girl couldn't find the back of her hand with a map, let alone Delmar, Iowa four hundred miles away."

Teresa pulled away from the table and said, "Do it yourself then and don't complain when you can't find anyone who will."

As she walked away, Emmett said, "Who in the hell do you think you're talking to?"

The kitchen doorbell rang and everyone stopped to stare. Mary stood and opened the door and there on the porch stood her younger brother Frank, handcuffed and standing next to a police officer.

She opened the screen door and the officer helped Frank down the two stairs to the kitchen and stood staring at the large gathering.

Emmett and Liam stood at the same time and said, "John Quinlan."

Office John Quinlan tipped his hat and said, "Emmett, Liam. I'm sorry to have interrupted folks."

Elizabeth stood and said, "What is it, John?"

"Ms. McGrath, I'm afraid I apprehended your son for possession of an illegal substance."

Emmett said, "What was it?"

"It was marijuana, Emmett."

Emmett said, "Why didn't you drag his sorry ass downtown?"

Officer John Quinlan looked a bit surprised at that and said, "Emmett, it was a small amount and I didn't think that was necessary."

Emmett said, "John, thanks for getting him home safely. I think we can handle it from here."

"Thanks folks. Again, I'm sorry to have interrupted."

Elizabeth said, "Don't give it a second thought."

John Quinlan took the cuffs off and left. Frank began walking to his room and Emmett was on him before he got out of the kitchen. They scuffled until they reached the top of the stairs to the dormer, where Frank roomed with his brothers, Sean and Mick.

Elizabeth said to the older boys, "Maybe you should stick around a bit before you leave. I might need your help."

By the time they had reached his room, Frank had had enough and pushed away from his dad, saying, "Knock it off."

Emmett said, "Oh, you think you're a tough guy do you? Come on, you want a piece of this?"

Frank stood eyeball to eyeball with his six-foot father. His dad had him by forty pounds but Frank was contemplating taking a shot.

"Smoking dope, huh? You jerk, John Quinlan should've thrown your sorry ass in jail."

"Oh, and this coming from a guy who drinks eighteen beers a day."

"Don't start with me, punk. First of all I'm over twenty-one and the last I checked beer was legal. Hope you enjoyed your private education because it's done."

Frank's heart sunk even though he knew this was coming, but his pride wouldn't allow his old man to see it and said, "Fine with me."

The fist came out of nowhere and knocked Frank on to his bed, nose bleeding. Frank got up and came after his dad when his older brothers Bill, Joe and Eddie made it to the top of the stairs. Before Frank's haymaker met its mark, the older boys got in between the two combatants.

As Joe and Eddie held Frank back he said in a fury, "Screw you, Dad. I never wanted to go to that hole anyway!"

Bill, holding back his dad's onslaught, said, "Frank, shut the hell up."

Emmett said, "Get him the hell out of my house. You're

done here, boy."

Joe said, "Dad, you don't mean that."

"The hell I don't."

Bill said, "Dad, let's go downstairs and cool off."

As Emmett walked downstairs with his three oldest boys he said to Frank, "This isn't over by a long shot."

Frank said, "Yes it is. I'm out of here."

Eddie ran back up the stairs, grabbed Frank by the shirt, eyes ablaze and said, "You better shut the hell up. We just saved your ass. You're the one who messed up here, so knock it off."

Frank said, "I've had enough of him knocking me around."

With that Eddie could say nothing – all the boys had all been in the same spot at one time or another. Frank sat, coming down from the adrenaline overload, put his head in his hands and cried.

Things quieted down and everyone save Frank ended up in the den. Emmett cracked another beer and Elizabeth said, "Honey, haven't you had enough?"

He said, "I'll tell you when I've had enough. Mind your own damn business."

Liam hated when his son-in-law drank to excess and talked to his daughter like that. He had spent plenty of time drinking to excess himself, but he was never a mean drunk. After a moment of uncomfortable silence, he said, "Emmett and Elizabeth, why don't you let Francis take me to Iowa. The separation will be good for everyone involved and it'll allow me to spend some time with the boy."

Mary said, "Mom and Dad, that sounds like a great idea."

Emmett said, "Anything to get him out of my sight."

Frank had walked silently into the kitchen now, heard the whole thing and was angry. He was a member of a clandestine group who called themselves The Booga Brothers. Four times a year they rented rundown halls throughout the city using fictitious names, hired local bands, purchased thirty five kegs from an unsavory bar owner named Red Finn and put fliers up at all the local high school hangouts. They'd charge five bucks a head and had a knack for disappearing ten minutes ahead of the local police. When all was settled up, each Booga Brother would net four hundred dollars or so, tax-free. Each event took months to plan and a no show meant no dough. Saturday night was the next party.

Frank said, "I'm not going anywhere this weekend. I've got plans."

Emmett stood, his older sons with him just in case, and said, "I'll tell you your plans – your decision. You either take your granddad to Iowa or you might as well walk out that door now and don't look back."

Frank knew that this was no idle threat and that he had been beat. He put his head down and walked back upstairs.

CHAPTER 2
THE HEDGEROW TEACHER

At seven a.m. on Saturday morning, Frank walked into the kitchen with a gym bag packed. His mother and his granddad sat at the table having coffee.

Liam looked up at his grandson as he dragged himself across the kitchen floor and said, "Ready to go, son?"

"I can't wait," He said, as if the acidic level of his sarcasm was forming sores in his mouth.

The sun glared unmercifully into the car. Frank adjusted the visor in the brand new 1977 Pontiac station wagon, his dad had recently purchased, as they headed east out of Omaha on I-80, crossing over the Missouri River into Iowa.

Liam said, "Son, I know this is the last thing you wanted to do this weekend."

Frank said, "You can say that again."

"But as long as we're going to be together – hey the speed limit is fifty-five son, you're going a little fast."

"Granddad, let me do the driving, okay?"

"I was just saying."

"Look, I know what you're saying. Drop it."

Liam smiled and said, "Okay, take it easy. You drive and I'll ride."

"Good."

"Anyway, can I ask you a question?"

"Whatever."

"Do you know why I wanted to go to Delmar?"

"Yeah, you get homesick and want to go home."

Liam laughed and said, "No, Omaha's been my home now much longer than Delmar ever was."

Frank said, "What then?"

"I'm dying."

"You're what?"

"I'm dying and there are a few things I want to do before I go."

"Right, Granddad, and so am I."

They drove east out of Council Bluffs, Iowa and the road split, I-29 going south to Kansas City and I-80 east to the Atlantic Ocean. Frank merged left and headed east, without knowing his world was about to change, forever. The sky above was blue and sunny, but looking east a line of dark gray clouds were making their way south and east of the northern jet stream.

After fifteen or so minutes Liam said, "What do you know about the Irish Frank?"

"Why?"

"It's a subject near and dear to my heart. It's another reason we're driving to Iowa and you may or may not know it, but the Irish are prone to storytelling at any given moment. And if you're not opposed I might tell you a story or two about the Irish."

Frank thought for a moment. He had never given the Irish much thought. His mom was Irish and a sweetheart, but his dad was also Irish and he was a mean drunk.

He thought about past St Patrick's days, the only time he ever paid attention to the Irish, when adults got drunk and acted like idiots. Arguments broke out and fights started – it never made much sense to him. To his simple seventeen-year-old sensibilities he formed the general opinion, based on that one day, that the Irish were loud mouthed, opinionated and argumentative drunks.

He said, "Look, Granddad, I don't know."

Liam said, "Come on son, you're not going to hurt my feelings."

Frank hesitated again, deciding whether he wanted to run for cover on this one or tell the old man sitting next to him what he really thought. Before he gave it any further consideration, he blurted out, "I think the Irish are a bunch of loud mouthed, opinionated jerks!"

Liam leaned back at the sudden and unexpected response and laughed so hard he thought he was going to faint. The air rushed forcefully from his lungs and he couldn't seem to get it back. When it finally returned waves of laughter filled the car.

Frank said, "What?"

His granddad could not respond from laughing. He reached down and pulled up his socks and finally gained control of himself. He knew well how his grandson felt but he wanted him to verbalize it, he just hadn't expected the candidness.

He said, "Tell me son, why do you think that of a whole race of people?"

Frank said, "Well, when you put it like that I guess they can't all be bad."

Liam said, "Of course not."

Frank said, "Its just that my old man is as Irish as they get and he's a mean drunk and a bigot and so are most of his Irish buddies. Those are the Irish I see."

Liam said, "Well, if it's any consolation, son, I understand. Your dad *is* rough around the edges and so is the crowd he runs around with, but that doesn't mean that we're all that way. No."

Frank said, "So you agree with me?"

Liam said, "About what?"

Frank said, "Some Irish are bad news."

Liam said, "Of course, to a degree. Now, I can't speak for other races of people, but the Irish are a dichotomy."

"A what?"

"A dichotomy. We're divided into contradictory parts. What you love about us you also hate about us."

"Like?"

"Well, let's see. Okay, I got it. Like your old man."

"Right," Frank said, once again the sarcasm dripping from his tongue like honey from a hornet's stinger."

"No seriously. He's a perfect dichotomy. He gets drunk, he loses his temper and he punches you in the nose. A true scoundrel, correct?"

"I wouldn't have been that flattering."

"But you should hear him talk about you when you're not around."

"What?"

"Yeah, you'd think you were St Patrick himself. And if someone were to do you harm or even think of it they'd face the wrath of Emmett McGrath."

"You're a lying sack of..."

"The hell I am. You want more contradictions?" Liam O'Conlan, on a roll now, his voice rising in octave as his heart beat faster, was talking his true passion, the Irish.

Frank said, "Sure," wanting to mollify the old man so he didn't have a heart attack on his watch.

"The warrior poet."

"My dad?"

"No, the Irish. Describe what you think of when someone says poet."

Frank thought for a moment and then said, "Some light weight who sits depressed in a coffee shop smoking cigarettes and writing."

"Great stereotype and a definition that is widely held and maybe for the most part is true, but in Ireland, historically the poet has always been held in high esteem and great influencers of the Irish psyche. The men who started the Easter uprising in

1916 in Dublin called themselves warrior poets. They wrote to make people aware and then they fought for their independence from England. Hells bells, these guys were a sorry assed rag tag army with the courage of Hercules and held off one of the greatest warring nations on earth at the time for an entire week!"

"Who was the warring nation?"

"The English, boy, the English."

Toys in the Attic, the latest Aerosmith tune, came on the radio and Frank turned it up. Liam smiled, caught his breathe and looked patiently out the window, seeing a sign for Atlantic, Iowa on the interstate. The song finished and Liam said, "Pull over, lad, I've got to go."

Frank thought, "Man, this is going to be a long trip."

He waited patiently for his granddad to get back into the car and they headed east.

Liam said, "Frank, have you ever heard of the Seanachie?"

"The what?"

"The Seanachie."

In a sarcastic drone Frank said, "No Granddad, I've never heard of the Seanachie."

"I didn't think so. Do you mind if I tell you what that is?"

Frank looked out the window at the cold, drab, snow covered Iowa farmland and said, "Your captive audience anxiously awaits."

"Look son, your sarcasm is not being lost on me. You're being a smart ass and I don't appreciate it. There was a time when people were lining up to hear my stories. And maybe, if you'd pull your head out of your stubborn Irish ass you might start to enjoy some of this. No wonder your old mad punched you in the nose, I might've done the same."

"Okay, grumps, I mean gramps."

Liam chuckled and said, "You just can't help yourself can you?"

"Well, when you make it so easy."

"Do you want to know or not?"

"Know what?"

"What a Seanachie is."

"Yes, yes I do," Frank said to keep from being punched in the nose again.

"Seanachie is Irish for historian. In ancient Irish times, the Seanachie held a place of great honor on the King's court, along with the poet and the Druid seer."

"The what?"

"Druid seer. Before Christianity came to Ireland, it was a pagan nation. They didn't believe in God as we know Him to be. The Druids were kind of a religious cult who practiced black magic. Anyway, the Druid seer was a high priest who was said to have the ability to see into the future."

"No lie?"

"That's right. Anyway, getting back to the Seanachie, the English invaded Ireland six hundred years ago and as they did wherever they invaded, they tried to Anglicize the invaded nation."

"Anglicize?"

"They would try to create a mini England, change the laws, the language, the culture to fit the Anglo Saxon culture whether they wanted it or not."

"Why?"

"Because they thought they were superior and cultured and all others were heathens, especially the Irish."

The first thing they did was change the system of law from the Brehon law to English law. This way whatever injustices they imparted they could justify in a court of law. Next they outlawed any form of school, reading or writing and finally they outlawed the Irish language."

"What do you mean Irish language, didn't they speak English?"

"Hell no. They spoke Irish and if anyone was caught reading, writing or using the Irish language in any way they were hung to death."

"What?"

"It's true. Anyway, so after the English showed up, Irish legend holds that the Seanachie felt so strongly about keeping the Irish history alive that they took to the road to tell the Irish story of her great past. They would hold court at the hedgerow outside local villages and that was how the great tradition of Irish oral story telling began. But Irish legend also held that these Seanachie had powers greater than mere mortals, being able to disappear in a flash when the English constabulary would arrive, or invading a villager's dreams to pass on a tale. The locals would swear that the hedgerow teachers had leprechaun blood running through their veins."

"Hedgerow teachers?"

"Yeah, some people began to call the Seanachie "hedgerow teachers" because that's where they taught. You see, throughout Ireland there are stone hedgerows that surround farms and villages. The Seanachie would show up outside a village and begin telling stories and people would gather around to listen."

Trying to appear disinterested, Frank said, "What do you mean they'd disappear when the constabulary came? Were they magic?"

"Many of the Irish would swear to it. You see the English were out to destroy all things Irish and they wanted no Irish history passed on. If they caught the Seanachie in the act they'd hang them in the village to rot. In reality, the Seanachie taught at the hedgerow in order to make a quick escape if need be. But the superstition held that the Seanachie could sense trouble and would be gone in a flash if the constabulary were near, thus the leprechaun blood. "

"You said something about dreams?"

"Yeah, they believed that the Seanachie could show up in a dream to pass on clan tales, you know, specific family history."

"And you believe this crap?"

Liam smiled and eased off into a snooze. Frank once again turned up the radio.

CHAPTER 3
HE'S IN

After about an hour Liam's snoring became interrupted by long pauses of no breathing at all. Frank became exceedingly alarmed and said, "Granddad. Granddad!"

Liam looked up and said, "Huh? What the hell? Where are we?"

"On our way to Delmar, you stopped breathing."

"Oh yeah, I didn't stop breathing. I'm alive and well so stop with the fussing. Let's stop and get a sandwich."

"Sounds good to me."

Twenty miles east of Des Moines, they pulled off the road at Highway 117 and drove a mile south into a small town named Colfax. There was a colorfully painted sign welcoming them to Colfax that read, "A Pleasant Blend of Town and Country." Frank thought, "More like 'A pleasant blend of depression and despair.'" They drove over the Skunk River Bridge guarding the small Iowa burg and the first diner on the left was a place called Poppy's. Liam pointed at it and said, "That'll be as good as any, maybe the only one."

A homely waitress in her early fifties came to their table and said, "Special is hot beef sandwich, mashed with gravy, green beans and a drink, $2.99."

Liam said, "I'll have the special and coffee, please."

She said, "Thanks sweetie. And you, honey?"

Frank said, "Cheeseburger, fries and a Coke."

"Coming right up, fellas."

Liam said, "So, let's see. What else about the Irish do you want to know?"

"No more, Granddad. Let's give it a rest."

The waitress set the drinks down and walked away. Liam smiled again as he poured cream and sugar into his coffee."

Frank said, "How can you drink that crap?"

Liam said, "One day you'll come to cherish a good cup of coffee."

"No way."

Liam said, "Okay lad, forget about the Irish. What if I was to tell you a story about a certain family, a mother, father, three daughters and two boys?"

"Yeah."

"They lived in a faraway country, over the sea. One day they woke up and all the food that they had harvested that year went bad and people ended up starving all over the country."

"What, like Uganda or something?"

"Yeah, okay, let's use Uganda. So this Ugandan farmer, his wife and five kids – let's say aged six through thirteen, all of them youngsters – have no food and little money and no way of feeding themselves."

"Sucks to be them."

"Yeah, whatever. Anyway, the father knows he has to make a decision as to what he has to do for him and his family to survive. Finally, he decides that he's going to take what little savings he had and put his family on a rickety old ship and move to a foreign country where life has to be better.

"Problem is he knows there's about a fifty/fifty chance that they'll all survive the trip alive. But he knows that if they don't go they have a one hundred percent chance of starving to death at home."

The waitress interrupted and said, "Gentlemen, enjoy your lunch."

Liam looked up at her and said, "Thank you."

"Sure hon."

Frank said, "Anyway, so they're getting on a ship."

"Right. Now after a few weeks on this crummy old ship the father dies from a deadly disease, the mother dies from the same disease the day they get to their new country and the kids are left orphaned in a strange land and know no one."

"That's the worst."

"That's exactly what happened to your great-great grandfather and great-great grandmother when they moved their family to America."

"We're Ugandan?"

"No, boy, we're not Ugandan, we're Irish."

"Why'd they come, then?"

"Potato famine, no choice."

"Serious?"

"Yeah. The youngest of those kids was a boy named Billy O'Conlan. He was six years old when orphaned in New York City. Before he died he was the largest landowner in Clinton County, Iowa, where we're heading now."

Frank stared at his granddad and said, "No lie? What happened to all the dough? We sure didn't get any."

"Well, I'm afraid that's a bit of my fault."

They finished their meal in silence, paid the tab and got back on the road.

The sky burned a bright blue as the wind blew the snow across the interstate. Eighteen wheel trucks passed them as if they were standing still and temporarily blinded them with the blowing snow. Frank thought, "Darn trucks."

Liam said, "Would you like to hear more?"

"You tricked me into this Irish crap. I'm not interested in hearing the confessions of an old man with regrets, you feeding me this crap about you dying, if you made some mistakes, so what? Who hasn't? Money's not everything."

"Okay, then forget it. I just thought that maybe we could pass the time. And yeah, I don't mind admitting it; I do have a few regrets, how about you, Mr. Skeptic?"

"Yeah, I regret getting busted with the dope."

"Do you regret that you smoked the dope, or do you regret that you got caught?"

"That I got caught."

"You're lucky it was John Quinlan who caught you, otherwise you might have gone to the can. That ain't a pretty place."

"How would you know?"

"I've been there."

"You've gone to jail?"

"Yep."

"What happened?"

"Oh, that's a stupid story about an old Irish guy with regrets, you wouldn't be interested."

"Wait a minute."

"Forget it."

Liam tuned the station to Lawrence Welk and turned it up.

Frank thought, "Screw him."

After about fifteen minutes, when he could not take another minute of the depressing music, Frank said, "Okay, I can't take anymore of this crap," And turned off the radio.

Liam said, "Paybacks are a bitch."

Frank caught himself laughing and said, "Okay, you got me. Are you going to tell me what happened or not?"

"Well, let's see. The episode involved too much drinking and doing some really bad things that I regret."

"What about jail?"

"Well, if I told you I went to jail without telling you the whole story it wouldn't make sense. Your great grandfather Billy O'Conlan was quite a guy."

Liam's words caught in his throat and the familiar tears of regret misted in his eyes temporarily blurring his vision. With that Frank looked over at the bent old man next to him and became uncomfortable.

Liam looked out the window and continued as if to himself, "I was raised in the lap of luxury and it still wasn't enough."

Frank said, "What's that suppose to mean?"

Liam lost somewhere in the past said, "Huh? Oh, yeah, right. Well, it wasn't as if I didn't know hard work; my dad worked us from sun up till sun down. But he made the assumption that we'd all want to farm, but that was the last thing I wanted."

Frank said, "What did you want to do?"

Liam said, "I wanted to move to the city, go to college, get a good job, you know get a little something for myself on my own."

Frank said, "And?"

Liam said, "My dad would hear none of it. But I digress. You'll have a better understanding of all this once you know my dad better."

Frank said, "What about jail?"

Liam said, "Hold your horses, boy, we'll get there. We've got a long drive ahead of us."

Liam coughed to clear his voice and straightened his pants around his thighs. Then thinking about what he was going to say wished like hell he had a glass of whiskey and started.

"Frank, can I trust you?"

With a bit of hesitation wondering what he was about to get himself into, Franks said, "Yeah, Gramps, I guess."

"There can be no guessing, lad, either I can trust you or not. What I'm about to tell you, I've never told anyone and never discussed with anyone. So I need to know if I can trust you to keep it quiet, even after I'm gone?"

Frank looked over at his granddad and saw the seriousness of a surgeon delivering bad news and said in a whisper, "Yes, Granddad, you can trust me."

He said, "Good," and then took the deep breathe of a sprinter before entering the starting blocks and stared out the window at dead cornfields.

Liam then said, "Frank, I killed a man."

Frank sucked in oxygen so hard and fast that it felt like a gulp and he got light headed. He said, "Granddad, no."

"Yes, it was an accident; I didn't mean for it to happen but it did. And that is one of the reasons we are heading to Delmar this weekend."

"Why?"

"You'll see."

The silence in the vehicle became unbearable and so the storyteller, the Seanachie began: "My dad, may God rest his soul, had a hard life. He was dealt a lousy hand and worked for everything he ever had. They left Ireland when he was only six years old, during the great famine, so he knew hunger. He was orphaned shortly after arriving in New York after both parents died during the trip. Within five years of being here two of his sisters died, so he knew great loss. He was in an orphanage for five years so he knew what it was like to be an outsider. As a boy of eleven he ran water and tools all day long to the men working the railroad, so he knew struggle and hard work. After that he became an indentured servant for a farmer in Clinton county, Iowa, working for no more than room and board, so he knew humility. On his eighteenth birthday he was given his own acre of land that he turned into a thousand, so he knew pride and gratitude. He then turned that into the largest farm in Clinton County Iowa so he knew wealth and prosperity. And with all that he never missed daily Mass the entire time I was with him, so he knew faith and he knew his God."

Frank said, "Come on Gramps, all this happened to one guy?"

Liam said, "Yep."

Frank said, "No way, you're making this crap up."

Liam said, "No I'm not. This was my dad, your great-granddad. The only reason I know all this stuff is because he'd never let any of us forget it. That's why he wouldn't entertain even discussing other options. To him it was preposterous, why would anyone want to do anything else?

"I remember working with him and at times he would just stop what he was doing to look around his large farm in awe of what he'd been given. He loved the feel of the soil beneath his feet. And the fact that it was his soil made it sacred to him. He loved the land, plain and simple. After all his poverty and all his experiences as an outsider, he couldn't fathom the idea that someone wouldn't love to work this land – that someone wouldn't consider it the same honor that he did. There were many times that I envied him, because he found his one true love, something that always eluded me."

"Even now?"

"Even now. But you have to understand that Billy also had never had the experience of being given something. He had worked for every square inch of his farm, and was glad to give it to his sons and daughters. It was his legacy. This was a man who had stepped off a coffin ship."

Frank said, "Whoa, wait a minute. What's a coffin ship?

"The years of 1846 and 1847 were the worst two years of the famine in Ireland. Over fifty percent of all Irish immigrants leaving Ireland during those years died on the ships before they ever reached their destination, buried at sea. So the Irish took to calling them coffin ships. The great Irish statesman of the time, Daniel O'Connell, called them ocean hearses. In 1847 it got so bad that Irish history books refer to it as black '47."

Frank thought for a moment and said, "Wow."

Liam said, "Yeah and within two hours of walking off that ship, your great-grandfather was an orphan with nothing, something he never let any of us forget. Yet by the time he died, he was the largest landowner in Clinton County, Iowa. The land was everything to him, which led to the falling out between him and me."

"What's that mean?"

"Hang on, I'll get there. After grade school and high school in the same one room schoolhouse, I craved knowledge, the knowledge that came from books and classrooms. I wanted to read and write. I wanted to study philosophy, literature, history and mathematics. I wanted to travel and go to college. You see, son; I was looking for my one true love, my reason to live. I was looking for that contentment that my dad had and I don't think I ever found it."

Liam stopped. The blowing wind and snow across the highway had worsened and the traffic blew past them mercilessly. He said, "It's painful to think back on those days."

Frank thought, "A bunch of sentimental garbage and he's unloading it all on me. This sucks."

Then Liam said, "Like I said, Billy and I didn't get along very well. Some of our stand offs were legendary around Petersville."

"Petersville? I thought you said we were going to Delmar?"

"We say Delmar because as a town it still exists, Petersville is no more than a church and a cemetery now. But at one time you could've called it a village and the farm was just outside Petersville."

"Okay, so your beefs with your dad?"

"Yeah."

"Worse than me and dad last night?"

"Huh? Well, as bad anyway. We couldn't see eye to eye on anything. We had some screaming matches and we threw a few punches. But it was different circumstances and for different reasons."

"Sounds familiar."

Liam looked out his window as if thinking about some place far away or maybe a long time ago. He smiled and nodded off to sleep.

Frank looked over at the old man who had just fallen asleep and thought, "Figures," and turned up the classic rock station that was playing the long version of the Loggins and Messina tune *Vahevala.* It was a jam session he never tired of and he figured that if Granddad didn't wake up or bother him, he had fifteen minutes of bliss coming out of the dashboard radio.

As Frank drove, the weather gradually worsened from blowing ground snow to big fat January flakes falling from the wintry Iowa sky. The mixture of heavy snow and blowing wind made driving miserable, but Frank thought, "At least it slowed down some of these maniacs out here."

After half an hour the combination of weather, people sliding into the snow-filled ditches and his granddad's erratic breathing that ranged from loud obnoxious snores to struggling guttural noises, to not breathing at all, were more than Frank could take. He pulled off at the next exit and shook his granddad awake.

Liam said, "Huh, where are we, son? And why did you pull over?"

Frank said, "People are sliding into ditches, the weather's getting worse and you stopped breathing again. I've had enough."

"Where are we?"

"About thirty miles west of Iowa City."

Liam said, "How about we make our way to Iowa City. If the weather doesn't break by then we'll get a room there rather than driving all the way to Davenport."

"Easy for you to say, you're not driving in this crap."

"Well, I didn't know you were such a candy ass. We can get a room in a no tell motel off 151 here, but don't blame me when the cockroaches crawl over you in the middle of the night."

The candy ass comment was all Frank needed to assess his level of testosterone, but the thought of cockroaches made the decision even easier.

They drove for fifteen or twenty minutes in silence. Frank, concentrating so hard on the road that he forgot about the radio; Liam, seeing the intensity with which the boy was focusing, didn't want to continue his tale while his grandson was white-knuckle driving. He would wait.

The weather started to improve. Soon the snow had stopped altogether, the wind calmed down and they drove out from under the cloud cover. The highway was clear ahead and the stars under the rural sky, far from the city lights, were sparkling and dancing in a soft rhythm like the backup singers for a traveling blues band. Frank's mood improved considerably and he even smiled, relieved that the worst seemed to be over for now.

Before Frank thought of turning on the radio Liam said, "Francis, do you believe in ghosts?"

"What do you mean?"

"Do you believe that ghosts come back to visit people or haunt houses or maybe buildings?"

"Well, I don't know. I've heard people talk about the ghosts who live in O'Connor's pub in the Old Market in Omaha. The owner has seen them when she's doing her books late at night after the place is closed. Yeah, I guess so. Why?"

Liam smiled and said, "I don't know, an Irish thing I guess. Hey, did I ever tell you about the time my brothers and I had a chance to play pro baseball?"

"No way."

"It's true."

CHAPTER 4
MR. HORSE SHIT, IS IT?

"I don't mind telling you that my brothers Vince and Gene and I were damn good baseball players. We played in a county league, playing teams from all over eastern Iowa. We developed quite a reputation for ourselves. Our team was always tough and the newspapers started to cover us regularly and people began to talk. Vince was a pitcher, Gene a first baseman and I was a catcher. Pretty soon we had scouts from Chicago, Cleveland and Boston nosing around to watch us play."

"Professional baseball scouts?"

"Yes."

"No lie, this is on the up and up?"

"On my honor, we were that good. This scout from the White Sox organization in Chicago asked our coach if he could talk to us after a game one night. He even made us a verbal offer"

The past was coming in crystal clear and, at times, Liam relished the memories, while at other times he loathed them. The bitter cold wind of Iowa in January beat without mercy against the windshield of the station wagon and its defroster was fighting a losing battle. Liam wrapped his gray cardigan tighter around his chest for warmth and said, "Let's see, the scouts name was Hershey, Todd Hershey. He cornered Vince, Gene and me after a game one night and asked if we were interested in playing pro ball."

Frank, still not convinced, said, "Come on Gramps, are you lying?"

Liam said, "On my mother's grave it's true."

Frank said, "How come I never heard this before?"

Liam said, "What have you ever heard about me?"

Frank said, "Nothing, really."

Liam said, "Because I haven't shared this with a lot of people. Too many regrets I guess."

It slowly began to dawn on Frank what was happening here, that it was almost sacred, how lucky he was to be here. He said, with more excitement now, "Okay, so you guys were talking to a real pro scout."

Liam said, "Don't get too excited, it doesn't end well."

Frank said, "What do you mean?"

"The man offered us a tryout, said we were good enough. But we all knew."

"Knew what?"

"That Billy would scoff at the idea and run the man off. And sure enough he did."

"What happened?"

"We told him about our dad, that he was the boss – that we worked the family farm and there wasn't a snowball's chance in hell that we'd be going anywhere. He was insistent on coming out and talking to dad anyway."

Liam stared out the window and laughed a bitter laugh at the thought of one more lost opportunity in what he considered a failed life.

Then out of nowhere Liam said, in a thick Irish brogue, mimicking his dad, "Baseball? Well for Christ sakes, a child's game? For me big strong lads? Are you serious, man? Give up their life's work to play a game? Have you looked around? Did you notice the farm when you pulled up in your big black Mercury? And just who do you think's going to till the soil next spring and reap the harvest next fall? A goddamn banshee? Mr. Horsefeed, is it?"

By now Frank was leaned over the steering wheel laughing, the air exploding from his lungs in gasps and spasms with nothing coming out and slapping his hand against it.

Liam now enjoying the floor, continued to his mimicry and said, "If you haven't figured that out, how can I possibly trust that you know even the first thing about baseball and 'tis only a child's game? The door is right behind you Mr. Horse Shit, is it? And don't be letting it hit you in the arse on the way out. But thanks for stopping by."

When the laughter stopped, the seriousness of the loss dropped on them both like a bomb of despair and depression. It left an aftermath that made the air in the car around them seem heavy and dull.

Liam said, "As funny as all that was, son, there was much truth in it. When we got home that night we told Billy that we had a scout ask us if we were interested in playing pro ball and that he was coming to the house to talk it over with him. He threw a fit."

Frank said, "Wow."

Liam said, "When Hershey left, my dad and I had another fierce argument. Words of hatred were passed. I hated him for the power and control he wielded over me."

A moment passed, both lost somewhere in their own minds when Liam said, as if to himself, "Maybe that's why I'm going back home?"

Frank said, "Why?"

Liam said, "To forgive and maybe be forgiven."

Frank said, "Come on, Gramps."

"No Frank, I was a spoiled little bastard and would say things that hurt my dad down to his very soul. It was a desecration of things he considered sacred and I did it just to hurt him. But you know, I really only hurt myself. And after I was done opening my big mouth and inserting my foot, it hurt me to see him and I wondered why I said what I said. I remember that night him subtly gasping, while holding back the tears that inevitably came with the painful memory."

There was a brief moment of silent reflection when Liam looked up and said in a whisper, "Jesus, have mercy, I was such a jackass."

Frank said, "Take it easy, Granddad. There's not a father and son in the world that don't have the occasional blow up. Your dad forgave you a long time ago."

"I don't know about that. But I'm hell bent to make it right before we go home."

Frank, not knowing what that meant said, "Anyway."

"Oh yeah. After the lousy fight we had, I immediately regretted my words upon seeing the stinging pain in my father's eyes. I remember we stopped and looked at each other, both of us kind of having the wind knocked out of our sails with those last remarks. It hurt Billy to be reminded of it and it hurt me that I said something so hurtful without thinking first."

Frank said, "What did you say that was so hurtful?"

"He was always reminding us that he came off a coffin ship with people starving all around him and that we should be grateful to have the things that we had. Being the spoiled jerk that I was and, of course in my fury, forgetting that his parents died on that coffin ship. I got fed up with hearing it constantly and told him that I didn't give a damn about some coffin ship and was I suppose to be sorry I was born when I was born? It was basically screw the coffin ships, screw Ireland and screw him. To make matters worse, regardless of how poorly I treated him he always had my back."

"What do you mean?"

"You'll see. Anyway Frank, for me, it was one more rung in the ladder of bitterness and resentment and one more tie in the railroad track heading out of town."

"You said your love eluded you, what did you mean by

that?"

"It did. I never found my niche."

"I think you turned a blind eye to it."

Liam looked at Frank and his eyes welled with tears. He quickly looked out the window to hide the emotion and watched the dark cornfields whiz by.

He quietly said, "Thank you."

The lights of Davenport, Iowa become visible and the sign for Highway 61 read one mile ahead.

Liam said, "Take Highway 61. We've got a room reserved at the Best Western there on the corner."

Frank could see the Best Western sign on the horizon and was glad. The muscles in his neck were sore from tensing up while he drove through the storm. He was hungry and tired and looked forward to his bed.

CHAPTER 5
THE ACCIDENT

Frank and Liam checked into their hotel room, went to the restaurant in the hotel lobby and had dinner. The Saturday night prime rib special had filled the place and they had to wait for a table.

When they were finally seated, they both ordered and Frank said, “Granddad, that is such a bummer.”

Liam said, “What are you talking about?”

“The baseball thing.”

“Oh yes, not one of the happier moments of my life. Look, lad, you have to understand my dad. He grew up in dire straights. Can you imagine how scared you’d be if you lost both parents and were orphaned in a foreign country? The United States was a far different country than it is today. Irish Catholics were about as welcome then as a liberal at a John Birch meeting.”

Frank said, “What?”

“Never mind. What I mean to say is that the vast majority of people on the eastern seaboard in 1846, when the mass immigration from Ireland began, were of Anglican and

Protestant roots."

"What?"

"A people whose roots came from England, a country that spent the last six hundred years trying to destroy the Irish, they couldn't decide what they hated more, an Irishman or a Catholic, and an Irish Catholic personified everything they found despicable. We embodied everything they loathed or feared.

"An *orphaned* Irish Catholic had it even worse because nobody, and I mean nobody wanted them, not even their own. It was a miracle that those kids ended up in an orphanage and not dead in the streets.

"For a man like my dad to have done what he'd done was nowhere near short of spectacular. But because he had, he figured that this is what *everybody* wanted. So when my brothers and I got the offer to play ball, it wasn't like it is today and, to his way of thinking, it *was* preposterous. He could never understand my desire to get off the farm and, of course, I was doing everything in my power to do just that. Because of this, drinking and gambling and ignoring my family and chores were my way out."

Frank and Liam finished their meal and sat in silence. With everything Frank had heard, he felt like he'd been in an all day history class, overloaded with information, brain buzzing and tired.

They went back to their room. Liam washed his face and came out of the bathroom in his striped boxers to his knees and spaghetti strapped t-shirt. He got on his knees, said his prayers and jumped into bed. Frank swore Liam was snoring before his head hit the pillow and thought, "If he breathes in starts and fits all night, it's going to be a long night."

Frank watched a fifties horror movie and called it a night. His Granddad seemed to be resting peacefully. He sat on the side of his bed and stared at the old man sleeping in the twin bed across the room. He thought, "I've known this guy my whole life and had no idea, none." He laid down on his pillow and fell into a fitful sleep, not totally oblivious to how his life seemed to be changing.

He came straight up in his sleep and didn't know where in the world he was. Liam sat in the corner with a glass of water on the tabletop as if waiting for the boy to wake up with a start at three o'clock in the morning.

Frank said, "Granddad, what time is it?"

"Just after three."

"What the hell are you doing?"

"I don't sleep well most nights and this is not most nights."

"What's that supposed to mean?"

"I'm facing some demons tomorrow I've been running from since 1926."

"And I suppose you want to talk about it?"

"It's one night. You can sleep anytime."

Frank reluctantly pulled himself to a sitting position, wrapped the blankets around him and listened.

Liam sipped his water, leaned back in his chair and squinted in the dimly lit room as if to better focus on the past and said, "I tried to get away from the farm, even temporarily. I went to St. Ambrose College in Dubuque, with the blessing of my mother, but I was always called home for the damn fall harvest or the spring planting. Each time I was called home the resentments grew. I felt like a mean brown trout on a line, my dad reeling me in.

"It was at about this time when the drinking and gambling started to become a problem. I'd developed a taste for these vices as a teenager, but when I started to need them more than I wanted them was when I knew I was in trouble.

"The money was always there and I loved to have a good time. I'd spend hours at the tavern in the evenings. It was then that I developed a reputation as a partier, gambler and yes, storyteller. The tavern owners in town loved to see me walk in because my storytelling got their customers to stick around and drink hours longer than they might have normally."

Frank said, "What? You'd just stand up and tell a story?"

Liam said, "No. There'd be five or six people sitting around and I'd be sitting there with them. One thing would lead to another, which would remind me of something and it would start."

"What would?"

"The Story. Pretty soon more people were sitting around and I'd be the only one talking in the whole tavern. I was shocked at times as to what came out of my mouth. I never knew where the stories came from or where they were going – it was as if they just took on a life of their own and people seemed to love them.

"It was also at this time in my life that I met the most wonderful person I was to ever know, Kathleen Mooney, your grandmother. I was working hard and playing hard, typical of a twenty-one-year old man. In that neck of the woods I was the epitome of the eligible bachelor.

"Kathleen had seen me around, but we had never talked. I had the reputation a rounder and kept my distance from the ladies, more interested in the inside of a tavern and the delights that lie there.

"Kathleen had graduated from a girl's high school boarding academy and was back in Delmar on the farm. Against her parents wishes she took a job at the general store in Delmar. Her mother was furious with her because she felt that it was beneath her. But Kath insisted saying she had to get out of the house, it was driving her nuts.

"One morning in early spring, just before planting, Vince, Gene and I walked into the Delmar General store. We had a list of supplies Billy had given us that we needed for spring planting. I walked up to the counter and said, 'Kathleen Ann Mooney, how are you doing on this fine spring morning?'"

"She responded with a nice hello and the sweetest smile I ever saw. Frank, it was the damndest thing. As the words fell off my lips, I was startled and wondering why in the world I just did that. It was impulsive and I was suddenly embarrassed.

"Vince and Gene stood staring and smiling. They knew I

could make an ass of myself when the time was right."

Frank sat wrapped in his hotel bed blanket and said, "Sounds familiar."

Liam said, "Yeah?"

"I do it about everyday."

"It's part of life, son. If you never take a risk, you never make an ass of yourself, but you never grow either. Anyway, for reasons unclear to me to this day, your grandmother took a liking to me, even if I was a bit forward. Then we had one of those awkward moments, when neither of us knew what to say."

Frank smiled and said, "Been there, done that. I don't understand girls."

Liam said, "Don't feel bad, son, you never will. Anyway, after she said hello and smiled at me, it was as if my tongue swelled up and I couldn't talk. Gene saved my fanny by stepping up and asking her to see her boss, telling her that we needed to buy some supplies. When she left the room they both jumped me."

Frank said, "For what?"

Liam smiled and said, "They knew if I was to pursue Kathleen Mooney, and I had every intention of doing so, that they'd get stuck with all the work. And, of course they were right. Once again, thinking only of myself, I was up front talking to your grandmother, while my brothers were out back, loading supplies and doing all the work."

Frank looked over at his granddad and said, "So you blew off your brothers, huh? Nice guy, leaving them with all the work."

As Liam swirled water in his glass he looked out the window at the predawn traffic on I-80, he smiled and suddenly looked like a prepubescent experiencing puppy love for the first time. He felt those pangs of first love that he felt first so long ago, and it felt good. Then a pain came over his face as he realized his love was gone and he would never see her again in this world. And the thought came, and not for the first time and not unpleasantly, that it would be nice to see her again even at the price he'd have to pay.

Frank, witnessing all of this said, "What?"

"Oh, I was just thinking, son."

"About?"

"That lunch, that first lunch, that first hour, that first moment I knew I would spend the rest of my life with your grandmother. Have you ever been in love, son?"

"No. But if I ever find a girl that I like, I'm not going to treat her like my old man treats Mom."

Liam nodded and started again. "By the time we had finished lunch, I had fallen head over heals in love with your grandmother and knew she felt the same way. I got her back to work on time and headed to the tavern for a little celebration. By mid-afternoon I found myself in the middle of another one of my stories. By the time I'd finished, the bar was full and it was after six p.m. I got a lift home and the family was in the middle of dinner.

"When I walked in, the room went silent and I knew I was the topic of conversation by the way people were avoiding eye contact with me. It wasn't good. But then the strangest thing happened."

Frank said, "What's that?"

Liam said, "My dad didn't explode on me like he usually would've. It was almost like he'd had enough, or maybe he'd just had enough that day."

"Enough of what?"

"Oh, our fighting and bickering all the time. I'm sure I smelled like a brewery when I walked in and so he asked me if I'd been at Sullivan's or Murphy's. I told him I'd been at Murphy's and that's when it happened."

Liam stopped; Frank looked up from his thoughts and noticed a look of wonderment in his granddad's eyes. They shone in the dim hotel room. One of those rare moments when the memories didn't hurt, it was as if he was actually back in that kitchen at that moment and he didn't want it to slip away.

He came to and said, "He then asked me if I was playing poker or telling one of my stories."

"I told him I had been telling a story. He then proceeded to tell the family that I had developed quite a reputation as a storyteller. He then told them about the Seanachie back home in Ireland and how he'd remembered them when he was little and the impression they had made even then. He said that the Seanachie were master storytellers, that they were something special and revered in Ireland, that his father was a hell of a storyteller and that he was glad that one of his sons had the gift."

Frank said, "Why is that such a big deal? It's pretty obvious that you can tell a good story."

Liam said, "Frank, first of all, my father rarely handed out compliments, so it really meant something when he did. And secondly, I had no idea that he knew anything about my storytelling or that anyone was even talking about it."

Frank said, "Who told him?"

Liam said, "Come to find out, Gene and Vincent."

Frank said, "That doesn't surprise me."

Liam said, "I guess not. But when he said that, I was struck. I sat in shock as he spoke, stunned at how flattering he had spoken of me. It was rare but it felt good."

Frank said, "Why is it so hard for you to see?"

Liam said, "See what?"

"That your gift is your storytelling, *your* life's work."

"It never made me a dime, how can that be my life's work?"

"There you go talking about money again. That has nothing to do with it."

"Spoken like a true neophyte."

"Like a what?"

"Never mind, just wait until you have kids and a wife, then tell me that. Anyway, we dated for six months when I finally had the nerve to bring your grandmother home for dinner. Billy loved her the minute he laid eyes on her; she won his heart.

Within fifteen minutes of her arrival on the O'Conlan farm she was considered family.

"I wish I could say the same about my first meeting with her parents. My reputation had preceded me and they were not happy with the prospect of their respectable daughter dating what they considered a bad seed. Plus they were lace curtain Irish and looked down their noses at me who they considered shanty."

"What's lace curtain Irish mean?"

"Frank, during the early days, the first Irish in this country to create wealth, get an education and create an upper-class for themselves were called "lace curtain" Irish by the shanty Irish. They could afford the lace and linen."

"Shanty Irish?"

"Yeah, the working stiffs, the blue collar Irish. The Mooney's were "lace curtain" Irish. My family created as much wealth as the Mooney's, but they always considered us shanty Irish. I guess because we worked the land and education, other than the basics, was not a priority for my father.

"When we were finally engaged my parents threw a big pig roast. I swear my dad did it just to piss off the Mooney's. He made us out to be hillbillies. The Mooney's, who were far more reserved and less accepting of me, had a quiet cocktail party, with a parlor quartet and hors d'oeuvres. Dad was ready to wear a pair of overalls when mom put a stop to that and made him put on a suit of clothes. Lord, I remember mom calling him a rascal and telling him to mind his manners."

Liam laughed to himself, or more like giggled, thinking back on those days of his youth. Then a pained look came across his face and he furrowed his brow, realizing that the trouble, that familiar struggle was as familiar today as then.

"During our engagement, I was in a predicament that I couldn't ever seem to rectify. I loved your grandmother, I loved my family and friends and I loved Eastern Iowa. But I hated farming. Problem was, it was all I knew and it was my only source of income and a substantial income at that. My discontentment grew and with it, my drinking and storytelling. I look back now and realize I was looking for some sort of solace and found a false solace in both."

Frank said, "I understand the hiding in a bottle, but a story?"

"Frank, it wasn't the drink or the storytelling, per se, it was the running, and I was a great runner. When life got too tough, or I had to make a decision, I ran away and drank, and with the drinking came the storytelling or maybe hiding in the storytelling.

"My longing for peace and contentment often led me down a treacherous and deceptively steep slope. Initial tranquility became lasting turbulence. If one beer was good then eighteen must be paradise. Losing at poker, night after night, meant my luck had to change.

"Then I met Kathleen Mooney and I was sure she would be my catharsis, cleansing my soul of all its iniquities. With her in my life, the drinking and gambling were sure to fall away like the last pebble of an avalanche coming to rest somewhere in my past.

"But rather than an avalanche coming to rest, the drinking and gambling were like an active volcano boiling over with frustration and ready to explode. The only consolation I found from this self-inflicted perdition was the storytelling. It seemed as if I would find myself lost in a vivid and yet lonely forest of history, fiction and poetic license. Confined with vines and downed tree trunks blocking my path and the only way I could find my way out was word by word, step by step, to *my* place in the universe. I never knew where and when the story would start, where it was going, and where it was to end, devouring me heart and soul and, at times, leaving me exhausted."

Frank, lost in his grandfather's oral artistry, said in a soft whisper, as if to himself, "I get it." His words seemed muffled, almost lost, in the muted shreds of the dust filled light, which filtered through the room off the dimly lit lamp in the predawn hours.

Liam said, "Get what?"

Frank coming out of sort of daze said, "Huh? Oh, never mind."

"Okay, so anyway, where was I? Oh yeah, one morning a few years after we were married, I didn't wake up until nine o'clock and I was just getting to my chores, way too late, when Billy drove up, he'd been at work since before sunrise.

"He walked into the barn as I was throwing hay and laid into me, wondering what the hell was going on. He told me I was drunk too much, gambling too much and staying out too late and that I was useless to him, my wife and my kids. My response to his diatribe was that I hated the damn farm, I hated the work, I hated him and I wanted out."

Liam put his head down and stared at the carpeting in the hotel room and said, "Frank, as much as Billy didn't understand me, he did love me and hated to see me deteriorate like I was. But I told him that he had enough dough to send me off to school to get an education and asked him why he was being so damned stubborn. And do you know what his response was?"

"What?"

"He asked me what guarantees he had, if he made that sort of investment in my future, that I would quit drinking and gambling."

"That's legit."

"Of course it was, but once again I was a fish on the line, powerless, there was no way out. He walked out of the barn that day and we didn't speak for a couple of months. Until the morning he bailed me out of jail.

"One evening, before spring planting, I was at Murphy's tavern and had been all night. I loathed spring planting; it was eighteen-hour days of pure hell for the likes of me. I left Murphy's at one-fifteen a.m.; I was just to the edge of town, and ready to get on the gravel road when I came upon a man walking there, I guess he was going to hoof it to Clinton to try and jump the rail. He was dressed in all dark clothing, wearing a long, well-worn coat and a beat up hugger cap. I was half in the jar anyway and didn't see him in time and hit him. The man went to the hospital morgue and I went to jail."

The sun was coming up in the east and began to permeate the room with what should have been the hope of a new day. Instead it brought a gloomy sunrise that shot cumbersome unwelcome rays into a room with a grave air about it. Frank sat with his back to the headboard on his bed, wrapped in his hotel blankets and stared at his granddad.

He said, "So you weren't kidding. You really did kill a man?"

The words hit Liam like a wooden bullet shattered by the explosion and hitting him with multiple splinters across his chest."

He said, "Yes. It was the worst moment of my life. I relive it everyday. I ask God to forgive me everyday and I ask the man whose life I took to forgive me everyday."

"Who was he?"

"I still don't know, I don't think anybody does. Apparently he was a hobo, as drunk as I was, stumbling for a train to get back on the road. At least that's the story the sheriff told your grandma and me."

"What do you mean, 'at least that's what the sheriff told you,' you say that like maybe that wasn't the truth."

Liam stopped before he responded and looked out the window at the gray day, the gray highway lost in a painful memory. Frank becoming aware of the hesitation looked over at his granddad and caught a slight wince as if he just received a small shock from some unknown friction.

Liam said, "Frank, before I answer that directly, you have to understand the Irish at that time in America. As I've mentioned before, when we came to this country we were not wanted and not liked. So we created our own communities, either small towns that we built or parishes in the city that we rallied around. Whichever the circumstance we understood democracy and the right to vote. So to protect ourselves we put candidates up and soon we were mayors and city councilmen and then we appointed our own police chiefs and Fire Chiefs."

"Granddad, what does this have to do with anything?"

"I'm getting there. The Irish who made the money usually got the guy into office that they wanted, one of their own. My dad gave a man named Red Shanahan enough money to get him elected Sheriff. The night that I hit the hobo, Red showed up at my parent's house after he took me to jail and the hobo to the morgue. The next day the story was that the hobo was hit by a passing train and they buried him in the cemetery in Delmar."

CHAPTER 6
THE CEMETERY, THE DEPOT, THE REGRETS

Frank and Liam showered, packed and went down to breakfast. After checking out, they filled the station wagon with gas.

It was just before six a.m. when Frank jumped in the driver seat and said, "Man, for being up most of the night I feel pretty good."

He looked over at the tired old man slumped in the passenger seat who was gently snoring. He thought, "Darn, I hate waking him but I don't know where to go."

He said, "Granddad."

Liam came straight up in his seat and said, "Sorry lad that just happens sometimes. Head north here on Highway 61 and in about forty five minutes or so we come to Highway 136 where you'll go east into Delmar."

"Gotcha."

"I know you don't like anyone telling you what to do, but watch your speed here on 61. These Iowa state troopers just love stopping out of state cars."

"No problem. Double nickels all the way."

Liam tuned it to a forties swing station that was playing Tommy Dorsey and his big band. Frank snapped it off and said, "Sorry Granddad, but I need more info."

"I'm tired son, give me a break."

"Come on, Granddad. You started it, now finish it."

"Good Lord Almighty, for someone who had no interest."

"You're the Seanachie."

Liam laughed and said, "Okay, okay. Where were we?"

"Your dad got the news of the accident early that morning from the sheriff, who banged on his door at 3:30 a.m."

"Your grandmother was sitting at the kitchen table, at my place, drinking a cup of tea when my dad knocked. She'd been waiting for him. Kathleen Mooney O'Conlan was prone to premonitions; she told folks it was a gift and a curse."

Frank said, "Premonition?"

"Yeah, if I'd seen it once, I'd seen it a hundred times. She knew things before she was told, or before they even happened. Her mother told her it was a gift from the old country, that it was a fairly common trait among the rural women there. Your mom's got it too."

Frank said, "I know all about that."

Liam said, "So you've been nailed by your mom for some stupid stunt you've pulled when there is absolutely no way she could've, would've or should've known?"

Frank said, "Man alive, it's eerie. Sean, Mick and I have talked about it."

Liam said, "And don't *I* know it."

They both laughed, sharing the same experience of getting caught, by women who had powers of the ancient Irish seer.

"Your grandmother knew when my dad walked in to tell her and she was very upset at him for deciding to leave me in overnight. But he was a stubborn son of a bitch, still trying to teach me a lesson, even at the age of twenty-six.

"The next morning Billy, Gene and Vince went into town to bail me out. Once again, Vince and Gene were there as a safety precaution and when Billy insisted that he and I ride together and that they take my car, they protested. But there was no arguing with my dad. It was ugly in the car ride on the way home, another of our infamous stand offs."

Frank said, "What happened? What was said?"

"My dad gave me the old 'I told you so' lecture. I was hungover and didn't want to hear it. Of course I never dreamed that the guy had died. When my dad informed me that the man had passed away I began to shake violently. Dad got worried and pulled over I jumped out and ran to the side of the road and wretched."

Liam put a hand over his heart and winced as if the sting of putting the awful memory to words had sent a shock of pain through his chest.

The day was now an overcast gray that hung lazily in the air and added to the sadness that Liam felt, reliving all the damage he had caused. He realized now that he had not made the amends necessary to release him from the shackles that cuffed him to the past, especially with his own dad and the regret was palpable. But the cold January wind had yielded to a southern front that had shrouded the landscape and had warmed the day to an almost record high for this time of year, and he rolled down the window as if to let the breeze clean the car of its remorse.

The cold hard flakes that had fallen yesterday gave way to a soft spray on the breeze that helped to lift their spirits a little. But it wasn't to last and the beast called winter was to bare its razor sharp teeth once again, changing their lives forever.

Liam took a deep breath, drank some fresh, hot coffee and continued, "When Billy was first given property from old James Fitzpatrick, he was given a choice of any acre on the farm. He picked an acre that had a spot with a small pond and some blue spruce trees around it. When life got tough and he needed time by himself this is where he went, this was his spot.

After the accident, and my breakdown, Billy spent every night that week around a small campfire, next to the pond in *his* spot. It was beautiful, quiet, serene and exceptionally private. He found time to reach out to his God, where he could feel the spirits of his dead father, mother and two sisters and they brought him comfort and peace.

"A week or so after the accident, Billy came by the house to visit your grandmother and me. He gave me an ultimatum."

Liam's hands balled into fists and his knuckles went white. His jaw clinched and tears ran down from his eyes.

Frank looked over to ask what the ultimatum was and the look on his granddad's face made him cringe.

Frank said in a soft, consoling tone, "It's okay, Gramps, we can stop if you want."

Liam said through gritted teeth, "No, lad. It needs to be said. But damnation if it doesn't still hurt like hell after all these years."

Liam pulled himself together, blew his nose, wiped away the tears and took a deep breath as if he were stepping back into the ring for the fifteenth round and didn't know he'd make it out.

He said, "My dad told me that the consensus of the entire family was that I was a drunk, that I needed to dry out and that he was sending me to the county sanitarium for a month."

Frank said, "And if you refused?"

Liam said, "That the farm would no longer be mine to work and that I'd have to take my family and leave."

Frank stopped him and said, "You're kidding, right?"

Getting worked up once again over the county hospital experience, that sometimes, even now, haunted his dreams, he said, with the same malice he had not intended, "Have I been kidding about anything up to now? Of course I'm not kidding. Of all the crap that I went through with Billy, it was the one thing I could never forgive him for. Frank, it wasn't like it is now."

"What isn't?"

"Being called a drunk. Today they're called alcoholics.

Back then they were called drunks and were people who were shunned. There was really no recourse for an alcoholic in 1926. It was the worse thing you could be called. I felt utterly betrayed by my family."

"What did you do?"

"What could I do? My back was against the wall. I had a wife and three youngsters to support, so I went."

Again there was silence in the car, overwhelming silence. Liam had another chest pain and found it hard to breathe. He thought, everything dies, all my brothers and sisters, my mother and father, most of my friends, all dead. So why don't memories die? And all the stinking pain that goes with them. His hands shook and he couldn't stop them. The tears fell and he couldn't stop them. The awful pain of those memories flooded his brain like a small cascade and he couldn't stop them either.

Then he stopped everything, a shudder ran through his frail eighty-three-year-old frame, and said, more to himself, "Maybe *that's* really the reason for this trip?"

Frank said, "What?"

Liam smiled at his grandson and said, "Maybe it's time, after all these years, to forgive my dad and maybe to ask for his forgiveness. But I've got to get this off my chest before I can do that."

Frank said, "Get what off your chest?"

"You'll see."

The rows of dead corn stalks ran together and became a blur, like the painful memory he now conjured. Liam thought, "I know why dad had done it? I killed a man, damn it, and my drinking was out of control. So why couldn't I forgive him? Aren't I supposed to be older and wiser? Then why the hell don't I have the answers? And why do I need to be forgiven? Damn lousy memories, why am I doing any of this?

Frank said, "Granddad?"

"Oh yeah, let's see, where were we? Dad came the next morning, with Vince and Gene, who insisted on coming. They thought sure I'd come out swinging. They were wrong. I came out, too exhausted to swing at anyone, with the black bags of no sleep under my eyes and a forlorn stare. I didn't look at any of them or acknowledge their existence. I walked to dad's car and got into the front seat. They dropped me off to a hell that I never knew existed. I'd heard stories, but none came close to the terror that subsisted within those padded walls.

"The inmates at that country club were on a scale from mildly insane to dangerously insane and they were all in the same room. I had to constantly be on guard to protect myself from attacks. I rarely slept or ate and, to make matters worse, I couldn't have visitors. I wanted to see your Grandmother, my kids, Vince or Gene. Anyone, but those bastards treated me like I was mentally insane. I descended on a road to hell by myself for a month. Yet, I knew I deserved this, hell I should've been in jail. But still I hated my dad for putting me into that penitentiary for the insane.

"The thirty days passed in slow motion as if the hours waded in thick molasses. Dad arrived one morning to pick up me. When I walked out of that hospital, the only delight I took was the look in dad's eyes when he first saw me. He actually winced. I had lost twenty pounds and had grown a full beard. The black bags under my eyes going in were now emphasized by how pale my already fair skin had become. To describe myself as a weak and bent old man at age thirty-three was an understatement."

Frank said, "God, Gramps. What happened in the car on the way home?"

Liam said, "Now, you have to realize something here. I'm an alcoholic and have been sober for over twenty years. But like most alcoholics, when I was drinking and causing all these problems, everyone saw the problem but me. But looking back, at the time, he did what he thought was best until he saw me come out of the place. Remember that people didn't know what to do with alcoholics at the time. He tried to reconcile things with me in the car, but the resentment and burning hatred that had descended on me wouldn't hear any of it.

"We blew up at each other again, I told him to go to hell and in his utter and total frustration with me he punched me in the nose. Nose bleeding and furious, I got out of the car and told him he could have his farm and his money because come hell or high water I was taking my family and leaving. I walked the rest of the way home. Gene and Vince tried to pick me up and I told them both if they didn't scoot I'd whip both their asses. They knew I couldn't take them both but that I was so mad that somebody'd get hurt so they left me alone."

They rode a while without a word; Frank listening to his granddad's heavy breathing as the story got him all worked up. He tried to relax as if letting go of some of the past, but couldn't.

Liam suddenly started to laugh and Frank thought, that's it, the old man's snapped.

Frank said, "What the hell's so funny?"

Liam said, "It's just that I was such a horse's ass and there's nothing I can do now but laugh. And I'm sick and tired of crying. Maybe its relief I'm feeling, getting all this off my chest

"I don't think my mother ever forgave my dad for what he did. Frank, my dad thought long and hard about what to do with yours truly. He didn't want to lose me, but he knew that I was an adult and had to make some decisions for myself. Thing is, to his grave, Billy never believed he was wrong in putting me in the hospital. I, on the other hand, would never forgive him for putting me there and now that I was leaving, wished I had taken your grandmother and the kids and had gone in the first place, instead of facing that hospital. I still have nightmares about that place.

"My dad and I hadn't spoken since I got out of the car on the day of my release. And because emotions still ran high, he thought a letter would be the best way to communicate with me."

As Frank drove north on Highway 61, Liam pulled a letter

out of his sportcoat.

Frank said, "That's the actual letter?"

"Yes, I saved it."

Liam read,

"Dear Liam:

I know you are unhappy and I know you are just stubborn enough to go. If it makes you feel any better your mother is furious with me over this whole ordeal. She will never forgive me and I'm thinking, neither will you.

Be that as it may, and as much as you disagree, I feel like I did the right thing whether you like it or not. I'm still not comfortable with your drinking and gambling habits.

After much thought, the following is what I will agree to do for you; again you decide what you want.

I will not allow you to sell your farm right away. The land is too valuable and is gaining in value every year. To sell now would be throwing good money after bad. There are plenty of farmers around here who would be glad to rent your land and your house. This will give you a nice annual income, whatever you decide to pursue. You will have the opportunity to sell your land when your youngest offspring turns eighteen. By then it will yield tenfold what it yields now.

Secondly, I will agree to give you the lump sum of five thousand dollars, whether you go to Dubuque or Omaha, which should be more than sufficient to get you started. It should leave you money left for your education or whatever you see fit.

Liam, I know there are unresolved issues and you have a great deal of animosity toward me. I reiterate, I did what I thought was best. I do not ask your forgiveness, nor do I think I need it. You are hardly innocent in all this and in your soul searching I believe you will arrive at that. I only ask for your understanding.

Your Father,

William

"Frank, the year was 1926 and within a month of receiving this letter, I made arrangements to rent my land and home to a local farmer and his young family, and left Delmar forever."

As they drove north Frank glanced to the west. There was a temporary break in the cloud cover catching the full moon hanging helplessly in the morning sky just above the western horizon, a transparent wafer ready to be consumed by the morning light.

Liam said, "Take this next exit right."

Frank said, "I thought you said Highway 136? That's another three miles."

"This is a short cut."

Frank got off where his granddad had told him and headed five miles northeast into Delmar, Iowa.

For some reason, after hearing all of this, Frank thought that Delmar was going to be spectacular. To his disappointment, it was just like any other small town in the Midwest. From a distance he saw the small water tower standing watch over the town. The word Delmar was written on it and it reminded Frank of the upper torso of the Tin Man in *The Wizard of Oz*, all silver with a red painted hat. There was Main Street, one bar, a Farmer's Supply dealer, with four large and four smaller grain bins he supposed were full of corn. He looked to his left and saw Delmar City Hall, which surprised him; it was a nice building and rather ornate for a town this size. As he scanned the town further he noticed a diner and St Patrick's Catholic Church, resting on a hill overlooking the small burg. What caught his eye, though, was the Orphan Train museum in the heart of town. He expected the rest but a museum in a town of just over five hundred people?

Frank said, "A museum?"

Liam said, "It's a museum now, but originally it was the depot where we left town. They call it the Orphan Train museum because in the late nineteenth century the orphan train came through Delmar."

"What's the orphan train?"

"From the mid-nineteenth century to the early part of this century, there was a mass immigration into the US from all over the world. Many kids ended up just like my dad, orphaned and unwanted in a strange country. So they got the idea of loading them up and sending them to rural America where they might find a nice home. Let's go have a look."

They took a left off of Main Street and headed north and then east into a gravel parking lot. They got out of the car and walked up to the platform where trains used to come and go. Behind it stood a small building, painted red and yellow and filled with mementos, old pictures and propaganda from an age gone by, but a time someone didn't want forgotten. Just to the south of the depot sat an old Chicago Central caboose that stood sentry over the Veterans Memorial Park that was across the street. The memories came flooding back for Liam. Overwhelmed, he sat down to catch his breath on the cement stairs that ran up to the front door.

Frank sat down next to him and Liam said, "It was the hardest day of my life – and I've had some hard ones."

"You mean the day you left?"

"Yes. Leaving home, friends, family to a place unknown and never once did I take any ownership in what I was doing. Frank, I blamed it all on my dad, it was all *his* fault. When in reality it was all my doing. I was the unhappy one, drinking and gambling too much, not my dad. I was the one with the problems, I was the one who killed a man and, rather than facing them, I ran. I once heard that fear is an acronym for fuck everything and run."

Frank, shocked at his granddad's last statement, began to laugh. He was a typical seventeen-year-old kid who was always delighted in hearing someone drop an F-bomb. But particularly so when it came from somewhere unusual and wholly unexpected, like an eighty-three-year-old man sitting with his bony ass on the steps of a train depot museum in the middle of nowhere.

Liam, witnessing his grandson's laughter and never one to shy away from a good laugh, joined him, and found that it eased the pain of the memory.

Liam said, "Boy was I a runner. When things got tough here I ran to Omaha as if all my problems would go away there."

"Did they?"

"Hell no, they got worse, until I realized that I was the one with the problem, not anybody else. But by then it was too late, the damage was done. That's why I have so many regrets, son. It wasn't just me who got hurt in this deal. Let's go, I want to show you something, show you why we came. Well, why I thought we had come, but now I can see that it was for far more than that."

"Who else got hurt?"

"Your grandmother, your aunt and uncles, your lovely mother, everyone around me for Christ's sake."

"Far more than what?"

"This trip is turning out to be far more than what I was planning."

They drove south and then east out of town on Highway 136 heading toward Clinton, Iowa. They were on a rapidly curving road for three or four miles when they suddenly came upon a painted, wooden arrow road sign pointing south with the word "Petersville" on it.

Liam said, "Take a right at the arrow that says Petersville."

They turned onto a hilly gravel road and journeyed up and down for three or four more miles further into oblivion. They passed several, well groomed, Iowa farm houses when off the horizon to the south they saw the steeple of a church.

Liam pointed to the steeple and said, "That's it, boy."

"What's it?"

"That's Petersville."

"All I see is a church, a rectory, a one room school house and a cemetery."

"Well, that's all that's left. The church is Immaculate Conception. That's where I was baptized and married."

"It's in the middle of nowhere."

The church stood on the southwest corner of a deserted crossroads, with empty cornfields as far as the eye could see. To the left of the locked church was an empty church rectory, made of the same dark red brick that held together the church, across the gravel parking lot stood a whitewashed, wooden, one room schoolhouse that hadn't been used in fifty years. Just beyond that to the South was a small cemetery.

The temperature had reached into the low fifties and the pewter skies hung so low and thick that it felt like they might wash their hair in it, Frank wiping it from his glasses and forehead.

Liam stood trembling on his walking stick. Salted tears and spitting mist flowed down his cheeks and onto the front of his jacket. His lip quivered and he let out an audible sigh. Frank had to look away; he never could take watching someone cry without joining them.

Frank looked up to the church with its tan stone foundation, red brick walls, beautiful stain glassed windows of saints and green slate roof, thinking the Irish always had to have something green. He then stared at the white steeple, shrouded in the mist and knew then that this was his place too. There was a large black walnut tree that defended the front of the church, making sure the Blessed Sacrament inside was kept safe from intruders.

Liam said to Frank, "This is where I went to grade school and high school and that..." He couldn't finish his sentence as he pointed to the cemetery. Frank grabbed him under his arm and they walked to the place that, Frank now speculated, was the very reason for their trip across Iowa. The thought crossed his mind, "The low lying clouds, the mist and the rolling hills, this is how he had always heard the old people describe Ireland, and this was why they must have stayed here."

A brown, rusted wrought iron fence protected the graveyard and the latch that held the gate shut was partially rusted and squeaked as it was lifted. He noticed the huge evergreen trees that stood as great Celtic soldiers in a large circle watching over the hallowed earth just inside the fence. The gate swung in and the moment they stepped on the wet, spongy sod of this antediluvian and sacred burial ground, Frank felt a sensation he had never experienced before. He was light headed and his heart seemed full and contented as if he were welcome here. He didn't walk but three steps when he saw the large tombstone that said, WILLIAM and KATHERINE O'CONLAN. Then he saw the tombstones of Will, Fiona, Cheryl, Francis, Margaret, Vince and Gene and their spouses. Liam was the only one left out and now Frank understood why he had to come back. He would be the only one not buried here.

With his glasses off and his hand over his eyes, Liam stood weeping like a dejected child. He crumbled to a sitting position and reached out for the tombstone of his mother and father. And Christ's agony in the garden flashed through Frank's mind like a strobe light making everything seem slower than it really was.

Then, as if Frank was not there, Liam said, "Dad, I'm so sorry for everything I put you through. And even after I left you still took care of me. I was such an ungrateful bastard."

Liam said this with such intensity and remorse that Frank felt his wound, intuitively understanding its depth and pain and discerning that the healing would come only by cauterizing deep to burn the cancer that infected his soul. With that the sky opened up and poured down waters as if from a baptismal fount from heaven pouring down to cleanse Liam of his most painful sin and cool the burn. He lay flat on the ground and continued his self-admonition purging himself of all his wrongs and begging anyone who would listen for forgiveness. And it came.

He stood up and seemed stronger and more determined than Frank had seen him yet on this trip. He said, as if nothing had happened and he wasn't sodden with mud and drenched to the bone, "Follow me, Frank."

Frank followed him to the back of the cemetery where they came upon a sepulcher. Written on the tomb were John and Nancy Power. He said, "This is John Power, the man who rescued my dad, my Uncle Pat and my Aunt Nancy from the orphanage in Syracuse. What a man he was."

"Tell me about him."

"All in due time son, all in due time."

CHAPTER 7
THE SCAM

They drove back to Delmar and Liam was feeling relief from a seeming gift of absolution given to him in the small cemetery.

He said, "Frank, we have one more stop to make, one I should've made a long time ago."

They drove north on 136 out of Delmar and came to another cemetery. Liam said, "Frank pull in here."

Frank said, "Where?"

"Here, the cemetery."

"Frank said, "What the hell?"

"You'll see."

They drove into the cemetery and all the way to the back where the road finally ended. They got out and walked in the soaking grass all the way to the back corner of the cemetery where and old grave with a decaying gray headstone that simply said, "Rest in Peace."

Frank said, "Who's this."

Liam said, "This is the hobo I hit."

Frank stood a bit awkwardly and Liam said, "Frank, why

don't you head back to the car and give me a moment."

After ten minutes or so Liam jumped into the car and said, "Frank, take me home."

Frank smiled and said, "Let's do it."

They drove the five miles down 136 in silence, Frank glancing occasionally over at his granddad, waiting for him to continue his tale or maybe fall asleep. Liam did neither. It was as if he were in a contemplative mood and trying to decide what he wanted to say next or maybe where he wanted to start.

They headed south on 61 making their way to I-80 West when Liam said, "Son, you'd think I'd learned my lesson, but no. I just knew in my head that Omaha was going to save me. But a move, geographically, rarely does that. I've learned in my old age that it has to be a move spiritually and internally; it has to be a fearless and moral inventory of ourselves. When we're ready to remove all those old and ugly character defects that cause us to stumble, when we're ready to admit our own faults and do something about them, that's when we finally come to happiness. Taking this sinful old world as it is and not as we would have it, but I wasn't ready to live life on life's terms, no no, it was all about me, during that time in my life."

Frank said, "You mean, when you and the family moved to Omaha?"

"Yes. During that time, I tended to make careless financial decisions. My dad was the businessman, I wasn't. After arriving in the city, I was having serious second thoughts that maybe leaving the farm was a mistake because the adjustment to the city was tough. It felt all wrong.

"We moved in to a rundown, cramped apartment, which was a difficult transition from the large farmhouse. In hindsight I should've just bought a house with the money dad had given me. After we were settled in, I found work downtown on the dock at Paxton-Gallagher, a local retailer, unloading merchandise for eight dollars a week. Soon the farm life didn't seem half-bad. But my stubborn Irish pride wouldn't allow me to return to the farm with my tail between my legs. You know the prodigal son.

"Again my thoughts began to wander to school. I'd see the students on the streetcar on my way to work and I pined for that life. But with the long days on the dock and a growing family, those thoughts were put on the back burner.

"As you know, I'd come from wealth, so the menial labor coupled with the lack of opportunity for school were hard to take.

"The crew that I worked with were hard working men but lacked education and literacy, leaving us with little in common. These guys lived for the barstool and spent their evenings there. I knew my tendencies and wanted to avoid trouble. Yet even then I denied any problem and so rationalized that one night of drinking and gambling a week wasn't going to hurt anyone. It didn't matter if I stumbled in on Friday Night, half in the jar, with a few hundred less in the family dole that was given to me before I left the farm.

"We would meet at one of two public houses downtown, Theodore's or Sullivan's. When I'd first arrive Friday night, I would sit at that barstool trying to figure a way out. I knew there was always a game in the back. When I was sober it was easy to resist; I would just walk away. But after a couple of cold ones my resolve lessened. I would jump in with both feet. I won sometimes, but lost most times and within a couple of years I had gambled away the majority of the five grand I'd been given to buy a house."

Liam hung his head in shame. Tears began to roll down his chin and leave dark wet stains on his pale blue dress shirt. Frank looked over at his granddad, but this time he didn't look away to keep his emotions in check. He looked back at the road, vision blurred with his own tears. And with his right hand he reached over and grabbed the old hand that involuntarily shook and held it tight, a moment of solidarity between an old scalawag and a young scoundrel. For Frank, an epiphany, that life was a lesson not just for the young, but for everyone willing to search for the truth.

Frank said, "Granddad, it was only five grand."

Liam said, "No son, it was much more than that. It was a selfish bastard who put his wife and kids, people who loved him unconditionally, at risk."

Then Liam laughed and said, "Thank God for Johnny Dooling."

Frank said, "Johnny who?"

Liam said, "Johnny Dooling. A guardian angel caught in the great abyss between heaven and hell, who showed up in my life just in the nick of time."

"When I began to see the ugly monster rearing itself once again, I felt myself being dragged back to that familiar and comfortable place. My universe, my hiding place, you know, my storytelling in taverns, losing myself there, finding my way out one syllable, one word, one poetic stanza at a time. When I was lost in that maze of history, fiction and creative license, magic happened and the weight of my world would slip away. I would turn the ordinary into the extraordinary and take the audience with me.

"Soon the word spread and by mid-week the boys on the dock would be asking me where I was going on Friday night. The place would swell to capacity and I would be the center of attention, holding court while patrons whispered their orders to the cocktail waitress, hanging on my every word; people buying me beers and the stories would go for hours.

"One night at closing time, after a few too many, I sat with a fellow named Jimmy O'Brien. I had gotten to know O'Brien through the taverns and thought he was a stand up guy only because he was an Irishman. Believe me this guy was anything but stand up, he was a mean son of a bitch and I was about to find out the hard way.

"I knew O'Brien was a sweet talker and a pretty boy. But what I didn't know was that O'Brien was a mean son of a bitch that would've sold his mom for a buck. During the day, he was a bag man for the local brewery."

Frank said, "Bag man?"

"Yeah, the brewery would give him a bag full of cash and he would drive around paying off tavern owners to keep their beer on tap, a totally illegal practice done under the bar. At night he was a runner for the Irish mob in town with ties to Detroit."

Frank said, "Why Detroit?"

Liam said, "At the time, the Irish mob controlled Detroit and their arm reached across the Midwest.

"The diversity of O'Brien's night job was what he liked most. He would run cash for the gambling operations, pay off dirty cops to look the other way, deliver messages to and from lieutenants, pimp for the prostitutes and bust a leg or two when a john got out of line or a deadbeat wasn't paying his gambling debts.

"O'Brien, as bad as he was, for some reason really liked me, he enjoyed my company and, like everyone else, was captivated by my outlandish stories. O'Brien, as busy as he was in the evening, would make a point to be around for my tales.

"One night after a story or two and the tavern had quieted down, he and I had a chat. I made the mistake of telling the man that I had plans to buy a house. He instantly wanted to know how a dockworker came by that kind of cash. I let it slip that I had some inheritance and, of course, his wheels started turning. He knew my fondness for a good game of poker, so he invited me to a game that following Friday night, said it was a bunch of hens.

"Being naïve to city ways, I didn't realize at the time he was playing to my ego. Plus, I learned later, all he really wanted to know was what kind of cash I really had. I spent the entire next week debating whether to get into the game or not. I hadn't won in a long while, my luck had been terrible, but to my gambler's sick mind, that *had* to change.

"The following Friday night I found myself in the back of Theodore's in a high stakes poker game. I'd brought my last hundred dollars with me. I never told the man that that's all I had left from my inheritance. I think he was thinking that I had thousands and he wanted a piece of that.

"As it turned out the whole thing back fired on him. That night I sat down with my last hundred bucks. I came to Omaha with five-thousand from the farm and my drinking and gambling whittled it down to a hundred lousy dead presidents. I told you I hadn't learned my lesson. I was out of control.

"Anyway, my luck changed that night for a lot of different reasons. The first is that I was just plain hot. I won nine hundred bucks that night and walked out of there with a thousand in cash. I never felt so good in my life, my luck was finally changing, but again not for any reasons that I was aware of at the time. O'Brien came in after the game and realized how I had skinned his flunkies and he was furious.

"The following Wednesday O'Brien came by the docks and invited me to Theodore's for another little game on Friday night with, according to him, a bunch of chumps. I thought, "Great," and just knew my luck would hold and I'd skin this cat for another grand or maybe two. What I hadn't figured out was what this cat was going to do to me when he found out I was playing on his money and his money only. He had nothing but a hundred bucks to squeeze out of me.

"Johnny Dooling overheard the conversation. He was a 130-pound Irish kid I worked with from the streets of North Omaha."

Frank said, "He was from North Omaha?"

"Yeah, in those days the Irish ran North Omaha."

"Wait a minute, I thought Sheeley Town was in South Omaha and that's where the Irish were."

"No, John Sheeley was a wealthy Irishman who made all of his money in meatpacking. All his meatpacking plants were in South Omaha and that's why they called that area of town Sheeley Town, but he lived out north in Sacred Heart Parish with all the rest of the Paddy's.

"Anyway, Dooling and I had been working together on the dock for the past few years and had gotten to be good friends. For his size he was a tough son of a gun and in his day he could go beer for beer with the best of them. And even though he was small, the few people who messed with him ever wanted a piece of him again. In his day, Johnny Dooling was the best pitchman in the city and his legendary card game scams landed him in jail several times. Finally, as he said, he saw the error of his ways and gave it all up. He'd been on the straight and narrow for over five years.

Johnny said, 'Liam what were you doing talking to a hood like Jimmy O'Brien?'"

"I said, 'He's not a hood. He helped me win nine hundred bucks last week in a poker game with a bunch of hens.'"

"Johnny said, 'Oh man, you won nine hundred bucks in one of his matches?'"

"I said, 'Yeah, my luck finally changed.'"

"He said, 'Your luck finally changed, huh?'"

"I said, 'What? A guy can't have a winning night every once in a while?'"

"He said, 'Do you know who Jimmy O'Brien is?'"

"I said, 'I thought I did.'"

"He said, 'Look Liam, he's the bag man for the Harms brewery during the day.'"

"'What's that mean?'"

"'That means the guy goes to the brewery, they give him a bag of hundred dollar bills. He then spends the day in the taverns insuring their beer stays on tap. At night he works for the Miller family.'"

"'Who?'"

"'Man alive, Liam, do I have to hold your hand?'"

"Embarrassed now, I said, 'You don't have to be such a hard ass, Johnny.'"

"Johnny said, 'Okay. Look Liam, I'm not trying to be a hard ass. You're my friend and I'm just trying to look out for you, okay?'"

"'Okay, sorry.'"

"'The Millers are the Irish mob out of Detroit. They have an operation here as well as connections back to the old county, you know, the brotherhood. Jimmy is nothing more than a henchman for them. He runs money and breaks legs when they need him to. He's a mean son of a bitch and not to be taken lightly.'"

"I was flustered and said, 'Well what happens if I don't show and just bank all my winnings?'"

"'Not a good idea, Liam.'"

"Then Johnny Dooling's face lit up like an octogenarian's birthday cake."

"I said, 'What?'"

"He said, 'Liam, my man, revenge is sweet.'"

"I said, 'What are you talking about?'"

"As we swept the warehouse and put away pallets, Dooling told me about his sordid past. How he had straightened out and had not played hard for five or six years.

"Dooling said, 'But before I went to jail for the last time, I took one last screwing from Mr. O'Brien. He was playing at the table I was working and I had these guys dead to rights. See, I can count cards and knew what everyone was holding. Didn't matter anyway because I had a full house, kings over jacks and nobody was going to do anything about that. It was pure luck, which does happen once in awhile. That's when the cops walked in, cops on O'Brien's payroll. There was sixteen thousand dollars in the pot. As they cuffed all the participants, O'Brien put the dough in a bank bag while we watched and he walked out the back door.

"Dooling said, 'Now I'm in the back of the paddy wagon with these fools and I'm thinking, how in the hell did he do that in front of the cops? He was gambling with the rest of us. I thought I was working the scam. I looked at my partner, he leaned his head to the cops and he said, 'They're dirty.' That's when the nightstick came down on his head and I realized that the son of a bitch had scammed me. The pot would have been my biggest payoff; I could've retired. Instead I end up in jail for six months and working on a dock for the rest of my life, all because I was out-scammed by that turd O'Brien. Liam this is just the opportunity that I've been looking for. Did O'Brien play last week?'"

"I said, 'No.'"

"Johnny said, 'Good, he's gotten too big for his own britches. Where's the game Friday?'"

"I said, 'Sullivan's.'"

Johnny said, 'Buzzers and mirrors'"

"I said, 'What?'"

"He said, 'The room is set up with small angled mirrors so a guy upstairs can see your cards. One of the chairs has a silent buzzer sending signals to one of the guys at the table. He doesn't have that set up at Theo's and he's not taking any chances that you'll take him again.'"

"I said, 'I'm in trouble.'"

"'On the contrary, you let me worry about that. You can introduce me as another chump to join the game. I'll play the part and we'll take them for everything they got. Understand one thing though; we play until closing, no matter how it goes. You have to trust me on this one. But I'm going to ask a couple of favors.'"

"I said, 'What's that?'"

"'I'm not going to let you piss away these winnings and I'm not going to listen to you whine about your bad luck. The old, if it weren't for your bad luck you wouldn't have any luck at all, crap. You have to promise you'll buy that beautiful Kathleen the house you should've bought her seven years ago and you have to promise you'll quit drinking and gambling.'"

"'Deal.'"

"'Bullshit, you look me in the eye and promise.'"

"'I promise.'"

Frank, totally mesmerized now, said, "Did you keep your promise?"

Liam said, "You'll find out. We smiled, shook hands and walked off the dock."

"Thursday, over the lunch hour, Dooling went to Sullivan's for a roast beef sandwich. When he was done he went to the rest room and from there slipped into the back room when the bartender was looking the other way.

"Under the round poker table, by the chair closest to the door, there was a silent button. The wire ran down the leg, across the floor under the carpeting and up the wall to the office upstairs where the mirror man worked. Dooling promptly disconnected the wire and smiled as he walked out.

"Friday morning came and I was as nervous as Monsignor O'Donnell hearing confessions in a whorehouse and that son of a bitch Dooling was smiling and acting as if it was any other day. The day passed slowly; Friday night couldn't come soon enough for either of us.

"The whistle blew and we headed to Sullivan's on the street car. On the way, Johnny explained how we were to work this thing.

"First of all he told me no drinking – we had to be sharp. Then he said something kind of funny. He said that he'd do the math."

Frank said, "What'd that mean?"

Liam said, "Remember how I told you he was one of the best pitch men in town?"

"Yeah."

"That's because he could count cards. He always had a pretty good idea of what everyone was holding. He told me that if he wanted me to take one, two or three cards, he'd tap me on the foot one, two or three times. And I knew enough about poker to know which cards to lay down and which ones to hold."

"So, you were nervous?"

"As a long tail cat in a room full of rocking chairs."

They both laughed.

"We walked into the back room at Sullivan's, I made some quick intros and the game began. It was five dollars to ante, no limit. It was another great night. I won a hand and then Johnny won and so on and so forth until we both had enormous amounts of cash lying in front of us.

"Now, the idiot who was the button man kept looking around nervously. He hadn't got a signal all night due to Johnny's handiwork earlier in the day. To see the look on the man's face, it was all I could do not to laugh. Finally, at one thirty, the men around the table threw in their cards and called it quits. Johnny and I were ready to bag our winnings and get the hell out of there when O'Brien walked in the back door. When he saw Johnny he pulled out a gun."

Frank said, "He what?"

"Yeah, the guy actually pulled out a huge hand gun and I about wet my pants."

Frank said, "No kidding?"

"Dooling, acting like there was nothing to worry about in the world, actually started filling a bank bag with our winnings. Here I am, sweating and shaking, looking at this gun and Dooling's filling the damn bag.

"But then O'Brien suddenly looked confused, like something was not right here and he hadn't figured it out."

Frank said, "You mean like why you and Dooling had all of O'Brien's cash?"

Liam said, "That'd be about it. But then I saw something that changed my mind about O'Brien."

Frank said, "What?"

"He smiled, but it wasn't a nice smile. It was a malevolent smile, as if he just figured out the problem, and it sent shivers up my spine. I knew at that moment that the gun he held was no ruse. He wouldn't hesitate to shoot someone and the atmosphere became so intense I couldn't breathe. He suddenly bent down and saw that his wire had been disconnected. When he stood upright he pointed the gun at Dooling's head and told him if he put one more bill in his bag that he'd blow his head off."

Frank looked over at his granddad and said, "You're really kidding me now, right?"

Liam said, "Lad, I wish I was. I still shake thinking about it. I was shaking and had been since I saw the gun. Before that I was having the time of my life. I'd never been in on anything like this before and when I realized what idiots these guys were, I couldn't believe O'Brien trusted them. But I never thought that people would start pulling guns either. Had I known I wouldn't have gone.

"But Dooling didn't even flinch, I was stunned, the son of a bitch kept loading the bag with cash and I was thinking, this is it, it's over, we're dead where we stand. Then like an angel of God, Officer Bill O'Leary, Lieutenant on the police force, followed by ten police officers with shotguns walked in and surrounded the table. O'Leary and his boys had been in the front room soon after Sullivan had cleared his customers away for the night and they heard everything. This was the real scam that Johnny had been planning without my knowledge. He'd been working with the cops to get O'Brien for a while now and this was the perfect opportunity. Johnny smiled as he continued to stuff his bank bag, picking up both his pile and mine.

"O'Brien was so mad by now he had lost his reason, turned and pointed the gun at O'Leary. The officer closest to O'Brien used the stock of his gun to knock his arm off course and the bullet went through the ceiling. He then put the butt of his gun to O'Brien's head and knocked him cold. They cuffed him and his boys and dragged them off in the paddy wagon.

"Officer O'Leary, Johnny Dooling and I stood in the back room after the commotion was over. O'Leary laughed and I looked at Johnny and said, "You mean you were in on this, with the cops?"

"'Johnny said, "Do you think I'd start bagging my winnings while a guy's holding a gun on me without some kind of back up?'"

"'I said, "Why didn't you tell me?'"

"'Would you've come?'"

"'Well...'"

"'See.'"

"I laughed and said, 'I was wondering what you were doing.'"

"Johnny said, 'He did the same thing to me when he scammed me, so I wanted to rub his lousy nose in it. Only I did it on the up and up with legit cops.'"

"O'Leary said, 'Well Johnny, a deal's a deal. You boys get the winnings, minus a grand for my boys, and I don't want to hear from either of you again.'"

"He walked out. Johnny and I laughed out loud and hugged both of us shaking from the adrenaline rush. Johnny didn't make it to work on Monday and I received a postcard from Miami Beach a month later."

Frank looked at Liam and said, "So, what did you do with the dough?"

"Kept my promise and the next month I bought Kathleen the house I live in now on North 42nd Street."

Frank said, "How about the gambling and drinking?"

"Never gambled another dime in my life after that night, it scared me straight. The drinking was a different story. I drank for another ten years until I hit my bottom. I was on the verge of losing the house, my job and my family when another angel of God entered the picture when he introduced me to a little group called AA and I've been sober since. It didn't mean my life got any easier, but it helped me deal with the demons that haunted me where I lived."

The wind began to pick up and dark cloud cover moved in. Then they heard the winter thunder that meant nothing but trouble in the plains. The rain soon turned to ice pellets that began to snap off the windshield.

Thanking God silently, they came to the I-480 and I-80 interchange meaning that were getting close now. They took I-80 south for another twenty-two miles toward Council Bluffs and east into Omaha. By the time they were within a mile of the Missouri River Bridge the highway had turned into glare ice upon which they crept, both sweating the last leg of their journey.

As they reached the bridge, Frank glanced quickly over his left shoulder to check his blind spot to make a lane change and when he looked forward again Liam screamed, "Frank, watch out!"

A semi truck in front of them had jackknifed on the bridge. As the trailer slid sideways it crossed both lanes. Frank slammed on the brakes to no avail and at fifty miles an hour and perpendicular to the trailer they slammed head on into its side, shearing off the roof of the station wagon as they slid under the trailer above. Frank heard a loud crunch and the windshield shattering, and then everything went black.

CHAPTER 8
THE PASSING

The next day was the longest day the O'Conlan clan had ever spent together as a family. Frank rested, teetering between life and death, in a coma in the ICU at Bergan Mercy hospital. They would only allow Frank's mother and father in to visit and even then for only short periods.

It was ten p.m. when they walked back into the waiting room to join the other nine children, cousins, aunts, uncles, friends and extended family. The ten o'clock news had just come on and as they all looked up, the commentator said, "In other news tonight, Liam John O'Conlan, eighty-three, of Omaha was killed late last evening on an icy I-80 Missouri River Bridge when the car, his grandson, Frank McGrath, was driving collided with a jackknifed semi truck trailer. McGrath survived the collision but is reported in critical condition at a local Omaha hospital. Weather and sports are next."

They all stared in awe at the finality of it all; no one said a word.

Frank knew he was lying down, but he had no idea where he was. He could hear a woman talking with his mother and father but he couldn't move a muscle or open his eyes to tell them he was okay. And for some reason this didn't seem to bother him.

At times he would lose consciousness and then suddenly be awake. At other times his mind would explode into incredible colors, like he had taken some kind of hallucinogen. And then for no apparent reason his life would suddenly flash before his eyes. He recalled hearing stories like this when people were about to die and so, he figured this was his time. But he would not go without a fight.

Then it happened. In some kind of sub-consciousness, he heard the heart monitor that they had hooked up to him send out a long, loud perpetual whine, informing anyone within ear shot of his heart failure.

Frank floated aimlessly above his body and watched as his dad raced to the hall screaming for help. He turned back and saw his mother on her knees, brushing his hair out of his face, rattling her rosary beads, begging for the Blessed Mother's intercession and he saw the silent suffering in her eyes.

His head suddenly jerked up as he was introduced to the most brilliant light he had ever seen. He was not blinded though, looking straight at it and was instinctively drawn to it by a will other than his own. He felt a love that was so intense he knew intuitively that, had he been in his body, it would have exploded into a million pieces. He raced toward it wanting nothing more than to be totally engulfed in it. He saw spirits there that he seemed to know and they were cheering when he stopped. He looked to his left and there stood Liam, laughing out loud and pointing. Frank was so overjoyed at this high he was feeling that he went to hug Liam and went straight through him.

Liam said, "Francis, you have to go back."

Frank said, "Right, I'm not going anywhere, this place rocks!"

Liam said, "Your time's not up, lad."

Frank said, “Don’t say that, Granddad. I want to stay here with you.”

Liam said, “Sorry, son, but we’ve still got work to do.”

Frank said, “What do you mean, we?”

Liam smiled brightly and said, “You’ll see.”

Then suddenly, as if by some supernatural slingshot, Frank was slammed back into his body. He opened his eyes and looked up as the doctor held the shock paddles staring intently at him.

CHAPTER 9
THE NIGHTMARE, THE GHOST AND THE FAILURE

Other than some seriously bruised ribs, a couple of broken fingers and some stitches on the crown of his head where it had hit the windshield, Frank was okay and really just glad to be alive. He was out of the ICU in a couple of days, out of the hospital in a week and within two weeks was catching up on lost time at school. But he was no longer the same loud, obnoxious teenager that had left for Iowa that Saturday morning two weeks ago. He was quiet and contemplative now and spent long hours reliving the time he spent with his granddad and the story he had told him. It had become a sacred memory for him and the more time passed and the more he thought about it the angrier he became. He was angry at the loss, angry at life and lonelier than he had ever been before.

And he was confused. Did he really have the out of body experience? Or was that all a bunch of baloney because of all the morphine they poured into him? But if it wasn't did he really see his granddad? And how about the words his granddad said, "Your times not up. We've got work to do?" What was that supposed to mean? How in the hell could *we* have work to do, the guy was dead?

He didn't say much at school and he didn't say much at home. He didn't wanted to talk about it afraid they would all think he was nuts. What? Was this some kind of sick practical joke God was playing on him? Or, more likely, some sick practical joke his granddad was playing on him and having a good laugh on the other side, the jerk.

His mother worried day and night about him. Frank McGrath was not the same boy.

One evening in mid-February, a month or so after the accident, Frank went to bed early. He had been depressed, his mom wanted him to see a counselor and he didn't want to talk about any of it. Frank was an avid reader and usually couldn't get to sleep without at least a chapter or two of some good fiction. But not tonight. He was so tired that his head wasn't on the pillow for thirty seconds before he emitted the first small snores of early sleep.

He could feel the ocean swell around him and the stench of human waste and rotting flesh became unbearable. Many people were dying in the hull; some had been dead for days.

They'd been at sea for three weeks since leaving Ireland. They were finally getting over the seasickness when their worst fears came true. A storm was pursuing them like Orion stalking his eternal prey. To keep the ship afloat, the sailors were forced to batten down the hatches.

The hull, where they resided, shoulder to shoulder, contained no lavatory. All forms of human waste were placed in open containers with no way of disposing it.

The food was rancid and water was scarce. The air was filled with typhus and to avoid it was to quit breathing. The hard rain and high seas started five days ago. They hadn't had a breath of fresh air or seen the light of day since.

Despair - or even worse – resignation, hung in the air. They'd lost their fight, their will to live. For five days the storm raged. By the fourth day the only noises heard above the rain and waves crashing into the ship were the screams of those who had gone daft, or the last scream of pain before death paid a merciful visit.

Most just stared at the floor or at the hatch in the ceiling above, praying that God would relieve them of their misery. Even death would mean liberation; no purgatory awaited any of these suffering souls.

These God-fearing people, wondering, for the first time in their lives, whether God existed and if He did why He allowed this.

A young mother lost her seven-year-old son; a nine-year-old daughter held her daddy's hand as he died. Grandma and Grandpa passed away holding hands, a best friend, an older brother, Mom. All dead. The storm raged, and still they wouldn't open the damn hatch. He felt his sanity beginning to waver. A panic began to set in, a need to breathe fresh air.

The storm was not letting up, perhaps worsening. The ship heaved and rolled in a sea bent on destroying them. As the vessel moved up and down in the violent waves, it moaned its understanding of their misery. Just then a ferocious wave hit the ship with such force that he fell from his bunk.

Frank found himself lying on the floor, wondering where the hell he was. Then the nightmare came to mind and he thought, "Man, what was that all about? It was so real." He stood up, brushed himself off and got ready to jump back under the covers, when he looked up and there he was, sitting at the foot of his bed, the ghost of his dear, dead Granddad.

Frank tried to scream but nothing came out. Feeling a sudden chill that shook him, he tried to jump under the covers but was frozen in his tracks. His eyes darted back and forth and the ghost sitting on the bed let out a warm friendly laugh that could have only come from his granddad.

Frank said, "Gramps, what're you doing?"

Liam said, "I told you we had business to finish, didn't I?"

Frank said, "Yeah, I guess so, but I didn't expect this. What business?"

Liam said, "I hadn't finished the story."

"So, that's what you meant?"

"Yep."

"And it wasn't all baloney?"

"What wasn't?"

"The out of body experience. I thought I was losing my mind."

"No, you're not losing your mind. We met there."

"So, you're telling me that I could've gone toward that fantastic light, but instead you sent me back to this misery for a lousy story?"

Liam laughed and said, "I was just the messenger. Story or no, lad, your time wasn't up. You were heading back anyway. I just thought finishing the story would make it a little more interesting."

"I thought you had told me the whole story?"

"I told you my whole story. But aren't you a little curious about Billy coming over from Ireland? How all that happened? There's some great stuff there."

"I never thought of that."

"What did you think of the nightmare?"

"Scary stuff."

"I thought it was a nice touch, a little precursor."

"You did that?"

"Yes."

"Thanks a lot."

"What?"

"Oh, I just love having the shit scared out of me."

"Come on lad, how do you think your ancestors felt. They lived that nightmare. That's why I did it; give you a small taste of what they went through."

"Don't do me anymore favors."

"Okay, smart ass, do you want to hear the rest of the story or not? I'm on borrowed time here, boy."

"Is the Pope Catholic? Of course I do."

Liam smiled and said, "Good, I thought you'd feel that way. Let's get down to business."

There was a rocking chair in the corner that Frank had never seen before. Liam sat in it, lit his pipe, blew a large smoke ring and began.

Liam said, "First of all, Frank, now that I'm on this side, I know the *whole* story."

Frank said, "What do you mean the *whole* story?"

Liam said, "Do you remember when you were a little kid and you wondered why people had to die, why the avacado pit was so big, why an ostrich or emu couldn't fly or why the sky was blue?"

"Yeah, I guess so."

"Well, now that I'm on this side of the fence, I know the answer to all those questions."

"What are they?"

Liam said smiling, "You'll just have to wait, kid. Anyway, rather than telling you the story, I'm going to take you there and let you see it for yourself. Take my hand. Come on, don't be afraid."

"Take me where?"

"Ireland."

"Right."

"I'm serious."

"What? We're going to fly or what?"

"Take my hand, Mr.Cynic and find out."

Frank tentatively reached out and grabbed his granddad's hand. He felt a warm peaceful feeling come over him and suddenly felt himself being drawn down a long tunnel and he could hear his granddad's soothing voice. When Liam let go Frank found himself standing next to his granddad in a small village in Ireland.

Liam said, "Welcome to Upperchurch."

Frank said, "Welcome to where?"

Liam laughed and said, "Upperchurch. We're in Ireland, son. This village is located in north central Tipperary County in The Republic of Ireland. This is where your ancestors came from."

Frank looked around. The village was at the bottom of what seemed like a large bowl with great hills all around them that reached into a wide open blue sky. It occurred to him suddenly how green it was. He had never seen shades of green like this which were highlighted by the blue sky. The beauty of this countryside was overwhelming; and unlike the rural countryside he had seen in the middle of the United States it was not flat and unending.

Frank said, "How do they farm this, it's so hilly and undulating, not flat at all?"

"It wasn't easy, son. But unlike the big farms back home that feed the world, these were small family farmers who consumed what they grew. Instead of hundreds or thousands of acres, they would lease one acre and try to feed their families on that."

"They didn't own their land?"

"No, that was illegal."

"Illegal for a man to own a piece of land?"

"It was illegal for an Irishman to own land in Ireland. That was part of the English law."

"Who owned it, granddad?"

"The English landlords. When England invaded Ireland and began to run things, the King of England sent Earls to Ireland and gave them large tracts of land."

"Earls?"

"Yes. These men were part of the English ascendancy or like the upper crust in America. They were from wealthy families and they were loyal to the crown in England. They were lured by promises of huge wealth to leave England and take up residence in these large agricultural estates which were taken from Irish families and given to them. They would raise sheep, cattle, hogs, horses and any number of crops similar to the big farms and ranches back in Iowa and Nebraska. Most of what they raised was exported back to England. In the process they became exceedingly wealthy, paid huge tributes to the King in England and became known as landlords. The land you see around here?"

"Yeah."

"As pretty as it is, you saw it right away, is tough to farm. The landlords wanted nothing to do with it so they leased it to tenant farmers. These families would get ten maybe fifteen acres. They'd grow some wheat, barley, potatoes, maybe some turnips and with a milk cow and a horse they could squeak out a reasonable living, but nobody was getting rich."

There was a chill in the air and as Liam spoke steam floated aimlessly away from his words.

He continued, "Then there was the subtenant and there in lies the rub."

Frank said, "The rub?"

"Yeah. These subtenants came to be known as croppies because they would grow and live off their crops, in this case the potato. They were the poorest of the poor in the poorest country in Europe at the time."

"Why were they called subtenants?"

"Well they would lease a bit of land, an acre maybe less from the tenant. Then they would grow as many potatoes as they could and try to survive on that, which never seemed to be enough."

"Why only the potato?"

"Well actually it started a hundred or so years previous to the great famine. The potato was introduced into Ireland and they found that of all the crops it grew more easily and with greater abundance than other crops and so they became increasingly too dependent upon that one crop. But with the croppy, even as hearty as the potato crop was, it never seemed to be enough."

"What do you mean?"

"They'd grow as many potatoes as they could and they'd store them in a cool, dry pits in the ground but they never seemed to last long enough to get them to the next growing season. They'd always run out of food, so away the men would go to do some illegal fishing, trapping and hunting, anything to feed themselves."

Frank said, "So let me get this straight, it was illegal to read and write, go to school, own land, hunt, and fish, speak their own language and all this in their own country?"

"Not only that but it was also illegal to be a Catholic in Ireland for oh three hundred or so years."

"Seriously?"

"Seriously."

"Hey, you said something about the rub?"

"We'll get to that. Three things occurred to cause the greatest famine Europe was to ever know. I digress, my father never referred to it as a famine. He always said a famine is when there's no food. He called it a potato blight."

"Well there wasn't any food was there?"

"There was plenty of food, son, just none for the Irish. The Irish believe that God sent the potato blight, but the English government created the famine."

"Why?"

Let me explain. The first of the three was a fungus."

"A fungus?"

Liam, now getting a bit irritated with the interruptions said, "Yes, a fungus. Some spuds were imported from South America that had a foreign strain of fungus. Once it was introduced to Ireland it spread like wildfire throughout the island, and for five years wiped out the only food source for the croppies who represented a vast number of people in the country at the time."

"What was number two?"

"They knew nothing of plant rotation. They grew potatoes on the same plot year after year after year. This caused the soil to be depleted of all its richness and nutritional value."

"Okay, so what could possibly be worse than those two."

"Well that's where the English government comes in. You have to understand the problem as the Irish saw it. It was their people, their families who either starved or immigrated while food was exported through the countryside as they watched. They blamed the laissez-faire doctrine of the English parliament."

Frank said, "Laissez-faire doctrine?"

"The English government, who loved the Irish to help fight their wars and pay their taxes, did little to help. They said God was punishing the drunken Gael and Celt for our sinful, godless ways. So they absolved themselves of their sins, washed their hands and looked the other way. This way they didn't have to see the famished throngs dying in the countryside, even while exporting food out of Ireland right under the noses of the starving."

"You're lying."

"As God is my witness. Remember the English landlords and their large farms?"

"Yeah, so?"

"That was where all the food was, but they exported it to England. They turned a blind eye to all of it. You see they lived these lavish lifestyles, many lived way beyond their own means. They had to export the food because they had large bills to pay. In their eyes the croppies were filthy animals anyway. So what's a few million filthy animals starving to death? Am I right?"

Frank said, "It couldn't have happened."

"I wish it hadn't."

"What about the rub?"

"Well here's the hard part. I talked about the English landlord, the tenant and the subtenant, right?"

Frank said, "Right."

"Well, it wasn't just the English kicking the Irish off the land. There was also the Irish having to watch as their Irish brethren, whom they leased land to, leave their land. It was every family for themselves and survival of the fittest. So there were situations in which an Irish tenant had to watch a subtenant go and could do nothing about it. It just simply came down to either feeding your family or feeding your neighbors family, who can blame anybody? But the Irish a hundred and thirty years later still struggle with it."

Frank said, "What year did you say it was?"

Liam said, "It's the fall of 1846."

Frank said, "Wow."

Liam said, "That's right, boy. You're about to receive a most amazing gift."

"And that would be?"

"You're about to experience, first hand, what happened to one family during the great potato famine that started in 1846. It's not going to be pretty, Frank, so hold on."

Frank said, "It seems awfully quiet, no one around."

"Oh they're around all right. Francis, the countryside is full of hopeless people. One would imagine screaming in the night, fighting and gnashing of teeth. When in reality, what exists out there is silence. It's the silence of the starving, the silence of the desperate, the silence of the bewildered who are still not sure that this is happening. It's the silence of the children, bloated, eyes black with question and cold as death. It's the silence of the insane whispering to themselves, crazy from grief and wondering why."

CHAPTER 10
THE KING, THE TALISMAN AND LEAVING UPPERCHURCH FOREVER

Liam stared off into the distance. The drawn lines on his face created by years of worry and hardship were accentuated as the weight of what he had just described settled there. In his mind echoed the silence of the starving and it touched a raw nerve deep within him sending shock waves throughout his body.

He leaned heavily on his walking stick in need of extra support at the moment and said, "Your great, great Granddad was a man named Aidan O'Conlan, he was Billy's dad. He had taken a wife named Maureen McNulty and she had given him five children, three girls and two boys.

"The summer of 1846 in Ireland, Frank, had been unusual. The first six weeks were sunny and warm, so the potato crop was planted and grew wonderfully. The last six weeks, however, cool and wet weather set in and refused to let up. The fungus made its way into the crop throughout the island and the cool, wet weather allowed it a comfortable living space to prosper."

Frank and Liam were suddenly at a small harvest celebration. They had four or five jugs of poteen—potato whiskey—some dried fish and a fiddler. The villagers gathered every year to celebrate the finished harvest of that year's crop. The lean summer months of illegal fishing, hunting, trapping and scrounging were over and the potato pits were heaping. It was the largest crop they had yielded in recent memory. They ate, they drank, they danced, sang and told outlandish and wonderful stories. But most important, they forgot, at least for a while, the difficult life they led.

The next morning they all awoke to an oddly familiar stench in the air. The intense odor became stronger and seemed to permeate the fabric of the countryside; a certain familiar fear surfaced from thirty years previous.

Frank said, "Gramps, what's that godawful stink?"

Liam pointed and said, "You're about to find out."

Frank and Liam watched as Aidan O'Conlan went to his potato pits to investigate the reek when the nightmare of his youth returned to haunt him once more. He was a young boy during the blight of 1830 when he first smelled that horrible smell, a smell he could never forget. He crawled from pit to pit pulling out one spud after another; each went black and mushy in his hands. The foulness on the air was the blight, the stink of their largest potato crop in years, spoiled.

Liam said, "Frank, for the Irish now, life went from normally difficult to unbearable. The landlords were throwing tenants out of their cottages all over Ireland. Your ancestors, the O'Conlans and McNultys could do nothing but watch and wait."

Frank said, "Gramps, who're the hard asses over there throwing people out of their homes?"

Liam said, "Black and Tans."

Frank said, "Black and whats?"

"English soldiers sent by their government. They do the dirty work for the English landlords who own the land. They'd been looking for a way to get rid of the Irish croppies, move them off their land. The blight gave them a good excuse."

"What do you mean good excuse?"

"Well, if the croppies could no longer pay the rent then the landlords could legally throw them off the land."

Frank said, "How's that supposed to solve the problem?"

Liam said, "That depends on how you look at it. In the eyes of the English government, the trouble was the contemptible shanty Irish. Getting rid of them eliminated their predicament. In the eyes of the Irish, the problem was the English tyranny. And because of it, they were now starving, had no money and were forced out of their homes and off their land."

"That is so unfair."

"Now you're beginning to get a glimpse of why the Irish felt the way they did about the English government. And still do up in Ulster."

Liam and Frank stood in the center of the village of Upperchurch in Northern Tipperary County when Liam turned to the north, pointed and said, "Up the hill about a mile is the O'Conlan plot, it's one acre that just produced a years worth of black potatoes and would produce no more...ever."

"Black potatoes?"

"Yeah, potatoes that were infected by the fungus, they rotted, turned mushy and became inedible. The source of the foulness you smell"

Liam then turned a bit to the northeast, pointed and said, "There across the fields to the east of the O'Conlan plot is the McNulty's place. They're in better shape, but not much."

"What's that mean?"

"Well our family, the O'Conlans, were subtenants or croppies, living off that one acre of land. They leased it from the McNultys who were tenants with ten or so acres that *they* leased from a man named Doyle. But it goes much deeper than that. Paddy McNulty and your great, great grandfather Aidan O'Conlan were best friends. And then Aidan married Maureen McNulty so they were now in-laws, it was all family.

Frank said, "So..."

Liam said, "So, let's just go see what happens."

The two found themselves in a thatched roof cottage on the side of a hill with a dirt floor. There was a large iron cauldron that should have been over a warm fire offering delicious aromas to permeate the place. Instead it rested empty, cold and neglected on the floor.

Four people sat at the small wooden table in front of them, two men and two women, dour expressions smeared across fearful visage.

Liam pointed and said, "Frank that's Aidan O'Conlan, my granddad and next to him is Maureen McNulty O'Conlan, my grandmother. Across the table is my great uncle Paddy NcNulty, Maureen's brother and his wife, my great aunt Siobhan."

Frank said, "Granddad?"

Liam said, "Shush! Listen! Learn!"

Frank's cheeks reddened at the reprimand, but soon settled down.

Aidan O'Conlan said, "I think our options have run out."

Paddy McNulty said, "So you're sending Nancy then?"

Maureen said, "Good Lord No, Paddy! We're not sending our thirteen year old daughter to America by herself."

Paddy said, "Others are doing that, I just thought."

Maureen said, "Let them."

Paddy said, "So Aidan you'll go and send for the family?"

Aidan shook his head soberly and said, "No Paddy. We decided we're doing this together or not at all." Paddy looked puzzled and said, "What then?"

Aidan stood and walked to a rear bedroom and came back with a long narrow item covered in a bed cloth. He put it on the table and uncovered it. There rested a long beautiful sword in a jewel encrusted scabbard.

Paddy stared in disbelief, almost reluctant to breathe as he ran his hands across the priceless talisman that rested before him and said, "So it is true then?"

Aidan said, "Aye, 'tis. It's been in the care of the O'Conlan clan for eight hundred and thirty two years now. We've kept it secret for obvious reasons."

Paddy said, "How did your people come by such a precious relic?"

Aidan stood and began to pace as if deciding where to start. It seemed to Frank that Aidan was on stage, like how he had imagined Liam telling the stories of his youth. He smiled knowing now where this storytelling all came from.

Aidan said, "As you know King Brian Boru rose up from our great province of Munster to become the last great Ard Ri of Ireland."

Frank said, "Ard Ri?"

Liam said, "High King, now shut up!"

Frank sulked once more at the reproof but soon was lost in Aidan's story.

Aidan said, "'Twas Good Friday in the year of our Lord 1014 that the Danes, or Norsemen as they were also known, rose up to fight once again. You see when Brian was rising to power he took his army to Dublin, sacked it and took it from the Danes and their King Sitric who at the time held the title as King of Dublin. Brian, now seventy-four and still as feisty as a young steed wanted to lead his troops into battle but was counseled against it by his advisors and so sent his very capable son Murdoch.

"History tells us that Brian made it clear to his enemies that he had no intention of fighting on Good Friday and the battle would wait until the next day. But legend tells us that the Norse god of war, Woden, visited the Danish troops on Holy Thursday eve to tell them that the battle must be waged on Good Friday, if so Brian will be slain, if not he will be unstoppable.

"So the Danes brought the battle early on Good Friday morning and the fighting raged all day and into the evening but in the end Brian's troops carried the day. Brian himself, however, spent the day in a tent on the edge of the battle field surrounded by a protective guard of some of his best warriors. But all was not well as their was a traitor in Brian's camp who gave away his position to a captain of the Norse guard named Brodar who just happened to be the brother of King Sitric and was looking for revenge."

Frank and Liam watched as Paddy, Maureen and Siobhan sat in rapt attention, caught now in the storyteller's web as he spun his yarn with precision and charm.

Aidan continued, "Brodar sprung an unexpected attack on Brian's position and a battle pursued in which Brodar gained access to Brian's tent. Now Brian was no soft King and he knew that his protective guard was under siege so he prepared himself in his tent knowing he'd been betrayed. Legend has it that he awaited his attacker with a sword in one hand and his book of psalms in the other. When Brodar made his way into the tent a vicious hand to hand combat commenced, each combatant knowing surely he was fighting for his life. Brodar struck the first mighty blow to the chest of the great king, but before he died he rose up and struck a lethal blow back and the two warriors died next to one another in the tent.

"What the history books don't tell us is that in the tent Brian had hung a great banner that held the coat of arms for the Dal Cais clan or the Dalcassians, in which Brian was a member. You see Brian was born Brian Mac Cenne'icligh which translates Brian son of Kennedy who was chief of Thurmond at the time.

"The great banner hung from ceiling to floor in the large royal tent and behind it was a young boy of not more than twelve. You see this boy was a page for the King and ran his errands for him; the boy's name was Rory O'Conlan."

Paddy said, "No."

Aidan said, "Aye. When things became quiet the lad slipped out and saw the two combatants who lay dying. According to family lore the great king looked up at the lad and said, 'Take the sword lad and fight to keep Eire free of foreign invaders' and then he died. Rory took the sword and walked out of the tent to find that everyone had either died or had left and the legend of the sword began that day. And we, as the O'Conlans, have been the guardians of the sword of Boruima, the cattle counter, ever since.

Paddy, with tears in his eyes said, "And you're willing to give that up?"

Aidan said, "Can we eat it Paddy? What lessons have we learned from Midas? Boruima said to use it to fight foreign invaders, a lot of good it has been for the last three hundred years. What good is Brian's sword to us but as a head stone over our graves if we don't sell it? Am I willing to give up this relic? As willing as God seems to be in giving up on Ireland."

Paddy said, "But still."

Aidan said, "But Still? Have you been listening man? I'll starve to death keeping this. Your landlord is Doyle. The dark man is of Danish descent; his people were Norsemen if the history books are to be believed. He'll covet this above all else. But I'm in no position to barter with him. He could simply wait us out and take it when we die. But it is my greatest hope that he'll pay our meager way to America with funds enough to get a start once there. Go to him and ask him then, time is not on our side."

Paddy stood and waited for a half a second as if there maybe some other way out and then walked away.

Frank and Liam watched on as Aidan, Maureen and the kids spent the rest of the day packing and readying themselves for the trip ahead. There was a certain, black aura that had settled on the O'Conlan cottage that would not let up. They could all feel it, yet no one mentioned it. In fact, no one spoke at all and the harder they worked the less their minds turned to the future.

Final preparations finished, cottage and children cleaned.

They were off across the fields to the McNulty's for 'The American Wake.'

Frank said, "Gramps, what's an American wake?"

Liam said, "You know how we wake people back home after they've passed away?"

"Yeah."

"Well, that tradition started here in Ireland. The American wake was a morbid Irish play on words. They held wakes for those leaving for America because, as in death, they figured on never seeing them again."

Frank nodded and said, "Makes sense."

Frank and Liam watched as the O'Conlans walked into the McNulty cottage for the party.

Frank said, "They seem to be holding up, considering."

Liam said, "Oh really? Have you bothered to look into any of their faces? Not one of them wants to be here. Their thoughts are a million miles away, Frank."

Frank looked closer for clues as to what his granddad was talking about.

Liam said, "See?"

"Yeah," he said absentmindedly, as if in a dream.

"No matter how bad things had gotten, Francis, not one of them ever thought the day would come when they would have to actually leave. It's way too big and way too scary for any of them to contemplate too much."

The two continued to watch the scene unfold as the drink began to flow and a fiddler played tunes both happy and sad. Toward the end of the night, as hard as they all tried, the gloom and depression was so palpable in that room that Frank felt as if he could reach out and touch it. Aidan, able to take no more, stood with the effort of someone who was being held down, gathered his family and went home.

Frank and Liam found themselves standing outside the O'Conlan cottage watching as the heavy rain that surrounded them attacked without purchase the cross thatched roof that Aidan was constantly mending.

Frank looked up and squinted at the thick black clouds as the heavy rain poured down on them and seemingly bathed them in the deepest, darkest sadness he had ever known. The one a.m. church bell reverberated throughout the village and surrounding countryside and the sound gave the impression of reluctance in moving through the heavy, malignant blanket of air.

Liam sensing Frank's despair took his hand and led him into the O'Conlan home. Everyone but Aidan tossed and turned in their beds talking to the demons that haunted their nightmares as they slept. Aidan rocked before the peat fire loading a bowl full of fresh pipe weed allowing his private tears to roll fluidly down his cheeks.

Lightning suddenly lit up the entire cottage throwing frightening shadows everywhere and, after a full count of four, thunder boomed and shook the ground. Some of the younger children screamed and Maureen got up to tend to their fear.

After settling them down she walked to the rocking chair that held her husband and put her hand on his shoulder.

Aidan continued to stare at the fire and said, "Maureen, I've always told you, they can take everything I've got but as long as I've got you and the kids, we'll make it through."

Maureen whispered, "Aye."

Aidan leaned forward, lifted a jug off the earthen floor and took a long pull.

Frank said, "What's in the jug?"

Liam said, "Poteen, potato whiskey. Normally Maureen would tell him to take it easy with the stuff. It's powerful."

Aidan went to put the jug back on the floor when Maureen lightly touched his wrist and took the jug for herself.

Aidan sighed and said, "And now they have."

Maureen felt the burn of the whiskey in her throat and said, "Aye, that they have, love, that they have."

"Well not everything." Aidan held up a sack of hundred pounds in gold coins.

Maureen said, "At what price, that?"

"What price can you put on our lives, love? The sword bought our freedom."

Franked watched as his great, great grandfather squeezed the arms of his rocking chair so tightly that his knuckles turned white and before he could comment Liam said, "Did you notice the rocking chair?"

Frank said, "No."

Liam said, "Go have a look."

Frank walked closer and knelt down next to Aidan and Maureen, almost embarrassed that he was invading a private moment between husband and wife. He studied the chair, not knowing much about quality woodwork, but to his uneducated eye it was magnificent. The wood was darkly stained with ornate carving; it had solid, even seams and rocked noiselessly with precise balance.

Maureen went back to bed and Frank stood up and stared into the face of his great, great grandfather. It was chiseled with too many worry lines for a face its age. But it was proud which made the tears that welled there much harder for Frank to take. His pipe rested at the corner of his mouth with such ease that it looked like it was part of his anatomy except for those particularly stressful moments when his teeth clamped down on it in an almost involuntary act.

Over the man's shoulder, Frank noticed a homemade oil wool throw that Maureen had slipped over him to keep him warm. And between his knees his hands rested on what Frank observed was a shelaighly, an Irish walking stick. Both items had been stored in an old wooden trunk, along with the prized sword, kept secretly in the bedroom corner like a crypt, now packed for the trip in the front room.

Aidan crossed his legs and tapped his pipe on his boot heel to re-load it once more. Frank smiled sadly at the man with too many cares and walked back to Liam.

Liam said, "The blanket he has on his shoulders?"

Frank said, "Yeah."

"It's what they called an oiled wool throw. They soak the wool in a special oil to keep the rain out and it was knitted with the O'Conlan stitch."

"O'Conlan stitch?"

"Yeah, most Irish clans had their own stitch. If a corpse showed up that was a stranger, they could identify him by the stitch."

"No lie?"

"Yeah and the rocking chair?"

"Yeah, nice work. Whoever did it must have spent a lot of time."

"It was built and carved by hand by Aidan's grandfather. It was an O'Conlan family tradition for a grandfather to build one for his oldest grandson. I'm sure the reason he squeezed the arms of the chair so hard a few minutes ago was because he realized he won't be able to take it with him tomorrow."

Frank sighed and hung his head. When he looked up again Aidan was lifting the jug to his lips once more.

Liam said, "Aidan wasn't a heavy drinker. As a matter of fact he wasn't much of a drinker at all. I'm guessing the jug and the pipe are bringing him a small amount of comfort in a world that held very little for him."

Frank said, "It's just so sad."

Liam, as if he had not heard a word Frank had spoken, said, "And the rocking chair, a tangible piece of family history, like everything else in the man's life, had to be left behind, there was just no getting around it."

Frank, looking on, felt the same despondency his great, great grandfather felt, as if it were his own to share like the blood that coursed his veins. Liam feeling the kinship and sensing his grandson's despair once again, put his arm around Frank and pulled him close.

In what felt like seconds to Frank, the night time fortress of darkness fell to the onslaught of day, but it brought with it no promise of better things to come. The light of the morning hung in quiet desperation now below the pewter sky. And the ugly grey gave the day its disposition, lightened only slightly by the bright shades of green in the surrounding hillside that fought to hold its own.

Aidan had finally fallen into a fitful alcohol induced sleep. Maureen slightly touched his arm and no more was needed to fully awaken him to his dread. She already had the children ready and he looked at her in wonder.

He said, “Are we really doing this?”

Maureen answered, “Don’t be second guessing yourself now. ‘Tis you who started this and now that I’ve finally set me mind to it, your questioning?”

Aidan said, “Not so much questioning as scared.”

She said, “Don’t you let the children hear you say that.” Then she stopped as if she couldn’t get her voice box to cooperate and finally said, “But, me too, Aidan. What’s out there waiting for us?”

He said, “You’ve heard the Seanachie, just like I have.”

She said, “What?”

He said, “Their talk of the coffin ships and the swindlers. A proud man would sell his soul for a watered down bowl of soup or a crust of bread these days. I said it last night and I’ll say it again, they can take all that I’ve got, just so they don’t take you and those kids.”

He stood a little wobbly, his head full, hugged her and said, “We’ll be fine, we will.”

Frank put his head down and walked out of the cottage. He felt sick to his stomach and needed some fresh air. Liam followed him to make sure he was going to be okay. To Frank’s surprise, when he walked out, the whole village was outside and lined up to say goodbye. These poor, hungry and scared villagers came to see the O’Conlans off. Frank sat down, put his head in his hands and cried.

Liam walked over to Frank, tapped him on the shoulder and said, “Frank, I’m sorry to bother you but you don’t want to miss this.”

Frank said, “Miss what, granddad? More bullshit? More

sadness? More despair? No thanks, old man."

Liam said, "We can't change the past, son. We can only..."

Franks said, "Stop it! Don't go getting all philosophical on me. I just think all of this really sucks."

Liam said quietly, "I couldn't agree more, it's horrendous, but it happened."

They stopped when the O'Conlan cottage door swung open and the O'Conlan family walked out led by Aidan.

Liam said, "Frank, do you know what stoic means?"

Frank said, "No."

"It means, tough, impassive, unemotional."

"So what's your point?"

"That would be a pretty good assessment of Aidan O'Conlan. He'd had a difficult life, full of heart ache and pain and any show of emotion was rarely part of it, even as a child."

Frank was studying his great, great grandfather's face as he listened to Liam describe him. Frank's features contorted in question and he said, "Granddad, what the hell? He's crying."

Liam said, "My point exactly."

Frank started to argue once more when the startling realization hit him. Suddenly the suffering that Aidan was experiencing reached out like cold, bony fingers around his throat constricting his air ways and he choked up.

Aidan, Maureen and their five children began their journey south to the port of Cobh where they planned to buy passage to America. They crossed the fields once more to say goodbye for good to the McNultys

Paddy, Siobhan and their children walked out to say goodbye.

Aidan said, "My guess is a couple of days walk to Cobh?"

Paddy said, "Aye, that's about right, maybe a little longer."

Aidan said, "Paddy, I left me rocking chair in the cottage. It's the only thing in there of value. Would you see to it?"

Paddy said, "Aye."

The two men stared at the ground and kicked pebbles like men do who are faced with the awkward, gentle moment.

Aidan finally said, "Och! Am I doing the right thing here, Paddy?"

Paddy said, "Can you feed your family here, Aidan?"

Aidan said, "No."

Paddy said, "Then you've answered your own question."

Aidan said, "Jaysus, Paddy, I don't want to go."

Paddy said, "There's no getting around it, man. The rest of us'll probably end up in a workhouse in Skibbereen before its over. That's no place for a man like you."

"But Paddy, you've heard the horror stories of the coffin ships same as me, right?"

Paddy put his head down and said, "Aye, I have. 'Tis a hell of a mess we've got ourselves in."

"Paddy, I never knew, in all me life, a cross this heavy. And you know the worst of the whole lot?"

Paddy said, "What?"

Aidan said just above a whisper," Saying goodbye to you."

They stared at each other for a moment and Paddy McNulty, with his shy grin, turned and walked away.

Frank stood as close to his granddad as he could, wondering how much more of this he could take and said, "What's Cobh?"

Liam said, "It's a seaport town southeast of here on the coast of County Cork. It's where they'll find passage to America."

Frank said, "So let me understand this. We walk two days to this port to catch a ride on a death ship?"

Liam said, "Yes, that would be about right."

Frank said, "And you brought me to this hell hole, why again?"

Liam said, "You'll understand when it's all over. Oh and by the way, what doesn't kill you always makes you stronger."

Frank said, "Oh great, by the time this is over, if I do happen to survive, I should be flipping Super Man."

Frank and Liam walked with the O'Conlans from a distance witnessing all the devastation around them. The smell of death and the screams of terror would haunt Frank's dreams for the rest of his life.

Liam continued to walk and Frank stopped dead in his tracks. Out of the corner of his eye he saw something under a tree. His curiosity piqued, he moved toward it. His terror complete, he ran back to the road, knelt down and vomited.

Liam ran back to him and said, "What is it, Francis?"

All Frank could do was point. Liam walked to the tree where a family of five lay in the shade, starved to death. Flies and maggots beginning the first stages of decomposition; the stench was dreadful.

Liam walked back to his grandson who was on all fours spitting the last of the bile from his mouth. He knelt down and put his hand on Frank's back.

Frank spoke while fighting back his gag reflex and said, "Son of a bitch, Gramps! That was the worst thing I've ever seen. What's with the green ring around their mouths?"

Liam helped Frank to his feet and said, "It's been called green mouth disease by the Seanachie, Frank. At the height of starvation during the famine, people went insane and tried to fill their empty bellies with grass. Their poor ravished bodies couldn't digest the grass and they'd find them starved to death with the green ring around their mouths."

Frank said, "But I've seen carts of food on this road?"

Liam said, "I told you, son..."

Frank cut him off and said, "Take me out of here. I want to go home, now!"

Liam said, "We're on our way, son. Just not the way you think."

CHAPTER 11
THE PASSENGER BROKER, THE COFFIN SHIP AND THE POEM

Frank remained silent as they continued their dark journey of horror called Ireland in 1846. He felt helpless and hated being here. They made their way to the port of Cobh in county Cork and watched as the O'Conlans settle down for the night.

Liam said, "Francis, I know you're upset. I knew you would be going in."

Frank said, "Why didn't you tell me about this before we came here?"

"Because I knew you wouldn't come."

"That's an understatement."

"Look Frank, with everything gained, there's a price to be paid. From the dregs of this god awful mess surrounding us, the Irish have risen to heights unimaginable. Running cities and states, police and fire departments, big and small businesses, one of us became the President of the U.S. for gosh sakes! Did you know that at forty-four million we're the largest single ethnic group in the U.S? Do you honestly think you'd appreciate what the Irish are around the world today if you hadn't seen what they went through to get there?"

Frank said, "Well, mom says we haven't had a pope yet."

Liam laughed and said, "No we haven't."

Frank said, "It still stinks, big time."

Liam said, "I know, but who knows why things happen? Life is hard and you take the good with the bad."

Frank said, "My life back home is a can of corn compared to this."

Liam smiled and continued, "You're right. Anyway, during the blight years between 1846 and 1851, the vast majority of Irish immigrants out of Ireland were croppies. Those were the people we saw on the road here, the Irish people with little or no choice but to immigrate. Never having traveled farther than their own village, when all was said and done more of them had seen cities like Boston, New York and New Orleans than had seen Dublin. They were easy targets for swindlers.

"By far the most typical way the Irish immigrated to America was one member at a time."

Frank said, "Why's that?"

"Lack of cash, simple as that. The one that went, man or woman, would go to America, get work, usually the most menial available, work that no one else wanted and then they'd send money back home for the next family member to go. It usually took years.

"The Seanachie told tales of overcrowded coffin ships, Irish and English swindlers and disease. Aidan knew it wouldn't be easy, but he had no choice. As hard as all this was he was grateful that he didn't have to leave his family and go alone and how lucky they were to make the trip as a family rather than one at a time."

Frank and Liam sat on the wharf in Cobh, where large ships moored and they looked out at the sea as it briskly made its way to land, lapping the shore and daring anyone, who might, to challenge it. To the east the sun began to edge its way upon the horizon. Liam turned around with a certain sense and saw that Aidan was rising to meet the day, quietly careful not to wake any of the rest of the family.

Frank noticed his granddad and followed his gaze until it rested on Aidan and he said, “Granddad, where’s he going?”

Liam said, “To see a shyster.”

“A what?”

“A pettifogger.”

“A what?”

“A con-man, swindler, cheat, scoundrel.”

“Okay, okay, I get it already. But why?”

“Why what?”

Frank rolled his eyes and said, “Why is he going to see a shyster?”

“He has to.”

“Thanks gramps that explains a lot.”

“The man he’s going to see is called a Passenger Broker.”

“What the hell is that? Other than a shyster, that is.”

“They were men, in those days, who sold passage on ships.”

“You mean like a ticket?”

“Exactly. But most of them were really just plain crooked.”

“Like what?”

“They’d sell tickets months in advance on ships that didn’t exist. They’d sell tickets on ships that were already over booked. Remember that they were dealing with naïve, small village people who’d never been away from home before. This was the type of person Aidan was going to see.”

Liam and Frank watched as Aidan walked through the ship yard in the port of Cobh and knocked on a door with a wooden sign that swung above it which read, ‘Passenger Broker’ and then beneath that in smaller letters, ‘Morris Stewart.’

Frank said, “He looks so alone, so out of place.”

Liam said, “He is, Francis. He’s got the weight of the world on his shoulders.”

The two walked closer and heard the, "What?" in response to Aidan's knock. They followed in behind him to be silent witnesses once more.

Aidan walked in and looked at the man sitting behind a desk piled high with paper. He looked up and down at Aidan with condescending scorn, showing his utter disdain of the Irish croppy. His teeth black, some missing, chewing on a mouth full of snuff. Next to his desk sat a brass spittoon spilling over with black wads of spit. He stood from his chair and said, "I said what?" grossly underestimating the man who stood in front of him.

Aidan stood and stared directly back at the man without a flinch.

"I'm searching for passage to America."

"So what? Who isn't?"

"Are you a passenger broker or not?"

"Can you read?"

"Aye."

"That's a first. So answer your own question."

"I don't like your tone of voice."

"I could give a damn what you *like* or don't *like*, grass eater."

Aidan turned around as if to leave and the passenger broker began to laugh, derision thick, until he realized that Aidan was locking the door.

"What the hell are you doing?"

"Making sure that we have a little privacy to our business."

"Have it your way."

Aidan said, "Oh, I will."

With one motion Aidan was across the floor, pulled the passenger broker from his chair and slammed him head first into the wall behind.

Aidan held him there and spoke with a strength and malice he didn't know existed within him, "Do you know the definition of desperation?"

He said, "Screw off, Harp."

Aidan smiled and grabbed the man by the throat and pushed until the air passage was constricted, "I'm going to ask you one more time, and then I won't be so polite. Do you know the definition of desperation?"

Morris Stewart's eyes bulged and his face turned red and he shook his head no.

Aidan lessened his grip so the man could get a bit of air and said, "That's okay because I'm going to tell you. Then we'll have better understanding of one another which will make doing business easier. Is that all right with you?'

The passenger broker shook his head in favor of anything that might get him out of this predicament.

"Desperation is when a man has everything taken from him... everything. He has nothing to loose. That is where I am and that makes me a very dangerous lad, do you understand?"

His eyes began to roll into the back of his head feeling as if his brain were about to explode. He had to focus on the question and once again shook his head yes. Aidan dropped him and he fell to the ground grasping, coughing and sputtering to gain precious air once again.

The man made his way to his desk once more and Aidan said, "Now, are you a passenger broker?"

The man unable to speak just yet nodded his head yes.

Are you selling passage for the ship in the bay, *The Clifton of Cork*?"

He nodded yes.

"How much for passage for one?"

He put up eight fingers?"

Aidan said, "How about passage for seven?"

He held up five fingers with a scared question in his eyes.

"Thank you, that's a fair price."

Aidan counted out thirty-five one pound gold coins and lay them on the desk in front of him.

Then he said, "How about food for the journey?"

The man shook his head yes and then screech whispered, "Six weeks at least."

"You mean on the ship?"

"Aye."

"How much for food for one to make the six weeks without starving?"

The man raised ten fingers.

Aidan said, "I like five much better."

The man raised seven fingers.

Aidan said, "Six will have to do."

The man gave a weak smile and gave in as Aidan counted out forty-two more gold coins.

Aidan watched as the man prepared the boarding passes making sure they had the official stamp making them legitimate. Something, the Seanachie had warned anyone who would listen that these swindlers omitted regularly, rendering the boarding passes worthless and leaving passengers stranded and their life savings gone.

Once they were stamped and complete they walked out together to the food stores.

Aidan picked out some salted beef, cabbage and oatmeal. They sacked it up and went out to the storefront to weigh it. Remembering the Seanachie talking about the short-weighted food scales, Aidan pulled a horse shoe hammer from the pack he carried in which he knew the weight and said, "Could you put this on the scale before you weigh me food."

The man winced and held up a hand as he adjusted the scales accurate to the ounce.

Aidan got his food and passes and said, "Pleasure doing business with you, Mr. Stewart. You might want to be careful of the next grass eater that walks in. Sometimes we can surprise you with our horns." He winked and walked away

Aidan walked back to camp with four burlap sacks of food tied to his pack and seven official boarding passes for *The Clifton of Cork*.

Frank noticed a more confident gait in his step, as if he felt good about himself for the first time in weeks because he hadn't lost his touch.

When Aidan arrived, Maureen had a fire started and was hoping to feed the kids on what Aidan had rounded up. She looked up at her husband, as he walked back into camp, with the love of a woman who would follow her man anywhere.

She smiled at him and said, "Well, are we going to the New World?"

"Aye, that we are lass."

He looked at her and said, "I think I was able to get enough for us to make it to America."

"You did your best, love."

Aidan O'Conlan sat quietly eating his watery porridge in the morning light, staring intently at his children as they ate theirs. He was thirty-five years old, his wife Maureen was thirty-four and the children were thirteen, eleven, nine, seven and five. They all stared back at him; he was their entire world. What he didn't know was that he could do no wrong in their eyes. They thought of him as a strong, smart man that could do anything. If he thought it was all right to get on that boat and go to America, well then it was all right.

Frank stared with love and admiration at this handsome young family. He was growing to love them more and more by the minute.

Liam noticed Frank beaming at the kids as if he would have loved to go strike up a conversation and said, "Frank, as we talked about on the way to Delmar, Aidan and Maureen had five kids. The one sitting next to her mother is the oldest. Her name is Nancy and she's the one who will marry John Power."

Frank said, "Where's he?"

Liam said, "You'll see."

Frank said, "She's beautiful, but I don't recall any blondes in our family."

Liam said, "None of your family is directly descendent

from her."

Frank said, "That doesn't make..."

Irritated, Liam said, "Pay attention! Next to Nancy, the one with chestnut brown hair, blue eyes and cheeks the color of a rose on a thorn bush is Molly Rose and thus her name."

Frank said, "Cool."

Liam said, "The one laughing is Moria. She's the third oldest and the gregarious one."

Frank said, "Gregarious?"

Liam said, "Outgoing, talkative, always smiling. The two boys she's tending to are Patrick and your great grandfather, Billy."

Just dawning on Frank who Billy was he said, "No kidding?"

Liam said, "No kidding. Pat went on to be a war hero in the Civil war and you know about Billy."

The day passed slowly on the beach and they could not help but to stare at the seven hundred and fifty-ton ship they were to board in the morning. It was neither the smallest nor the largest of the ships hauling immigrants to the New World. They all took solace in the fact that it seemed to be in a good state of repair but that was all the solace they took.

Frank said, "We're not getting on that pile of junk, are we?"

Liam said, "You bet we are. I hope you have a strong stomach and don't mind cramped spaces. Remember your nightmare?"

Frank said, "No way, gramps! Ain't no way you're putting me through that again."

Liam lit his pipe, blew a large plume of smoke into the air and said, "Well then, I hope you're a strong swimmer."

A huge bell suddenly rang out and startled Frank who said angrily, "What the hell is that?"

Liam said, “Time to board the ship.”

Frank said, “I told you, I’m not getting on that pile of garbage and that’s that.”

Liam, with a confident grin, said, “Yes you are,” and walked away.

Frank watched him walk away and then saw passengers getting in line. Some cried, others wailed, still others dropped to their knees in quiet prayer.

Maureen O’Conlan walked a few feet from the line and dropped to her knees. She prayed for a moment and then she leaned forward and kissed the soil. As she came up the salted tears commingled with the salted sea spray to blur her vision. She tasted the mixture as it dripped on to her lips, a bitter reminder.

She came back to stand next to Aidan and put her arms around his waist and cried. Frank thought, “If they’re going I’m going.”

As they boarded the ship, they were all packed in below deck. Claustrophobics would have walked from the ship and starved. People had only a space of three foot by six foot in which to lay their head, five to a bed.

The captain ordered the anchor to be pulled up and the ship began to sail away from Ireland to the unknown. Aidan hung his head in what Frank guessed was total despair.

As the ship sailed from port that first day, the seas were calm and the sky was blue and Aidan spent it on deck reading.

Nancy approached him, holding Billy’s hand and said, “Da, what’re you reading?”

“A book of poetry by the great Irish saint and poet, St. Colm Cille.”

Frank said, “Who’s Colm Cille?”

Liam said, “Listen and find out.”

She said, “Why are you reading a book about St. Colm?”

He said, “Well, the very same thing happened to Colm

that's happening to us, only different circumstances."

"Like what?"

"Well, like many Irishmen, Colm had many great qualities but he had a few bad ones as well. His greatest weakness was his bad temper and, because of it, battles took place and men died. One battle in particular caused him to be exiled from Ireland forever."

Nancy said, "Exiled?"

Aidan said, "Aye, it means they made him leave Ireland."

"Oh."

"During Colm's time in Ireland there was a High King named Diarmuid. He and Colm never got along very well and had many heated arguments. One day a man named Curan showed up at Colm's monastery seeking sanctuary."

Billy said, "Da, what's sanctuary?"

Aidan smiled at Billy and winked at his older sister, pleased with the attention span of this five-year-old.

"Well, in those days and, come to think of it even today, a man can show up at a church and ask for protection and a place to stay. While there, no one, not even the law, can enter and take him away. It has to be negotiated. It's a long-standing tradition that originated in Ireland. That's sanctuary.

"Anyway, like I said Curan shows up and asks Colm for sanctuary in his monastery."

Nancy said, "Why, what did he do?"

Aidan smiled, tickled that these kids were so interested in the story. It also took his mind off the present.

"Curan was the son of Aed, the King of Connaught."

Nancy said, "Da, I thought you said Diarmuid was the King?"

He was," Aidan chuckled, "But he was what they called the Ard-Righ or High King. There were also kings for each of the four provinces, they answered to and paid tribute to the High King, Lord over the whole island."

They both said, "Oh."

"Do you understand?"

They nodded their heads.

"Okay. Anyway, Curan killed the son of Diarmuid's Stewart in a rugby match and this made Diarmuid angry. Curan, afraid for his life and rightly so, ran away and requested Colm's help. Now sanctuary was a tradition that not even a High King interfered with. But Diarmuid had a temper not unlike Colm's, and was so furious that Curan was taking refuge with Colm and that Colm was allowing it, he ordered his soldiers into the Monastery to forcibly apprehend Curan and then ordered his death. To Colm, this was an unforgivable offense.

"Colm was so outraged at this that he travelled to his home in Tir-Connaill where he told the story to his family and friends. The princes of Tir-Connaill and Tir-Eogain put together an army and they joined forces with King Aed's army and went to battle against the High King Diarmuid at a place called Cuildremne. When the battle was over they had defeated Diarmuid, but in the process three thousand men lay dead on the field of battle. The Seanachie attribute all responsibility to Colm for these deaths."

Nancy said, "Did Colm kill all three thousand men?"

"No."

"So why does he get all the blame?"

"Because he started it. If he'd held his temper no one would've died."

She said, "Oh."

"Shortly after the battle the high members of the church in Ireland held a synod, a meeting, at a place called Taillte where they tried to excommunicate Colm."

Billy said, "What does that mean?"

Aidan said, "It means they tried to kick him out of the church. But the attempt failed, due to the efforts of St. Brendan. But Colm couldn't live with himself, so he went to see St. Molaise of Inishmurry to confess his sins, seek absolution, and be given a penance fitting the sin. Now Molaise knew how much Colm loved Ireland, but he also knew how serious his sin was so for his penance ordered Colm into exile with orders to never see Ireland again."

Nancy said, "So Colm left Ireland for good, like we are now?"

"Aye and here's a poem he wrote about it. It's how I feel right now and why I was reading this book:

"There is a grey eye
That will look back upon Erin:
Which shall never see again
The men of Erin nor her women.

I stretch my glance across the brine
From the firm oaken planks;
Many are the tears of my bright soft grey eye
As I look back upon Erin

My mind is upon Erin
Upon Loch Lene, upon Linny,
Upon the land where Ulstermen are,
Upon gentle Munster and upon Meath

Melodious are Erin's clerics,
Melodious her birds.
Gentle her youths, wise her elders,
Illustrious her men, famous to behold,
Illustrious her women for fond espousal.
Carry my blessing with thee to the west
My heart is broken in my breast:
Should sudden death overtake me,
It is for my great love of the Gael.

Were all Alba mine,
From its centre to its border,
I would rather have the site of a house

In the middle of Derry.

Beloved are Durrow and Derry
Beloved is Raphoe with purity
Beloved Drumhome with its sweet acorns,
Beloved are swords and Kells.'"

With that Aidan hung his head, trying to hide the tears. With her free hand Nancy reached for his hand and let him finish. Billy said, "Da, what's Alba?"

He smiled again as his tears stained the wooden deck and said, "You were listening after all, weren't you?"

"Aye Da, I loved it."

"In the time of Colm, Alba was the name of Scotland. It was there that he took exile and did missionary work for the church."

They all stared quietly looking out over the horizon until they saw the land of Colm's fierce love quietly disappearing on the line that joined the earth and sky.

Billy said, "Da, are you scared?"

Aidan said, "No." Then he squeezed both kids in a fierce hug, belying what he said and felt.

They looked up in time to watch Ireland disappear, like a lover who knows now that it's over, never to see her again.

Frank and Liam watched, as the ship pitched and rolled on the sea that seemed to devour the last sight of the Irish shoreline.

Frank said, "How could this happen?"

Liam said, "You're now beginning to understand the great sacrifice all of these people made for us."

Frank said, "Gramps, I'm sorry but I can't go down in that hull. I've seen it and I'm not going down there."

Liam shrugged and said, "Fine with me. Stay up on deck

and see what the ocean has to say about that."

He walked away and heard Frank say under his breath, "Jerk."

The first dreadful days of the journey were spent getting used to the high seas. No one was to escape the awful seasickness and very few could hold any food down.

Storms would develop on the ocean and last for days. To avoid taking on too much water, the captain ordered the hatches battened down. This meant that the passengers were locked in the hull of the ship and could not go up, even once a day, which meant no fresh air and no sunshine. To make matters worse, there were not enough lavatories to accommodate all of them even during fair weather. So when they were stuck in the hull for days on end, during one of these storms, they had to use buckets, pans and any other type of container they could find and could not dispose of them until the storm was over.

The compartment, as large as it was, was wall-to-wall people and had turned into an arena for contagious germs and contaminants.

The stench that spewed forth was so dreadful that when the storm blew over, the captain would offer the sailor willing to open the hatches a one-pound note, usually finding that brave soul vomiting in the ocean at the task's completion.

Days turned to weeks and the first month of their journey came and went. Aidan had lost fifteen pounds from a frame that was already fifteen pounds underweight. At first it was from eating half a meal once a day to ensure Maureen and the kids got their fill. With the terrible conditions, however, he had lost his appetite altogether.

He walked a little slower, his speech was slurred and his vision became blurry. He found his children to be a small bit of heaven in what otherwise would be termed hell.

When the weather cooperated, the children spent as much

time as was allowed on the deck. It was precious few moments they got to spend up top looking at the ocean and the beauty of it all.

Aidan, meanwhile, began sweating profusely and took on a powerful thirst. He had contracted typhoid fever and was in a rapid decline. He was dehydrating – not a good thing considering the stiff rations that had been placed on fresh water. The mariners had unknowingly filled rotten wooden kegs with water in port and found after a month that half the water supply had leaked from those casks.

Aidan began to dry heave, as he had nothing in his stomach. He lost even more weight and, in his weakening condition, was in no shape to fight this deadly and contagious disease. Maureen waited with him as he lay there shivering in a cold sweat.

Frank had never experienced depression like he knew now. He found he could do nothing about it and at times hated Liam for doing this to him. He felt helpless and wanted to run, wake up, be back in his room, safe and warm under the covers.

He wanted no more of this; he struggled day and night and began to hate a God who would allow anything so foul. But he knew in his heart that this had to happen, that there was a bigger picture.

He watched as Maureen stood a silent vigil over her husband. When no one was there her shoulders heaved with grief. Her suffering became his and he wanted to go to her to support her and hold her. He became so engrossed that he even tried once to no avail.

Liam simply said, “You can’t.”

Aidan looked up at his wife and said, “Ma, I got the chores done as Da had asked. Paddy wanted me to go fishing with him. Do ya mind?”

Maureen trembled and, as the tears rolled off her cheeks, she rubbed the Claddaugh, her Irish wedding band, on her wedding finger, a habit she developed when stressed. Aidan gave it to her the night of their betrothal and she cherished it.

Maureen said, as if in a prayer, "God in heaven he's losing his mind, he's dying and I can do nothing about it."

She put a cold wet cloth over his fiery forehead and said, "I feel so helpless, Aidan. I love you so much and have no idea what I'll do without you. How am I to take care of these children by myself in a new country? I keep wondering what I did to anger God so much, it must've been a mortal sin of the grandest scale and I'd confess it if I knew what it was."

She looked down on her husband in his restless sleep and said, "God my heart aches and I'm so homesick I can't concentrate on anything, but I can't let the children know. We've never asked for much have we lad? What I wouldn't give for our cottage and kitchen, me cauldron over the fire. They weren't much but they were home. And I hate this awful place, full of sick and dirty people who don't deserve this either. It's all so unfair."

She knelt down beside her husband who had been finally blessed with a moment of restful sleep. She kissed him on his cheek and fell asleep upon his breast.

His chest heaved and she woke to watch as he winced in pain and fell back into a restless sleep. Aidan was in and out of consciousness all night and Maureen wouldn't leave his side.

The cold night air of mid-March cooled the ship and Maureen knew that was a blessing. She wrapped Aidan in as many blankets as she could find to try to keep him from shivering. Soon after, he would become uncomfortably hot and start sweating.

The next evening as the sun went down; a lone fiddler began to play as he did every night at this time. Aidan lay still for a half-hour or so and enjoyed the music. Suddenly he let out a loud spastic cry and his body convulsed in pain. He looked at Maureen as if he had something to say, but couldn't.

He smiled because his pain had disappeared. He then arched his back and took a last deep breath. His vibrant spirit pushed forth from his frail and now empty shell, he stopped for a moment and stared briefly at his unseeing wife. He beamed a brilliant smile and yet, somehow sad, departed by some will other than his own.

Frank said, "Why did you do this to me? Just take me home now!"

Liam said, "Is that what you really want? We can, we can go right now. But once we do, it's over, we can't come back and I'll have to leave. Then you'll never really know how it happened. Sure you know the ending, but what does that get you? Would you read the last chapter of a good novel or watch the last five minutes of a good movie?"

Frank said, "All right. Screw this." And he walked to the deck to see a full moon glisten creating a narrow path to the horizon on a smooth midnight ocean and cried.

Liam gave him a half hour and walked up to join him.

Frank said, "Gramps, did you see that?"

Liam said, "See what?"

"I could've swore I saw his spirit leave his body. Was I seeing things or did I see what I thought I saw?"

"I think you saw what you thought."

"So now what? How much more misery do we get to watch? How many more people do we *get* to watch die?"

Liam said, "A lousy attitude isn't going to help any."

Frank said, "Do you blame me?"

Liam said, "No, I guess I don't blame you, it's not easy, none of it is. Now take my hand."

Frank said, "Where are we going?"

Liam said, "You'll see."

The two suddenly were standing in the workhouse in Skibbereen. It was past mid-night and people slept anywhere they could find a spot.

Frank's gag reflex kicked in once more and he dry heaved as the smell of human decay, unsanitary disposal of human waste and body odor combined in the air to overwhelm him.

Frank said, "Where are we?"

Liam said, "Workhouse, Skibbereen, West County Cork, Ireland."

Frank, still trying to control his gag reflex said, "Workhouse? Skibbereen? What the hell? First we're on a death ship, now we're back in Ireland?" He gagged and his eyes teared over and not from emotion.

Liam said, "I know it's hard to take some of this. But how would you have liked to live it?"

"I wouldn't."

"Then consider yourself blessed and quit your complaining."

"Hmph."

Liam, not paying anymore attention to the whining, said, "When the blight hit, by the fall of 1846 things were so dire that the *Board of Works* in Ireland instituted what they called *relief works*. People were put to work building roads and such. They lived like prisoners in a building like this and traded busting rock and building roads all day for a couple of pints of watery soup and some crusty old bread."

Frank said, "Why?"

Liam said, "No choice. Do it or die."

Frank said, "How about leaving?"

Liam said, "No money."

Frank said, "That would do it."

Liam said, "Are you finished?"

Frank nodded sheepishly.

Liam said, "Good, because this is important. Do you recognize this man?" Liam pointed at a man sitting on the side of his bed, hair and beard all grown out and scraggly, unwashed and skeletal.

Frank said, "No. Should I?"

Liam said, "Yes, you should. It's Paddy McNulty."

Frank said, "That's not Paddy McNulty." And like he had done with Aidan in his rocking chair moved in for a closer look and winced when he recognized the man and said, "Holy smokes."

Liam said, "Shortly after the O'Conlans left the McNultys were kicked off their land and ended up in this work house. Frank, Paddy McNulty had become a shell of a man, mentally, physically and spiritually. Like I said, the workhouse in Skibbereen meant trading days of meaningless drudgery for watered down soup and stale bread.

"He grew to hate the English, God and himself. At one time, he and some of the other men rose up and struck for better working conditions and more food and were almost shot. At least they felt like men for a while.

"His thoughts often went to Aidan, Maureen and their kids, wondering how they were getting on. Out of habit he prayed for them, though, as the long days passed he questioned God's existence more and more.

"As you can see, Frank, at thirty-five he was a bent, gray, half toothless old man and the bright blue skies of early spring didn't have quite the same meaning that they once did for him."

Frank, unable to keep his eyes off Paddy McNulty and the substantial physical change in the man said, "Granddad, he looks like he's about half dead. God, he must be miserable."

Liam said, "Not much for him to smile about is there? He's lost family and friends to death and immigration. Ireland has been decimated due to hunger and disease, the hope is all but gone for the man."

Frank looked over the whole workhouse and its occupants; they suddenly seemed to him like they were moving in slow motion as if they were in a mini series on TV and the actors were submerged in water and trying to walk in ankle deep mud. When the night finally consumed the day, sleep, for the workers was an endless display of fits and starts, constant hunger keeping any of them from solid rest.

Frank walked outside to Liam's side who was lighting up

his pipe once more and said, "What's that smell? It's different from the stench inside and somehow more permanent. It's coming from that big hole over there." And he started to walk toward the large pit of death.

Liam grabbed his arm and said, "Don't, son! That's a mass grave."

Frank said, "A what?"

Liam said, "So many people died so fast that they couldn't bury them one at a time. So they dug large holes, blessed the bodies and threw them in. Then they covered them with lime to cover up as much of the smell as they could. But, as you've noticed, when there are so many, the smell still emanates and is an almost unbearable odor."

Frank said, "It'll be hard to forget."

Liam said, "Anyway, Paddy McNulty thought of himself as well as the people in this workhouse and throughout Ireland as people who refused to give up on their faith but had no hope. He wasn't sure what kept him moving anymore, because he had no faith in God now and he had lost hope long ago. He knew death would be a certain gift."

Liam walked Frank back into the workhouse and stood next to Paddy, he woke in the middle of the night, in the workhouse in Skibbereen. He was drenched in sweat and came straight up in his bed when he saw the illuminated figure floating above him. He shook his head and wiped the sweat from his eyes, grabbed his spectacles on the floor next to him and the ghost came into focus.

He looked around the dormitory of the workhouse to see if anyone else had noticed.

Aidan smiled at him and said nothing.

Paddy said, "My God, Aidan, you didn't make it."

"On the contrary, my friend, I did make it. No more hunger, pain or sorrow."

"Well blessed be the Holy Trinity and all that's good. Your

wife and kids are on that boat by themselves. They'll never survive."

"Maureen will be joining me soon enough."

"Aidan, why are you telling me such awful news? Am I to get on the next big boat and go after those children?"

Frank didn't know whether to cry at the news of Maureen's impending doom or smile at Paddy's eagerness to get on the next coffin ship and go after the O'Conlan children.

"No, Paddy, I'm here to let you know that I'm all right. Maureen will be all right and the children will be in good hands. You'll be hearing from Nancy soon enough."

"Oh, Aidan, you don't know how I've missed you and our life together in Upperchurch. It wasn't much but it was sure as hell a lot better than this misery. I may as well have gotten aboard a ship and left old Ireland as homesick as I feel. But surely I didn't think you'd pass so soon. It must have been some sort of torment on that ship."

Aidan waved as his spirit faded from sight and Paddy cried, "Aidan, me friend, please don't go, please."

Somebody from the other side of the dorm shouted, "Keep it down, we're trying to sleep down here."

To which Paddy said, "Awe, shut your gob."

He didn't sleep for the remainder of the night.

Frank and Liam were suddenly once again back in the hull of the *Clifton of Cork* and Frank didn't know which was worse, this hull or the workhouse. He suddenly jumped and grabbed Liam's arm. It was March 15th; two days before the feast day of St. Patrick, when Maureen let out a wail that had become all too familiar on the ship. The music stopped, and as was the fashion, the men took off their caps and everyone lowered their heads. This became a daily occurrence, but never taken for granted as anyone could be next.

Maureen lit one of the candles she had made in her kitchen in Upperchurch. The vanilla smell of the candle brought her back home so abruptly she had to catch her breath. She felt her heart pound. All night she stood a silent vigil over Aidan's body. As her children slept, she prepared his body for its ocean burial.

As the sun ascended over the water, her children began to wake and come to her side. First Moria, then Molly Rose, Nancy, Pat and finally Billy.

Maureen, pail and sickly with a sort of maddening glint in her eye, said, "So, this is it, then?"

Nancy said, "Is what it, mam?"

"We'll be handing him to the ocean and that will be that? No requiem Mass? No grave to visit? No flowers to place? Hardly a proper or fair way to say goodbye."

Nancy began to cry and said, "Oh, mam."

In a short desperate gasp, almost a whisper, as if to herself, she said, "What did we ever do that was so bad as to make God hate us so much?"

Nancy blew out the candle her mother was holding. She noticed that the wax had run over the side and on to her hand but she seemed numb to the pain. She was sweaty and hot so Nancy went to get her a scarce but cool drink of water.

Maureen began to speak and Nancy said, "Shh, you've had a rough go. Drink this, it'll cool your throat."

Maureen smiled weakly at her oldest.

Nancy, following her mother's instructions, asked Mr. O'Casey and Mr. Berigan if they would be pallbearers and if they could round up four more men. They would carry Aidan to the deck on his mattress covered in his disease-ridden blankets. There they would hold a short service and bury him at sea.

The women began preparing the body in earnest, while the men stood waiting. When the women were finished they all blessed themselves and began the rosary.

After they concluded, Patrick O'Casey, a big man, put Aidan upon his shoulder to carry him out of the hull. The rest of them carried his mattress and blankets. The men and women formed a line on both sides while the women wailed in grief for the departed. When they reached the deck, Maureen had asked them to lay him down for a moment. She had found a small piece of twine and tied her Claddaugh around his neck.

She kissed his cheek and whispered to him, "No mistake, Aidan O'Conlan, I love you."

The tears ran down her sunken cheek and dropped off her jaw onto his cold, waxy face. She sat on the deck inconsolable while the pallbearers rolled him to his watery grave.

Frank watched closely as Molly Rose, Moria, Pat and Billy all hugged and cried, trying to find some relief, none daring to watch. Then he looked over his shoulder at Nancy who stood apart from them on an empty water barrel and looked out to sea with a stern look on her face, contemplating. He walked toward her and stood next to her wanting to reach out and hug her.

Liam said, "Frank, you can't."

Frank looked back at his granddad with contempt and said, "I know, damn it!"

Liam said, "Watch your..."

"No! I won't! Do you think that I'm some kind of damn zombie with no emotions, no feelings?"

"No, I..."

"No, you didn't. Look at her. She just came to the realization that she'll never see her dad again. No tears, though, are there? And do you know why?"

"Why do you think?" Liam said, trying to be as gentle as possible.

Staring down at his great, great Grandmother he said, "Because, even at the tender age of thirteen she's smart enough to know now that her mom's sick with the same crap that killed her dad. Just look at her, granddad."

They both looked at Maureen wilting on the deck the deck

like a pale and gentle flower not strong enough to survive the latest summer drought.

They then looked back at Nancy as she wondered for the first time what they would do without their mother. She looked on as the white, rolling wake of the ship enveloped her father's corpse, watching the lifeless vessel disappear beneath the surf.

She held St. Colm's book of verse and read aloud, not caring who heard, "There is a grey eye that will look back upon Erin: Which shall never see again the men of Erin nor her women.'"

Nancy then stared out at the ocean, the mist pelting her face, her salty tears indistinguishable from the spray in both appearance and substance. She watched as the waves were choreographed in a complex dance, moving effortlessly to a musical din that only they could hear.

Liam looked at Frank and said, "Francis, you're a lucky boy."

Frank, with clinched jaw, said, "You can go to hell."

Liam grabbed his grandson by the shirt and pulled him close. Fire burned in the older man's eyes after having had enough and his brow furrowed in anger. He said, "Do you have any idea the gift you've been given here?"

Frank stood in defiance and said, "Gift? This is a gift? If this is a gift take it back! No wonder I hate the Irish and being Irish, it always has to be so harsh. Some gift. Let's just call it the Irish gift." The sarcasm not lost on the strong ocean wind and rain.

Liam raise his hand to smack the boy then thought better of it.

Frank said, "Just like the Irish, huh gramps? Always ready with a fist."

Liam turned to walk away and then turned swiftly back, grabbed Frank by the shirt and pulled him so close that Frank could smell his sour breath above that ocean breeze and said, "Wake up, boy and quit acting like a damned spoiled brat! This *is* an Irish gift, you're just too damn self-centered and pig headed to see it. The world is a hard place that devours the weak. You think you've got it so damn bad because you have a hard father. Well now maybe you're figuring out just what bad really is."

With that Liam walked away.

CHAPTER 12
THE ANGEL OF MERCY AND THE ANGEL OF DEATH

The ocean hearse heaved and rolled, creaked and groaned as if mourning all her dead. The floating mortuary continued to plough through her salt water cemetery leaving behind unmarked graves in her wake and no hope for those who survived. What she did not leave behind was helplessness, hunger, disease and despair; all of which blew like the wind in her mast keeping her afloat and pushing her toward her destination of provincialism, intolerance and utter disdain and discrimination of the Irish falling sick off the boats daily.

Maureen sat desolate on the deck and began to shake with involuntary jerks and starts. The children circled around to make sure she did not hurt herself. She would let no one else near.

At the sight of this, Frank now knew anguish and was unable to communicate it.

Liam came up behind him, gently rested his hand on

Frank's shoulder and said, "Maureen felt like she was going crazy. She now concluded that she was about to join her husband and had no idea what she was going to do."

Frank said, "Don't tell me that."

Liam nodded softly and looked on.

Maureen looked up after a long while and Nancy offered her a hand. She took it and the rest of the children rushed to help. She was no longer shaking cold because she was now overcome with fever and heavy sweating. She stood feeling dizzy and faint. They all helped her down below to her bed where she stayed until they docked in New York.

After they buried Aidan at sea, the days crept by and Frank felt as small and useless as a single drop of water in the vast ocean that surrounded them. The O'Conlan children had all gathered below deck weak and fed up, when Billy heard a faint, "Land ho!"

He looked up and said, "Did ya' hear that?"

Pat said, "Hear what?"

Billy said, "That."

As he said it, they all heard the voice. "Land Ho!" screamed the sailor from the crow's nest again.

There was a clamor in the hull as the entire lower deck screamed for joy. The ghosts of this ocean going coffin and the trail of dead spirits that followed it from Ireland had haunted them long enough. They wanted nothing more than to get off.

Liam and Frank, who were sitting by Maureen's bed, stood up as people do at a wake. She had been in and out of consciousness since Aidan passed. The girls had tended to her the best they could. But with the little they had there was little they could do.

Nancy knelt down beside her and said, "Ma, did you hear?"

"Hear what, honey?"

"They've spotted land. We're no more than a stone's throw from America."

Maureen smiled and squeezed her hand.

Liam said, "She tried like hell to be strong but knew she was dying. She was torn. She felt so sick and tired that death seemed a blessing; the thought actually thrilled her.

"But she also realized the awesome responsibility she had. She was taking her five children from the only home they'd ever known to a strange land. If she died, what was to become of them? Her rosary never left her hand and, when she was conscious, her prayer never ceased."

The *Clifton of Cork* finally struggled into New York harbor after two long months at sea like a whale who had escaped the deck of the harpooner's boat, but not without its wounds. The immigrant's patience were to be tested once again as it was more than six hours after the anchor was set before they could escape their prison bars.

In the hull of the ship, the O'Conlan children gathered around their mother. The kids were frightened; they sensed their mother's demise without uttering one syllable of it. And their anxiety heightened and their patience was frayed as they pined to get their mother and themselves off this floating charnel house.

As the sick Irish immigrants were leaving the ship, they were welcomed by an angry mob of Yankee Protestants who threw apples and tomatoes and hurled insults at them.

Frank said, "What the hell?"

Liam said, "Remember the hotel restaurant in Iowa where we had dinner?"

Frank said, "What's that got to do with this?"

Liam said, "I told you that in 1846 the U.S. was a country populated by white Anglo Saxon Protestants."

Frank said, "Yeah."

Liam said, "Their roots were the Mayflower and England. They didn't like the Irish or Catholics when they left England and they still didn't when the Irish Catholics came to America. Even after all the Irish had been through on the death ship, this was their welcome to America. Now watch this."

Frank looked to where Liam was pointing and another angry mob was moving in to do battle with the group that had been harassing the immigrants as they left the ship. A small riot broke out, fists flying everywhere.

Frank said, "What the hell's going on now?"

Liam said, "Those are the Irish that already lived here coming to the docks to take care of their own. They meet the coffin ships as they dock to make sure the immigrants get off in relative safety."

Frank looked on as the skirmish let up and the Yankees scattered. The Irish then moved in to help whomever needed their assistance getting to dry land.

Suddenly, without any warning what so ever, Frank found himself next to Liam on the other side of the dock, watching a nun, he didn't know, tending to sick and hurt people coming off the ship.

Irritated, he said, "Granddad, would you please stop that nonsense."

Liam smiled and said, "What nonsense?"

Frank said, "Don't go there, you know exactly what I'm talking about, this crap of you taking me from one place to another without warning. I think you're beginning to enjoy my frustration."

Liam said, "Okay, lighten up, I'm sorry. But I have to admit that I *do* enjoy your irritation, I can't help it."

Frank said, "Thanks a lot. Who *is* this?" pointing at the nun on her knees helping people in front of them. Liam said, "An Irish immigrant during the famine of 1830 and now a Sister of Charity here in New York. Her name is Sister Mary Therese."

They watched as she put a cold cloth on one man, gave a child a cool drink of water and spoke soothing woods to a mother of a small baby. She then looked to her left and noticed the O'Conlan children laying their mother down in the dirt of the harbor and she went to them.

After checking Maureen's vital signs she looked up and saw that the children were all in tears. She said in a mild brogue, "Come children, there's room over there, let's get her away from the fighting."

Before they lifted her she said, "And where might your Da be?"

Nancy said, "We buried him at sea two weeks ago."

She sighed with sorrow as she stared at them and said, "Let's see what we can do for your mother."

Maureen's breathing was labored and sometimes it seemed to Frank that she stopped breathing altogether. The nun left for a moment and then brought back fresh water for Maureen to drink and a cool cloth for her burning forehead.

Maureen looked up at her and in a delirium said, "And where might we be?"

Sister Mary Therese looked at her gently and said, "New York Harbor."

Maureen said, "And who might you be?"

"Sister Mary Therese."

"You're a pretty one, Sister."

"Thank you, mam."

"Is there a priest nearby?"

Sister Mary Therese understood. Maureen was looking for Unction and confession. In southern Ireland a priest was usually a few minutes away.

She said, "No mam, I'm afraid not. But I can bless you and know that God has already forgiven your sins. You lived your penance on that awful ship."

Sister Mary Therese took the jar full of water, blessed it, poured it over Maureen's head and prayed.

Maureen said, "Sister, why do you think God abandoned us?" But before Sister Mary Therese could answer, Maureen's eyes opened wide and she winced her last breath and died in the dirt of New York Harbor.

Frank's eyes widened and he felt a wall of panic and anxieties build up inside of him that made it extremely hard to catch his breath. When he could finally talk he said, "She didn't. Granddad, tell me she didn't die."

Liam nodded gently and said, "I'm afraid so."

Frank kicked the dirt and felt hatred for his granddad for the first time for bringing him here. He thought, "No one deserved this, no one." He then looked at the children.

Moria turned to Nancy feeling a fierce anxiety not meant for any human being, let alone a nine-year-old child. She said in a low haunting whisper, "Sweet Jesus, Nancy, tell me what we're supposed to do now?"

Even in a whisper, her voice cracked with panic and the tears stained her cheeks, people moving all around them.

"First Da and now Ma," she said, choking on her tears. "How could they leave us all alone? I want to go home." She convulsed in spasms on the ground, wracked with pain.

Nancy, a thirteen-year-old and a child in her own right, had no answers for her sister. She felt the same loss, the same pain and had to physically fight to control the panic that wanted to consume her.

She was so moved with pity for this helpless child lying on the ground that she forgot about her own pain and went to comfort Moria. Nancy sat down next to Moria on the floor, wrapped her arms around her and held her close. She didn't have any answers but she did have compassion and gave it freely.

She then felt the arms of Molly Rose as the three sat consoling one another. Giving each other all they had, which, for the moment, was enough.

As if by instinct, Pat and Billy went to the side of this woman, this nun, this stranger, for comfort. In her eyes, even though the scene had become familiar, it was, for the moment, surreal. As much faith as she placed in her omniscient Catholic God, she never understood why this was allowed to happen. What did the Island of the Saints ever do to deserve this?

Frank looked on not knowing whether he could watch anymore, let alone understand how these children actually lived through all this. He said, “Nice life. Nice fricking life.”

Liam said, “Watch your mouth.”

Frank looked at his granddad with belligerent eyes and said, “What’d you expect me to say? That this is all wonderful? Forget you.”

Liam said nothing. He stared solemnly as this death waltz, like a requiem mass, too familiar, too common, play itself out once again, seeming to get under his skin. He knew this was going to be hard, but he didn’t know how hard.

Sister Mary Therese went to the hem of Maureen’s long cotton skirt and lifted it slightly off her leg and began to tear away at it.

Nancy said, “Sister, what’re you doing?”

She ripped the hem and twenty-three gold coins fell to the ground. She looked up at Nancy and said, “Your folks weren’t the first Irish immigrants to sew money into their clothes, ‘tis a fairly typical practice.”

At the mention of her folks, tears burned their way down Nancy’s hot, red cheeks. But she persisted and overcame her desire to break and Frank sensed an almost fierce need rise in her to put herself away and take care of her siblings.

She said, “What do we do now?”

Sister Mary Therese knelt before the courageous young girl, handed her the coins, looked her in the eye, held her shoulders softly and said, “There’s an orphanage in the city.”

Nancy said, "No, no, no, not an orphanage. I won't, we won't."

The nun pulled the panicking girl to her breast and whispered, "Sshh, it's going to be okay, I'll see to that."

Nancy said, "No, sister, they'll split us up."

Sister Mary Therese said, "Listen to me, now. I'll do everything I can to see that that doesn't happen. I'll use this money to buy fresh under garments for you all and material to sew new outfits. But you've got to trust me."

Frank and Liam walked into the orphanage behind the children and Sister Mary Therese. Large rooms with hundreds of beds lining the walls were filled with sick and crying children. Nuns dressed like Sister Mary Therese, only they donned long white aprons from breast to floor, went from bed to bed tending the children and nursing them back to health. rank's stomach sunk and his heart gave way to a feeling of homesickness that was close to debilitating, as if he thought about running from all of this but that his legs would not carry him. He looked with a certain understanding at the children and couldn't help but wonder why.

Sister Mary Therese, sensing their panic, knelt in front of the O'Conlan children and said, "Okay, gather round. Things are not as bad as they seem."

Molly Rose said, "Yes they are."

"Okay children, they could be better, but we must put on a brave face. This'll only be temporary."

Frank watched vicariously as the O'Conlan children held hands together. They seemed to him like an antiquated weave so well worn that if one thread were removed it would fall apart.

Frank, in a trance-like state, looked at his granddad took his hand and began to recite:

"My Life is but a weaving
between my God and me
I do not chose the colors
He weaveth carefully.

Often times he weaveth sorrow
And I in foolish pride
Forget he sees the upper
And I the under side

The dark threads are as needful
In the skillful weavers hand
As the threads of gold and silver
In the pattern he has planned

Not till the loom is silent
And the shuttle cease to fly
Will God unroll the canvass
And explain the reason why."

Liam looked at his grandson with intense pride as Frank, poem finished, knelt down and cried.

Liam said, "What was that, son?"

Frank said, "A poem by a holocaust survivor named Corrie Tenboom."

Liam said, "Yeah?"

Frank said, "Yeah. Mom had it memorized and used to recite it to us as kids. Still does when she thinks we need it."

Liam said, "Huh."

The two watched as the O'Conlan children became like the other faceless souls occupying little bodies, abandoned by parents who died trying. They put one foot in front of the other becoming mindless, like the living dead, to protect themselves from the ruthless realities that existed in their world, which tried desperately to consume them.

That evening Liam and Frank watched with heartfelt

gratitude for the first time on this journey. Sister Mary Therese sat in front of a sewing machines, working the pedals, sewing outfits for the O'Conlans and repeating endless Hail Mary's and Glory Be's for all the Irish orphans unwanted by most everyone.

An older nun walked into the room and said, "Sister Mary Therese, your request has been approved. All the O'Conlan children will be relocated together in our orphanage in Syracuse."

Not even looking up from her work at the machines she said, "Praise Jesus."

CHAPTER 13
THE LETTER, THE POTEEN AND THE SMALL POX

Frank said, "Maybe there is a God after all."

Liam said, "Maybe. Hey, we need to go somewhere and I'm giving you fair warning so you don't go getting all huffy with me."

Frank said, "Huffy?'

Liam smiled and said, "Yeah, huffy."

Suddenly Frank and Liam were back in the village of Upperchurch, where this all started five years ago and the villagers were rebuilding the village, trying to put their lives back together during the first years of the worst famine Europe had ever known.

Frank looked on as Paddy McNulty sat with his wife Siobhan. He spoke and she just sat and stared, acknowledging nothing and no one.

Frank said, "What's with her?"

Liam said, "You'll see. Frank, Paddy McNulty continued to endure the potato blight and famine, a five-year span of time that would seem to move as slowly as an endless age of suffering. A melancholy and contemplative man by nature, he spent a lot of time thinking about his current situation – that of Ireland, his family and friends. Things had been bleak for so long he found very little to smile about. But at least he and his family survived the workhouse and had finally made their way back to Upperchurch to start all over.

"What he was most reflective about these days was the night Aidan visited him in his dreams. He'd spent a lot of time thinking about it and shared it with no one. Hell, he didn't know for sure whether it actually happened.

"Paddy had two thoughts that were causing him grave anxiety and constantly nagged at him since Aidan's visit. First, Aidan's prophecy of Maureen's death and second, if true, what would happen to the children if orphaned in a strange land, making them vulnerable to any sort of perniciousness."

Frank said, "What the hell does perniciousness mean?"

Liam said, "Well, let's see. Destructive, lethal, deadly, fatal, harmful..."

"Okay, okay, I'm sorry I asked."

Liam continued, "Paddy had many hardships in his life; not the least being the famine and seeing dear loved ones leave the island forever. But he simply could not let himself even begin to believe that those beautiful children were in America under those circumstances. Aidan said a letter would be forthcoming and Paddy knew that once the letter arrived, it would validate the apparition and bring anxiously awaited news. It arrived six weeks after his visit from Aidan."

Paddy said, "Siobhan, we finally got word from the O'Conlans. Apparently they made it to the shores of America. Do you want me to read this to you?" She did nothing but stare endlessley.

Paddy said, "Okay, here goes:

May 12, 1846

My dearest Aunt Siobhan and Uncle Paddy:

I am sad writing this letter. The last few months since we left Upperchurch have not been happy. There is no easy way to say this, so here goes.

Da died on the boat. He got the famine disease. We buried him at sea March 15, 1846, two days before the holy feast day of St. Patrick.

Mam got the same disease, we think from Da, it was terribly catching and she never left his side. There was little food or water on the boat. By the time we arrived in America she could not fight it. Mam died April 3, 1846 in the dirt of New York Harbor.

When we got off the boat we met a Sister of Charity. Her name is Sister Mary Therese and she is from county Mayo. She helped us as much as she could with mam but it was too late.

She put us in an orphanage in New York City for a month or so and then she was able to get us in an orphanage all together in a place called Syracuse, New York, which is where we are now.

I'm saddened though, because we'll never see Upperchurch again, or any of you again. We all get desperately homesick and would even be willing to get on one of those awful boats to come home.

But we all know we would all be a far greater burden than help back home.

One bright spot is that Syracuse has a large Irish population. There is actually a large Irish neighborhood here called Tipperary Hill. The orphanage is located near there.

However, even amongst our own people, we orphans are looked upon as a burden. They're all having a hard time making a living and five kids without parents are not welcome. But the nuns have been great. We're separated from the boys and only get to see them once a day, but everyone is getting along well.

I will continue to write.

With all of our love,

Nancy, Molly Rose, Moria, Patrick and Billy."

When Paddy finished reading the letter, Frank and Liam watched as he quickly wiped the tears from his eyes as he looked at Siobhan. She on the other hand was not hiding her grief as she wept openly, emoting openly for the first time in a year.

Liam said, "Frank, unrealistic as it was, Paddy always secretly felt he'd see them again one day. But that dream was now dashed. He felt so hopeless and lost; life would never be the same again.

"But Paddy took solace, however, in the other villagers who were in the same circumstances. So he went to share the news with them."

Frank said, "You mean misery loves company?"

Liam said, "I never thought of it like that, but I'd have to say no. He leaned on the other villagers and they on him for support. This went way beyond the American version of misery.

"Before this all started, Frank, there was a pub in Upperchurch called Paddy O'Quinane's. For obvious reasons it shut down during the blight. So when the villagers were in need of the occasional pick me up they gathered in one cottage or another, depending on who got to widow Killarney that week."

Frank said, "Who's that?"

"Who, widow Killarney?"

"Yeah."

Liam said, "I'm sorry, I got ahead of myself. Poteen is what the Irish call potato whisky. It was distilled throughout Southern Ireland and was illegal because the crown in England couldn't collect any tax on it. But like anything, some distillers were better than others were. These distillers were slick and smart. It was widely believed that they were related to the leprechaun because they could feel trouble long before it was met. If the constabulary was sniffing around they could tear down their still and be gone in the blink of en eye."

Frank was now laughing, a rare light moment and it felt good.

"Anyway, no one knew who the distillers were and they had widows selling their mash because the English wouldn't suspect it. But as hard as the villagers tried, they couldn't get it out of the widows, because it was a source of income for the little old women that would dry up if they opened their mouths. So the distillers knew they could trust these widows and count on them to be discrete.

"So Paddy found out it was Kevin Power who had the whisky and it was off to share the news. This time they held a wake, but it was the real thing. They had no bodies to prepare but they had memories and rosaries and they planned on getting the most out of both."

The next day, Frank and Liam watched as they all gathered at Holy Ghost Catholic Church where Fr. Finnerty said a requiem mass in memory of the immigrant parishioners that had passed. Then they gathered at Kevin Power's farm afterwards. The wake went into the wee hours of the morning; some of the more ardent mourners watched the sun come up on their way home.

Frank and Liam sat on a stone hedgerow on the outskirts of Upperchurch and were laughing at the stragglers, impressed with their stamina. Liam filled the bowl of his pipe, lit it and blew a large white plume of smoke into the humid morning air and then said, "Frank, Nancy O'Conlan, in every sense of the word, except the physical one, became a mother at the tender age of thirteen. Even though they were, by now in an orphanage in Syracuse run by the Sisters of Charity, she was the one who made sure they were all up, fed and ready for school. She made sure they were clean, with teeth brushed and hair combed. She was the one who made sure their clothes were washed and darned. She was the one who made sure they were fed at dinner and that they all did their homework at night.

"She discovered that being an Irish Catholic immigrant was a difficult chore. She found that her kind was not welcome and that the Yankees were fairly direct about it. She also realized that it was even worse to be the orphan children of Irish immigrants, treated poorly by not only the Yanks, but also by the Irish as well. Irish Catholic immigrants had their own problems; they didn't need the problems of some out-of-luck children.

"As a result, Frank, Nancy made sure that her brothers and sisters went out to face the world clean and well fed. This way no one would mistake them for the orphans that they were. If others were to find out it would not be because they looked the part. She was proud and would not allow any of them to look shabby.

"She was darning and sewing more than she wanted. She was doing laundry and dishes more than she wanted. These chores were after she came home from doing laundry, dishes, darning and sewing for wealthy Yankee families who treated her as less. When doing these menial tasks she would daydream of the man who would come and take her away. She could picture him and dreamed of falling madly in love.

Nancy decided to go to work and forego her education so that the youngsters would benefit. With what little she earned, and as much as they needed, she still found enough money to send back home to Uncle Paddy and Aunt Siobhan.

"Billy and Pat often came home with cuts, bruises and torn clothes from fighting. Every day was an endless proving ground for Irish kids and these two held their own. After six months of taking on and whipping every kid who challenged them, they were finally accepted and even began to make a few friends.

"Molly Rose and Moria couldn't be more different. Other than the fact that they could have passed as twins, they were like night and day. Molly Rose was quiet, studious and reserved, while Moria was outgoing, boisterous and gregarious.

"However, they were best friends and were always

together. The only difference was that you usually heard Moria before you saw her. She was always telling stories and playing pranks, Molly Rose, as quiet as she was, had a huge laugh and Moria got no more satisfaction than to make Molly Rose laugh.

"They made many friends and Nancy became somewhat jealous. She was working hard both in and out of the house and there was little time to make friends or socialize. She didn't have time to think about it much, but when she did it made her sad. That's when she became lost in her daydreams to take her away from the burdens, someone her age should not have to face. Life just wasn't fair. But her suffering now would prove to be to her benefit in years to come. The O'Conlans had been in America now for nearly three years. They were growing up and growing accustomed to their new life. Things were going pretty well for them, probably too well. They should have known better.

"Frank, Molly Rose, beautiful and quiet, was growing into a young lady. She had suffered many things in her short fourteen years. After three years in America she was finally allowing herself to feel a glimpse of happiness and joy. At long last, she was feeling comfortable; her stomach didn't hurt anymore from anxious thoughts. She was sleeping well at night. That's when she woke one morning with an irritable rash and headache that began to nag at her day in and day out. Once the fever set in, she went to the doctor at the orphanage. His diagnosis: small pox.

Frank said, "What's small pox?"

Liam said, "You wouldn't know, would you?"

Frank said, "No."

"During the earlier part of this century we wiped out the disease with vaccination. But before that it was a highly contagious and deadly disease."

Frank said, "No, Not Molly."

Liam hung his head and said, "We'll get to that, son."

CHAPTER 14
THE SECOND MIGRATION

Two Years Later 1851
Upperchurch, County Tipperary, The Republic of Ireland

Frank hung his head and the tears came. He hated to show emotion, but was unable to stop the flow within him.

Liam said, "You okay?"

Frank said, "No."

Liam gave him a few minutes and then said, "Remember the cemetery in Petersville where I showed you Nancy and John Power's gravestones?"

"Yeah."

Liam said, "Take my hand, you've met Nancy, let's go meet John Power."

The clouds of northern Tipperary County rolled and shifted like deep dark ocean waves in threatening blacks and grays and contrasted with the green rolling hills which gave the Emerald

Isle its name. Lightning split the early morning calm and Frank counted five before the thunder that rumbled deep within his chest clapped so loudly that even after expecting it, he jumped. The skies opened up and poured down on them in sheets so heavy Frank found it hard to breath and had to turn his head as if someone a story above them were simply pouring barrels of water on them and laughing at their discomfort.

After a few moments the rain lightened to a small deluge and Frank looked at his granddad and said, "Do you do this shit on purpose or are you just oblivious?"

Liam, who had been more than a bit surprised himself at the unsettling weather, started to laugh at his grandson's indolence and said, "Frank, this too shall pass."

Frank said, "Right. Anyway, you were saying something about John Power?"

Liam said, "Oh, yes, I almost forgot."

Liam stopped for a moment, rubbed his chin to get his thoughts together, smiled and said, "Frank, the Power lease was as far south of Upperchurch as the O'Conlan lease was north. John Power was the youngest of five boys. Kevin Power was his father and there didn't exist a more stubborn man in all of Ireland. People had been starving all around him for the last five years and because of a family business the Power clan ran they would not starve during the famine. That doesn't mean that times weren't tough it just meant they'd survive."

Frank said, "What business?"

Liam said, "Bootlegging the best Poteen in Tipperary County, maybe the whole Republic."

"Potato whiskey?"

"You've been listening. Kevin Power perfected a triple distill method that lads came many miles to purchase. He was also a genius when it came to distribution without paying the crown in England one schilling in taxes. He had old widows, who needed the money and were able to keep their mouths shut, selling jugs out of their cellars. He was able to put some money away and when the famine hit they were able to withstand the worst of it. But no potato meant no way of making the poteen and there wouldn't have been anybody to buy it anyway. But after five years of bad crops they finally had a descent one growing and Kevin Power was looking forward to getting the family business stoked up once more.

"But I have to tell you his youngest son, however, had different plans. He dreamed of leaving the farm, leaving the poverty and making something of himself. He knew for certain that America held great promise and he wanted to test those seas.

"John Power loved his father, loved his family and loved Ireland as much as any Irishman. But he felt he was a burden to all three. He knew that being the youngest of five boys meant that he'd get no land. So he began to scrimp and save as best he could. On occasion he'd do meager jobs and run errands for a land agent of a local landlord.

And, once in a while, his old man would throw a coin or two his way for his work on the farm. John Power had a secret mission that he'd not be talked out of.

Frank said, "What's a land agent?"

"They were people who worked for the landlords. They were hated because they collected the rent and mostly harassed people."

"So what was John Power doing with a land agent?"

"Let me explain. Kevin Power's landlord was a man named Anson Merryweather. Merryweather's main estate was south of Upperchurch around a town called Cashel where the land was flat in Tipperary and good for large plantations. He also had land around Upperchurch, Holy Cross, Thurles and Templemore all towns in northern Tipperary. But Kevin never dealt with Merryweather, he had his dealings and paid his rent to a man names Martin O'Hurley who was the land agent for Merryweather.

"John Power left Ireland in 1851 and just a year before in 1850 Martin O'Hurley died of a sudden heart attack. The O'Hurley clan had been land agents for the Merryweathers for three generations so when Martin died the job went to the capable hands of his son Matthew.

"Now unbeknownst to the Merryweathers, the O'Hurley clan, who called Upperchurch home, had republican leanings for many more years than they were land agents. It worked out well because Upperchurch, Holy Cross, Templemore and Thurles were all hotbeds of nationalism and Republicanism. This whole area was home to the Northern Tipperary brigade of the Irish Republican Brotherhood the I.R.B or NORTIP of the IRB as they were referred to locally. Throughout his life Martin was able to move freely within these communities, pass on tidbits of information as well as run and hide firearms in and around the Merryweather estates for the brotherhood in Munster, the province that Tipperary was in."

Frank said, "Province?"

Liam said, "Yeah, the country of Ireland has four provinces each consisting of the many counties. Anyway the Fenian blood ran thick in Matthew's veins as well. So when the brotherhood approached him after his dad died, he was game.

"Now, Anson Merryweather didn't hesitate to give the position to Matthew after his father was gone. He had a good head on his shoulders and, since the O'Hurleys had been working for the Merryweathers for over a century, knew the job. John Power and Matthew O'Hurley had a relationship based on mutual needs and interests. Power would run errands for O'Hurley and O'Hurley would lend Power books to read.

"When working for O'Hurley, Power would, on occasion, run into Paddy McNulty and ask if Nancy O'Conlan had sent any recent letters home. He dreamed of getting to America and seeing her again, having fallen deeper in love with her since she went away. Even though she was five years younger, he remembered her as a beautiful lass when the O'Conlans left. She became his reason for existing.

"He remembered with a heavy heart all the families leaving the village. But it was when Aidan and Maureen left that he experienced the quiet desperation that had fallen on most all of

Ireland. When the village of Upperchurch found out that Aidan and Maureen didn't make it, their grief was powerful. John's first instinct was to jump the first ship and save the children.

"The day he'd heard Paddy read Nancy's first letter home he went to the farthest corner of his father's farm, sat under a tree and cried. He didn't want any of his brothers to see him crying, but only a stone would feel no emotion after hearing what'd happened to her since leaving home.

"Most of his friends were gone now and the village was almost non-existent. He hated the idea of telling his father of his plans to immigrate to America and put it off as long as possible. He was twenty-one years old, wasn't married and wasn't interested in any of the local girls."

Frank said, "He sounds like a fairly decent guy."

Liam said, "You haven't heard anything yet." He pointed to the two men as they were beginning to converse and said, "Watch this and listen."

John Power and Matthew O'Hurley huddled together on a rural road just south of the Merryweather property as if they were in some kind of secret conclave.

John said, "Matthew, what do you think it's like in America?"

Matthew said, "They say it's a grand place. Wide open spaces the likes of which islanders like us could hardly imagine."

"Do you think a croppy like me could do well there?"

"John Power, there's not a doubt in my mind that a man like you would do well there, or anywhere you chose. Why? What's on your mind?"

"That there's nothing left for me here. I'm a burden and it's time for me to make a life for myself. I want to go in the worst way."

"It's more than that, isn't it lad?"

Power hesitated and said, "Aye."

"What is it then?"1

"The love of my life is in an orphanage in New York and, for the last five years, I've been dreaming of her. I want to take her away from there and make a life with her."

"What are you waiting for, man?"

"My Da."

"What about your Da?"

"He'll never let me go. He's nothing if he's not stubborn. He says the Powers are Irishmen and Ireland is where we'll stay. He doesn't understand."

"Have you talked to him about it?"

"No."

"Then I suggest you do. We Irishmen are independent thinkers and cherish freedom above all things. But John, you have to live your life as you see fit. Some day your Da will be gone and then what?"

"What do you mean?"

"I mean that your da is living his life as he sees fit and I suspect he'll understand when one of his sons, who's a grown man, makes a decision about his own life."

"I love my Da."

"Of course you do, lad, and he loves you. I know your Da and I know he's a stubborn man; but I also know your Da to be a fair man. Go talk to him. If he resists then you have to make a choice. My guess is he'll respect you for wanting to make your way in the world."

When they were finishing they heard a horse and rider approaching. They looked up the road to see Miles Merryweather, son of Anson, riding toward them.

Frank said, "Who's that"

Liam said, "Miles Merryweather, born to a legacy of English ascendancy in Ireland, son of Viscount Anson Merryweather. However, his father thought as much of his son as most people did — a pompous, patronizing, pain in the ass. The Viscount sent him away to school and was making secret plans for him after his education was through. He wanted him nowhere near the family business."

Frank said, "Huh."

Before Miles reached them, Matthew said under his breath so only John could hear, "Nobody told me this horse's ass was coming to visit. Keep your mouth shut, John."

Miles reached them and said, "Matthew, I've been looking for you. What are you doing talking to the peasants? We've got work to do."

"Miles, your father and I discussed what he wanted me to accomplish for him this week and he mentioned nothing about you."

In the arrogant disdain of many in the English ascendancy Miles said, "Whom do you think you're talking to? And whom do you think you work for? Your plans just changed."

O'Hurley said, "I work for your father and my plans change when he says, not you."

O'Hurley was a tall, well-built, muscular man and typically was of a pleasant nature, but it took little to rile him.

Miles Merryweather, on the other hand, was a slender man, all of five-foot two inches tall with a high, squeaky voice. He had been harassed his whole life by those bigger and stronger and, as a result, he hated everyone, especially those who he considered in his employ. He would approach no one outside the manor without his mount; it was the only time he could look down on anyone.

Before O'Hurley knew it Merryweather had struck him across the face with his leather riding stick and said, "If you work for my father then you work for me. You're little more than a common laborer and you'll show me the respect that I deserve as the son of a viscount and you *will* do what I tell you without question. Do we understand one another? Hmm?"

Merryweather then looked at a stunned John Power and said, "What are you looking at, peasant?"

Power smirked awkwardly and said, "I'm looking at you."

Merryweather said, "Well I suggest you look elsewhere, this is none of your damned business."

Power stepped forward and O'Hurley stepped in his way and said, "John, don't."

Merryweather said in a high and sarcastic voice, "Oh and what? We're going to have a brawl are we?"

Power pushed on O'Hurley who held him back and said, "There'd be no brawl here with a runt like you."

Merryweather said, "Clever. You peasants really are a rather clever lot. Let's see, you're clever at making unwanted babies, clever at being unable to feed them, clever at being out of work misfits and making an awful mess of things throughout the countryside with all your starving, what. But you always seem to have enough grain to make your tax free whiskey, don't you?"

O'Hurley was now holding back Power with all his might and Merryweather sitting atop his horse laughed and continued, "I'm rather struggling deciding what you unfortunates do best. Let's see, is it screwing, starving, fighting or drinking? Oh and I almost forgot you're a damn fine lot at waiting around for handouts from those of us who work for a living. You do that pretty well too, hmm? I'm sorry for the insult then, you're not totally useless. Doesn't that about sum up you Catholics, screwing, starving, fighting, drinking and handouts?"

Power moved in closer and Merryweather was now beside himself with glee and mimicked a drunken Irish brogue, "No wait! Let's not eat! We won't have anything with which to make the whiskey. Fuck the women and children, let's get drunk!"

Frank McGrath, a white middle class American, who had never experienced racial discrimination before, was now watching a blatant episode and he could feel the hair rise on the nape of his neck. He felt that familiar buzz of heat in his cheeks before a fight and shear hatred and loathing welled up in him that seemed to take control and he understood now why one man might kill another. And a certain perspicacity finally crashed in on him like a tsunami on dry, crusted earth, why African Americans rose up in the 1950's after having had enough of racial discrimination, hatred and misunderstanding.

Liam felt his grandson tense up and he put his arm around his shoulder and said, "It doesn't feel very good does it?"

Frank said, "What doesn't?"

Liam said, "Prejudice. Racism."

"No it doesn't. I've never wanted to kill a man before now. I honestly think I could kill that bastard."

Liam said, "Well then I'm glad it was John Power standing there and not you. Watch."

Power, in a raw fury, threw O'Hurley to the ground and with a swiftness and strength that surprised Merryweather, pulled him from his mount and held him off the ground while Merryweather struck him ineffectually with his riding stick and screamed.

O'Hurley grabbed Power and said, "John, put him down, he's not worth it."

Power came to his senses, put Merryweather down, grabbed the riding stick and held him by his throat against his horse.

Merryweather, gagging, said, "O'Hurley, you lay one finger on me and I'll see to your termination. As for this brute, I'll see to his hanging."

O'Hurley smiled and said, "Miles, as usual, you're right. John, back away."

Power, shocked at this, backed away from the small man.

Merryweather said, "That's better. Now, would you give me my riding stick please?"

O'Hurley said, "John, would you give me Mile's riding stick and then would you grab the rope from his saddle?"

John smiled and said, “With pleasure.”

The blood drained from Merryweather’s face as O’Hurley slammed him to the ground.

Merryweather said, “What the devil are you doing? Unhand me, you brute.”

The two men laughed at the wormlike figure writhing in the dirt. They pulled his arms above his head and then tied his hands together as well as his feet. O’Hurley picked up the small man like a ten pound sack of spuds and laid him perpendicular to the horse on his saddle, resting him on his stomach. Power then tied his hands and feet together beneath the belly of the horse.

Merryweather screamed, “You bastards, you’ll see a firing squad for this.”

O’Hurley pulled a handkerchief from his back pocket, stuffed it in Merryweather’s mouth and said, “Och, shut your gob, you’re squirming like a tadpole.” He grabbed the riding stick, spanked Merryweather several times on his buttocks, leaving large, well deserved welts and then slapped the horse on his rear with his large hand and watched him bolt through the countryside. The two men laughed until they were in tears.

Power said laughing, “For a small man he has a large mouth. Matthew, I hope this doesn’t come back to haunt us.”

O’Hurley said, “Are you serious? His father would’ve done the same. I’ll probably get a raise. Now go talk to your Da while you still have him. You’ll be fine.”

Frank said, “Gramps, was that guy for real?”

Liam said, “You bet he is. You haven’t heard the last of that horse’s ass. This guy had some serious problems.”

The month was May, the year 1851. The sun was just peeking over the eastern horizon like a shy child reluctant to meet new company. A cool breeze was blowing the early morning haze to the ocean while the green, rolling hills of Northern Tipperary anticipated the late spring morning, which brought with it the sheen that they so desired. Kevin Power was up as were all the boys, getting the necessary chores done before starting in on a long day in the peat fields, the ball and chain of their existence.

Kevin was talking with his oldest son Seamus when John walked in and interrupted.

"Da, do you have a minute?"

"Aye, what is it?"

They walked into the farmyard out of earshot from any of his brothers or mother. He stood for a moment and stared at his father. He was sick knowing he was in for a fight and that was the last thing he wanted. But he was a man and this was his proving ground.

John started sheepishly, "Da, I don't know any other way to put this."

"What is it, lad?" his dad answered impatiently.

He said, "Da, I've decided to make me way to America." He then waited for the wrath of God to come down on him.

Kevin Power, cantankerous, irascible and stubborn, even by Irish standards, stopped and stared at the ground around him. He would begin to talk and then would stop. He did this several times as if what he was about to say could not be retracted and he needed to get it right, that it deserved deeper contemplation.

After a few more moments of this, he looked up at his son and his pistol blue eyes gleamed with a love John had never seen before and he said, "You're a full grown man, John. You've made me very proud and the stubborn old fool that I am never allowed me those words."

He stopped once more then said, "I... " His voice caught in his throat and the tiniest tear formed in the corner of his eye.

John took a step back, he had never seen this kind of emotion from this tough old man and he didn't know how to react.

Kevin said, "I've seen it in your eye, I have. And don't you know I knew, with all your running around for Matthew O'Hurley, saving your pennies? And I have to admit I'm a bit ashamed that I don't have more than a wee bit of coin to send with you. Though, I know you'll be grateful for any that I have to give."

John said, "Da, you've already given me enough. I wasn't asking for anything more than your blessing. 'Tis plenty."

Kevin said, "Och. Me blessing 'tis the least I can give. I just wish I had more to offer you."

John stepped forward tentatively and with an awkward motion put his arms around his father. The gesture was returned with a fierceness that John had not expected. Kevin Power then turned and walked away and didn't look back, his shoulders heavy with grief as the drudgery of the peat fields once again offered him his daily bread.

Liam and Frank watched as the Power men came in out of the fields around 6:30 p.m., tired, dirty, and hungry. They went to the well, cleaned up and went inside to eat a meager dinner.

After dinner, Kevin Power walked outside and came back with a jug. The boys looked at one another, then their mother, eyes locked in question. The poteen, because it had become so scarce, was brought out only for special occasions and never to the dinner table. No one could guess the significance. He stood at the head of the table and asked his wife, Mary Clare, to gather some clean jars for he and his sons.

She brought one extra and he looked at her with question and she said, "Do you think I'll be left out?"

The only person in Ireland that could put Kevin Power in his place was his wife Mary Clare. He said, "I didn't think."

She said, "No you didn't."

He smiled at his thoughtlessness and filled the jars for all of them and then raised his glass, taking a long pull without saying anything. The boys did nothing except watch in amazement as he brought the glass down from his lips. His hands trembled as he refilled his glass.

"I've got both good news and bad news. The bad news is that your baby brother, John, is leaving us for America and you all know what that means."

The boys stared at John in disbelief. Other than Seamus, who was the oldest and would get the lease, all of the boys wondered who'd be the first to go, but none of them were surprised it was John. He was restless and spoke about it the most. It also meant that each of them would now have a shot at going.

Seamus looked up and said, "Da, you said good news as well?"

"Aye, the good news is that your brother John will have an opportunity to better himself by immigrating. But don't fool yourselves, this'll be no easy chore. He's been saving his money and I'm giving him some meager inheritance to take with him. He'll go first, he'll gain employment, he'll save his money and he'll send back money for passage for any of the rest of you who want to go. He'll also send back money to help us with our needs. You all know how scarce coin is around here.

"Lads, tradition tells us that the land goes to the oldest son. So Seamus will be getting the land, 'tis no great benefit this inheritance. The benefit has and always will be in the poteen. The spud is coming back and we'll soon be back as strong as ever. But I'll no longer be getting in the way of you lad's futures. If you must go, then you must. But if you stay I'll make sure you're taken care of."

They all sat quietly sipping their poteen, wondering what this meant to all of them. Pat, Clem and Tom were secretly disappointed that Seamus got the land simply because of his time of birth.

John couldn't be happier, but he didn't realize how difficult it would be to leave this land of green rolling hills, stone hedgerows, sunshine and damp, cloudy days. He also didn't realize how hard it would be to say good-bye to his family.

His mother, Mary Clare, a proud, independent woman, finished her jar, the dishes, walked out beyond the yard behind the barn, put her hands to her face, fell to the ground in utter despair and wept.

Frank and Liam watched as Mary Clare walked from the cottage and then stared as the men continued to talk.

Frank said, "I can't imagine having a conversation like that back home, talking about brothers and sisters leaving home for good, never seeing mom or dad again. This is insane."

Liam said, "Yes it is, son. And it happened over and over again all over Ireland. It's important for us to understand where we came from, to know the sacrifices that were made to get us where we are and to never, ever forget."

Liam leaned back a bit, lit his pipe and blew a couple of outstanding and carefully practiced smoke rings. His eyes gleamed as if he were really looking forward to an upcoming event and said, "Francis, John Kevin Power left Ireland in 1851, five years after the death ships had begun to set sail. He was a simple, God-fearing, rural Irishman, naïve to the chicanery that existed in the outside world. Yet somehow knew he was in for the trip of his life, even with the thoughts of danger, there existed the thrill of the unknown and the excitement of an adventure.

"For as long as he had prepared for this day, he had not prepared himself for the strength he would need to actually leave. He took solace in the fact that he may see Pat, Clem and Tom again at sometime in America. But saying good-bye to his Mother, Father and oldest brother Seamus, knowing he would never see them again, sliced at his heart leaving a gaping wound that he wore openly on his face.

"He made his way to Galway City on the West Coast of Ireland. He put one foot in front of the other and the thought of Nancy O'Conlan and her sisters and brothers on the other end of his journey fueled his resolve.

"When he finally reached his destination he found a seaside pub called "The Rooster." He was thirsty and hungry so he made a quick count of his money, took a deep breath and walked in.

"He ordered a pint of strong ale and noticed a group of sailors in the back drinking and carrying on at a pitch a couple of decibels above the rest of the crowd."

He said to the bartender, "Who're they?"

"A bunch of sailors blowing off steam. They got into port this morning."

"Navy?"

"No, merchant sailors, back and forth from America, moving merchandise. The stouts on the dock load 'em and unload 'em and these lads sail 'em, pain in the arse, all of 'em, if you're asking me, nutty as a bunch of damn squirrels after a couple of months at sea."

Power said, "Och. Looks like they're having fun, nothing more."

"Fun? Come on back around ten this evening. If they're not trying to get laid, they'll be looking for a fight. The stouts'll come in looking for a pint after unloading ships all day. They'll get all pissed up and then pissed off that these sailors are trying to pick up all the local gals and they'll all bust the place up sure as I'm standing here. And guess who'll be cleaning up afterward. I don't get paid enough for that."

John said, "Maybe I'll stick around, it might be fun to watch, something new."

The bartender said, "You're new around here?"

John said, "Aye. I'm making me way to America."

"Well you've come to the right place."

"What do you mean?"

"Seaport and all. These merchant ships are always looking for able-bodied men."

"Seriously?"

"Aye."

"I thought I was going to have to buy me way."

The bartender leaned over the bar and said, "You don't want to do that."

"Do what?"

"Buy your way. You'll want to stay as far away from those damn passenger brokers as you can. They'll screw you as soon as look at you and then you'll end up on a cattle ship in worse shape than the live stock."

The bartender nodded his head to the back of the pub and said, "You see the sailor over there, the tall one, red hair, beard, standing in the corner by himself?"

John looked over his shoulder and said, "Aye."

"He's in charge. He's not like the rest of these Yahoos. He's here to make sure his crew makes it back to the ship in one piece. Go have a chat with him. From the looks of it he'd have no problem finding work for you."

Power looked at the man standing behind the bar and said, "Thanks, mister, thanks a lot."

The bartender nodded his head and said, "Glad to be of service."

Liam tapped his pipe on the palm of his hand, took a small pocketknife out, scraped the bowl, and reloaded it before lighting it again.

He said, "Frank, John Power spent the next six weeks on a merchant ship working his way across the Atlantic Ocean on his way to New York. An English company owned the ship and the crew was a tough lot from all over Europe. They worked hard, drank hard and occasionally fought hard. Power mostly kept to himself dreaming about his new life, worrying and wondering about the O'Conlans.

"He met two Irishmen on the ship who had family in America and they promised introductions when the ship docked. Power didn't know what to expect when they got to New York but was dumbfound when he walked off the ship into New York Harbor. The large number of people was mind-numbing. He didn't know there were this many people in the entire world and was glad for the Irishmen he had met who would make some introductions.

"The welcome to New York was nowhere near as unfriendly as the reception most of the immigrant ships ran into because it was a commercial ship, but the size and scope of the city was enough of an unfriendly welcome as to put a scare in Power.

"The introductions were made and he was suddenly whisked off into a nightmare of people living on top of one another, babies crying, people screaming, men fighting and drunks wobbling to and fro. Trash lined the gutters of the streets and the stench of humanity was everywhere. He found himself in the bowels of an Irish slum in the Bronx. He felt a sudden pang of anxiety, wishing only for the wide-open space of the rural countryside he had grown up in and questioned for the first time whether he had made the right decision.

"Prostitutes were hustling him, swindlers trying to persuade him to throw dice with them and pick pockets moving in for their daily wage when he came to the realization that this was survival of the fittest.

"All he had were the clothes on his back, the money he had brought with him and the money he had made on the ship. But any anxiety and fear left him as he took a long hard look around and realized he saw no one he couldn't handle if he had to."

Liam stopped talking and Frank looked around as if coming out of a dream. He saw John Power standing with a group of Irishmen who had circled up and were talking. Power looked mystified like he just realized that in this mass of humankind he was completely and utterly alone, but then he smiled as if it became quickly apparent that it didn't matter because right here, right now, he was with his people once more and once more it was the Irish against the world.

The men were talking amongst themselves, smoking cigarettes and passing around a bottle of whiskey, apparently making a decision of some kind. Like all immigrants they spoke a mixture of their language back home and English, the language of their new home.

The bottle was passed to Power and he took a pull of the first aged whiskey he had ever tasted. He swallowed with pleasure and began to feel more at ease. He stood four to six inches above the rest of the immigrants in the circle and after a moment or two, once he started to pay attention to the conversation, he realized they were talking about him.

The leader said, "They don't have anyone other than Red Mahoney and with this newcomer we could double our money."

The leader's crony, a little pot-bellied man who kept looking up at Power as if sizing him up said, "Aye, double our money."

Power suddenly realizing they were all looking at him said, "What?"

The leader said, "Fisticuffs, lad. You ever boxed?"

Power said, "No."

The leader said, "We think you'd be good. What do you say?"

"You mean in a ring?"

"No, just a bar room laddie."

Power looked puzzled.

Ignoring him, the leader looked at the men around him and said, "How much money do we have?"

They ponied up ten dollars, grabbed Power under the elbows and began to walk him through the crowded streets. They broke through and walked halfway down a city block and cut into an alley. As they walked some of the men screamed to the bystanders, "We've got a contender!"

Frank said, "Granddad, what the hell is going on? Is he going to fight?"

Liam said, "Watch and see, lad, watch and see."

Frank said, "You can be such a turd."

Liam put his head back and laughed like he was just glad to be part of all this.

Pretty soon people were walking out of doors and joining the throng and by the time they reached their destination it was a small mob.

Power was rushed into a huge bar room that looked more like a big warehouse. It was full of people who began to hoot and holler in anticipation.

The leader looked at Power and said, "Take your coat off." John said, "Wait a minute."

Someone handed him a bottle of whiskey, he took a long pull and suddenly the crowd parted into a large circle and the biggest man that John Power had ever seen walked into the opening and said, "Who's the new meat?"

The crowd roared.

The leader said, "That's Red McMahon. Never been beat. Now listen to me, don't waste your time on the body, a steam ship couldn't hurt him. And don't bother hitting him head on, I've seen lads hit him with heavy oak chairs and he just smiled. Your only shot is to catch him from the side and break his jaw. He's slower than a two toed sloth but he can take a punch like no man and there's your advantage."

Power said, "What is?"

"He likes to wear his opponents down by taking punches until they can't lift their arms. Then he moves in for the kill. So move to hit him on the side of the jaw where you might break it, it may not do a damn thing but its all I got, and one last thing."

Power nodded intently.

"He's as dirty as the hull of an ocean hearse. He'll gouge your eyes out, bite your ears off and then punch and kick you in the stones until they pop, he will. The man's got eight kids and a wife at home and a wins worth five American. He's above nothing to win the purse. Stay away from him." Power said, "Easier said than done."

Power reckoned that the man had him by fifty pounds, but the sinking feeling he had upon his initial observance of the large Irishman began to vanish as he watched the slow, almost lethargic motion of the big man as he swung his large arms at an invisible target.

Power walked toward his opponent and as the crowd circled up its roar became deafening. Red Mahoney smiled at him. Power noticed that Mahoney had maybe five teeth and his eyes reminded him of staring down the shaft of a double barrel shotgun, dark and black. Power realized now that he was going into battle and he felt reluctance for the first time. His heart began to pound and doubt crept into his mind

Frank was beside himself with excitement. He had been moving at an incredibly fast pace with Liam to keep up with Power since his arrival in New York. Now he was jumping up and down screaming for Power and not even trying to converse with his granddad as the roar made it impossible. He watched as Mahoney came at Power, stepped forward and lunged, swinging wildly. Power ducked with ease and the slow moving arm missed its mark by a long shot. Power came up and reciprocated with a crushing left hook hitting Mahoney in the side of his left lower jaw. There was a pop that Power felt but couldn't hear. He followed that with a right jab that had the force of all his weight behind it, his wet bare knuckles slid off Mahoney's lower chin and slammed into his throat smashing the big man's Adams apple to the back of his esophagus.

Mahoney took a step back, wild-eyed and slobbering. He grabbed his neck, gagging for breathe and fell to his knees. Power, not realizing his opponent was nearing death, moved forward and smashed one bare fist after another into the dying man's face before Red Mahoney hunched over dead before he hit the canvass.

The crowd was in utter shock. The only sound that could be heard was the corpse of Red Mahoney as it bounced with a thud on the wooden barroom floor. Silence. Two friends of the big man rushed to him and felt for a pulse, there was none. The leader pulled John Power's hands over his head and the crowd erupted once again, only this time they were chanting, "Power! Power! Power!"

CHAPTER 15
THE ORPHANAGE

Frank watched in amazement as the crowd carried John Power into the street in a sort of sick celebration over, not just a boxing victory, but a man's death. The barroom emptied into the street and in the quiet aftermath Frank said, "Granddad, is that guy dead?"

Liam said, "Yes, he is."

"And they're all celebrating?"

"Not all of them, look."

Frank looked over as Red Mahoney's recent widow and his eight children cried while friends and family struggled to get the large man's corpse removed.

Liam said, "Frank, the word spread throughout the Irish slum and soon Power was being compared to the ancient Irish war hero, Cuchulain, who had, over the years of storytelling, reached mythological proportions.

"Strangers were shaking his hand, patting him on the back and buying him drinks. For two weeks he could find no peace. He was never alone. He fought every night; only a few men ever went more than a round or two with him. He'd collect his pay and go home. In two weeks time he had fought fifteen times, had not lost a fight and had made five bucks each bout.

"After a few days and given a chance to gather his thoughts, he began to fill with incredible remorse for killing Red Mahoney. He had no intentions of doing so; hell Power thought they'd be carrying him out. But the remorse only got worse when he found out about Mahoney's wife and kids. His plan all along was to find Nancy and get to Syracuse and he wanted that desperately now. So when the celebrity died down a bit he developed a plan in his head to take care of things. The idea was to make a quick exit and escape his new found infamy.

"Early one morning he went to the flat where Mahoney's wife and children were staying and knocked loudly. A petite Irish woman came to the door and looked up at Power, recognizing him at once."

Frank watched as Power began to speak to this little woman but his voice got caught in his throat and it seemed like it surprised him. When he finally found his voice he said, "I'm John Power."

Mrs. Mahoney said, "I know."

Power said, "I'm sorry to bother you so early in the morning Mrs. Mahoney."

She said, "I was wondering that myself."

He said, "I'm leaving New York and couldn't go without talking to you first."

He heard a baby crying in the background and a small voice say, "Ma, who is it?"

He said, "Anyway, I had no intentions of hurting, let alone killing your husband, Mrs. Mahoney. It should've been the other way around."

She said, "It was as it was, Mr. Power."

He said, "Well, I just wanted to tell you that I'm sorry it worked out the way it did."

She nodded as he held out his hand in an offering of some kind. She looked up questioningly as he put seventy-five dollars, his winnings, in her small palm. He then wrapped both of his large hands around her small fingers as if she might, in her Irish pride, decline the gift. When she didn't struggle he said, "I think you need this more than I do."

She looked at him as tears of gratitude welled in her eyes and said with simple dignity and grace, "Thank you, Mr. Power, thank you."

Liam, who had been strong throughout this entire journey, wiped a tear away and said, "Frank, that morning he slipped out of the large tenement building that had been his home since he had arrived in America at around three a.m. and was gone.

"After walking several miles west, the sun began to climb out over the eastern horizon to his back. His progress was slow so he decided to put his thumb out and see if someone might pick him up and give him directions."

Frank, looking on with the intensity of a student engulfed in the subject matter, watched as after a half-hour or so a man in a flat bed, horse drawn buckboard stopped and said, "Get in."

He jumped up smiling, put his hand out and said, "I'm John Power."

The man grasped Power's hand and said with a deep, unfamiliar accent, "I'm Jerzy Zwierzchowski."

Power said, "Where are you from with a strong accent like that?"

Zwierzchowski answered, "I could ask you the same."

"Aye, I guess you could. I meant no offense."

"None taken. I'm from Warsaw, Poland."

"I'm from a small village in Ireland."

"You just arrived here then?" Jerzy said, looking at his pack.

"Aye."

"Where can I take you?"

"I need to get to Syracuse, New York, wherever that is."

Jerzy smiled and said, "I might lose my delivery job if I drove you all the way there."

Power smiled back and said, "I didn't mean ..."

Zwierzchowski cut him of and said, "I know, I know, I make little joke. I have a brother who lives in Buffalo now and he worked the Hudson River north to the Eerie Canal and then worked a barge on the canal to get to Buffalo. He still works on the canal. I'm going to Jersey City and go over the Hudson River. I can drop you at there, the steamboat men are always looking for men to work."

"Aye, that would be grand."

Frank found himself, without warning, standing in an orphanage, much like the one he had seen in New York City. Startled and irritated by the sudden change he didn't bother to ask where he was. He turned to his granddad and said, "Damn, Gramps, why the hell do you insist on doing that? Where's John Power and why aren't we with him?"

Liam simply pointed and Frank turned to see Nancy, five years older and looking much more mature, saying goodbye to Billy and Pat who had both shot up in the five year span. But Frank also noticed that they all seemed old beyond their years, like youth that had seen and experienced things from which they should have been shielded.

Frank said, "Where's Molly and Moria?"

Liam said, "You'll see."

Frank said, "Where are we?"

"Syracuse, New York."

"What's this place?"

"Sisters of Charity orphanage where Sister Mary Therese brought the kids."

"Where's John then?"

"He worked his way up the Hudson River on a steamboat and then he worked a barge across the Eerie Canal. He'll be here shortly."

"Where was Nancy going?"

"A couple of years ago, after Mass one Sunday, she met a gentleman by the name of John O'Hanlon. O'Hanlon was the proprietor of a local pub and the two hit it off immediately and he became like a father figure to Nancy and all the kids.

"Anyway, Nancy was sick and tired of the way she had been treated as a housemaid for the wealthy snobs she had worked for so when O'Hanlon asked her to come to work for him, running his kitchen, she jumped at the opportunity. Nancy was heading off to work at the Pub when she was saying goodbye to the lads."

Frank nodded his head glad that Nancy got a bit of a break when he looked to the foyer of the large Victorian home that the nuns converted to an orphanage and saw a familiar figure walk in.

Frank said, "That was quick."

Liam shrugged and said, "The power of a good dream. When he got to town he asked directions to the orphanage. Let's watch."

Sister Mary Therese, who was walking to teach a class, saw the tall worn stranger standing in the entrance and said, "How is it that I can help you? Are you lost?"

He said, "That all depends."

"On?"

"On whether I'm where I think I am."

"And if you're not?"

"Then, indeed Sister, I'm lost."

"Where do you think you are?"

"Syracuse, New York."

"Go on."

"The Sisters of Charity orphanage in said city."

"Well that solves it then."

"Solves what?"

"The question of whether you're lost or not."

He stared anxiously at her and said, "Well?"

"Well what?"

"Am I lost?"

You are not. Mister?"

"Power, John Power."

"Well now that that's settled, how may I help you Mr. Power?"

"I'm looking for some children that I believe are here."

"We have many children here, do you have a name."

"O'Conlan."

Her heart skipped a beat and she said, "Where in Ireland are you from, Mr. Power?"

"A small village named Upperchurch in North Tipperary County."

At that moment another nun was walking past and said, "Sister Mary Therese is everything okay?"

"Yes, I mean no. I mean, Sister Marie is there a chance you could take my math class in five minutes?"

Seeing the concern and confusion in Sister Mary Therese's eyes she said, "Of course I can."

The two women exchanged knowing looks. Sister Marie took the work plan and quizzes from Sister Mary Therese and walked away, the latter said, "Mr. Power please come with me."

They walked into a large cafeteria styled kitchen that was void of occupants and the nun said, "May I get you some tea?"

"That would be grand."

She came back ten minutes later with cups, saucers, a tea pot, cream and sugar all on a tray and then sat down.

He looked at the nun after they had prepared their cups and said, "I'm guessing that I have found the right place."

She said, "Aye," keeping her eyes down, staring at her tea as it steeped to a deep golden brown liquid, steam rising to the air, the china keeping her hands warm.

After a few moments he said, "Can I see them then?"

"First I'd like to know what your business is with them."

Not willing to come right out and say that he was in love with Nancy for fear that she might not feel the same way about him he said, “Our families were close in Upperchurch. I remember, and not with fondness, the day the O’Conlans left Ireland. We all knew on that day things had changed forever. Then we found out that Aidan and Maureen had died and were devastated. It was then I told myself that I’d come to America and I’d find them. I wanted to come anyway, it was just the added motivation that I needed.”

She stared at him, familiar with the tale of death, destruction that tore families and a country apart, a story common with all Irish families who left Ireland because of the blight. She said, “Nancy is at work. She works at O’Hanlon’s pub down the street and the others are in school,” the half truth stung like salt on an open wound, she caught herself before she winced.

CHAPTER 16
THE PUB

Liam and Frank followed as John Power walked in to O'Hanlon's Pub and the proprietor himself was behind the bar pouring shots and pints and telling stories. He had the whole pub laughing.

Power sat on a stool at the bar, smiled and listened to the end of O'Hanlon's tale.

John O'Hanlon noticed the new face sitting at the bar, walked over and said, "What can I do for you, lad?"

"Is Mr. O'Hanlon in?"

"I'd be him."

"Me name's John Power."

O'Hanlon reached out shook Power's hand and said, "What can I do for you, Mr. Power?"

"I was told Nancy O'Conlan works here."

O'Hanlon looked at Power with an arched eyebrow. With what Nancy had been through, he had grown to be more of an overprotective father than employer.

John O'Hanlon was a bundle of energy and when he was behind his bar he never quit moving. At the mention of Nancy

O'Conlan he was stopped in his tracks and stared at Power in much the same way a father would in sizing up the date who had just stopped in to pick up his daughter.

With an intended edge to his voice, but louder than he wanted, he said, "Who told you that?"

The patrons sitting at the bar stopped their private conversations and stared. Power, in an unusual mode of self-consciousness, stuttered as he glanced down the bar at these strangers, who sat there and said, "Well, uh, Sister Mary Therese at the orphanage."

"Where you from, lad?"

"Upperchurch."

O'Hanlon, an Irish immigrant from Templemore, just north of Upperchurch, like most of the Irish at the time in Syracuse, fared from Tipperary. This fact alone was the only thing that boded well for Power at the moment.

"What do you want with Miss O'Conlan?"

Liam laughed at the confused look on Power's face.

Frank said, "What?"

Liam said, "Look at Power, he's confounded, a situation foreign to him. He had given no thought as to what he would say to Nancy when he saw her, let alone this father figure bearing down on him from behind the bar."

Frank began to laugh now while he watched Power's face go from pink to red and began to stutter once again inaudibly.

O'Hanlon, with no intentions of letting Power off the hook on which he'd hung him, stared.

Power said, "Mr. O'Hanlon, we grew up together in Upperchurch, er I mean..."

"You mean what?"

John Power had never anticipated this confrontation and felt like a troubled grade school child in the principal's office for some unknown offense. For the men sitting at the bar, it was a sight for sore eyes. The short, squat figure of old John

O'Hanlon on his throne behind the bar staring down his opponent, his superior physically, and not backing off in the least. Nancy, hearing some commotion at the bar, went to see what all the fuss was about.

Nancy stood and stared at John Power and he stared back. They were transfixed on one another.

John O'Hanlon looked startled and said, "Lass, do you know this scoundrel?"

Nancy said, "Aye."

John Power, relieved with her answer, stood, removed his cap and said, "Nancy O'Conlan?"

O'Hanlon said, "I thought you knew the lad?"

Nancy said, "Aye, Mr. O'Hanlon, but it's been five years and people change."

Then she looked at Power and said, "Aye, I'm Nancy O'Conlan."

He smiled brightly and said, "I'm John Power."

She said, "I know."

He said, "I'm glad to see you're doing well. When your letters stopped coming we didn't know."

A tear came to her eye and she said, "There's a reason for that."

He said, "I didn't mean to upset you."

She said, "You didn't."

The regulars all knowing Nancy's story, the bar went quiet with fraternal desperation, each immigrant sitting there empathetic through a different version of the same experience, while Power fumbled with his cap, not knowing what to say.

Nancy said, "Mr. O'Hanlon, would it be okay if I took a few minutes to visit with Mr. Power?"

O'Hanlon said, "Aye lass, if that's what you want."

She said, "'tis."

O'Hanlon softening up a bit upon seeing the tears said, "Why don't you find a private table in the back. What can I bring you?"

Nancy said, "Whiskey."

O'Hanlon's eyebrows rose once more and then he smiled. He looked at Power and said, "Nothing better than good Irish whiskey, huh lad?"

Looking at the bottle of dark liquid on the bar, Power said, "I tasted it for the first time in New York. I'm still partial to the whiskey we drank back home, widow Killaney's poteen. They say it was triple distilled, widely agreed it was some of the best potato whiskey in the Republic."

He winked at Nancy who also knew it was Kevin Power who was responsible for the poteen and the secret was kept even America.

O'Hanlon said, "This is made with barley, not potatoes, you'll grow a thirst for it. You two go and I'll bring over a bottle."

She said, "Thank you Mr. O'Hanlon."

"My pleasure, dear."

They walked awkwardly to the back of the pub, found a table and sat. John Power said after a moment or two, "Nancy, I know it's been a long time since we've seen each other and even then we didn't know each other very well. I was your age now when you left the village and you were a lass."

"Aye."

Power paused for a moment and then said, "I still feel like I know you."

"How's that?"

"Well, your Uncle Paddy and Aunt Siobhan shared your letters with the village and I didn't miss one."

She let out an audible sigh at the mention of her aunt and uncle and said, "God in heaven how I've missed them."

"And they you. Paddy's a big reason I'm here now. It was a mighty sad day when your family left Upperchurch. It was the first sure sign that things were desperate for us all. The entire village was at a loss; it was just like losing family.

"Anyway, when your letters came, everyone would wait for Paddy and Siobhan to share the news with the village. When the letters stopped coming we didn't know what had happened."

The tears returned once again and John O'Hanlon set down two glasses and a bottle on the table and quickly walked away.

John poured two fingers in each glass and to his surprise the whiskey rested not a half-second in the glass before Nancy picked it up and took a long pull. He smiled slightly with empathy.

She said, "As you know from me letters home, Da died on the boat and was buried at sea and Ma died the day we landed with as much dignity as she could lying in the dirt of the harbor. I was only thirteen and when Ma died I thought I was going to lose me mind. Molly Rose, Moria, Pat and Billy all were looking to me for help as if I knew what I was doing. Blessed be the Holy Trinity but I was lost and homesick. If it hadn't been for Sister Mary Therese I don't know what we'd've done.

"We all ended up in the Sisters of Charity orphanage here. No one wanted us, thank God, we were outcasts."

"What do you mean, thank God?"

"They would've wanted one of us, not all of us. We were too old and there were too many of us. So there we stayed, all of us together, until..."

The tears came in torrents as if Nancy O'Conlan were finally given permission to grieve. John Power held her hand with gentleness and let her exorcise the demons that haunted her every step, never allowing her a moment's serenity.

When she got her voice back she said, "All seemed to be going well. We'd been together under the guidance of Sister Mary Therese. Molly, Moria, Pat and Billy went to school and I decided to go to work. It'd been almost three years since we were poured off that godawful ship and life had become a bit more bearable. We were getting over the homesickness that kept us up at night, getting over life without Ma and Da, or getting used to it anyway. I should've known things were too good. Then two years ago Molly Rose came down with the smallpox and took on a fever they couldn't break.

"When we buried her, Moria was so distraught that she quit

talking and we found her passed away in her bed sixth months later. Natural causes, but I believe she died of a broken heart."

Power looked off in thought and then said, as if to himself, "So that's what it was."

Nancy said, "What?"

"Sister Mary Therese told me you worked here and then seemed really tentative when she talked of the rest, now it makes sense. She didn't want to be the one to tell me about your sisters, she must've thought that was your place."

"Moria took the death of Ma and Da the hardest. After three years, just when she was getting over it, Molly Rose died and it was more than she could take."

Frank's heart broke again and again. He trembled visibly, hung his head and cried unashamed, wishing for all this to stop. He felt a kinship to the two girls, fell in love with them and felt as if he had lost two of his own sisters.

Liam put his arm around Frank once more and pulled him close, feeling a sense of guilt, knowing how hard all this had been on the boy. There was nothing he could say to take away the pain so he held him close in a show of solidarity.

Nancy and John sat for a moment gathering their thoughts and sipping their drinks. They sat swirling their whiskey watching it line the glass, thinking about those two beautiful girls.

Nancy broke the silence and said, "I don't want to talk of this anymore. Tell me about you? And tell me about Upperchurch? I have so missed everyone."

John took a drink of his whiskey and said, "It's not all good."

She said, "I didn't expect it to be with the famine not letting up."

John said, "Being the fifth boy in a family of five boys, I knew there was nothing for me in Upperchurch. With the famine throughout Ireland, I knew there was nothing for me there either. I was a burden and I wanted to come to America. So five years ago I started secretly saving money, doing odd jobs around the village. I never let Da know because he had no intentions of letting me, or any of my four brothers, get on one of those coffin ships, or so I thought. He always said, 'if one of me sons is going to die, it'll be right here on Irish soil, not in some damned ocean hearse or some alley in America.' And once we received the news about your parents, his resolve to keep the Power family together was greater than before.

"After five years of bad crops, landlord evictions and ridiculous taxes from the 'so called' crown, his resolve lessened. To add salt to our already open sores, we began to see carts of bacon, barley, lard, cattle and sheep coming through Upperchurch daily. They were heading for export to England out of Cork and Galway while we starved. When this began, he became deeply depressed and took to the poteen more and more.

"The last straw was when Paddy McNulty's son, Eamon, out of shear hunger jumped one of these carts for food. He was shot in the leg by one of the British guards and then hung with a noose around his neck until dead from the big oak tree in the middle of Upperchurch."

Nancy said, "They hung me cousin, Eamon McNulty?"

"Aye. Then, just to teach us all a lesson on brotherly love, they posted two guards to leave him hang there for two days.

"Matthew O'Hurley spread the word throughout Thurles, Holy Cross and Templemore as to what had happened. The NORTIP brigade started moving guns in at night and at dusk on the second night they moved in, shot the guards, cut down Eamon and then hung the two guards from the same tree. Then they waited. Matthew O'Hurley held a meeting with the Republicans and the villagers at Padraig O'Cuinneain's pub. More arms were supplied, more men came and within twenty-four hours a small battle pursued leaving twelve black and tans and six villagers dead.

"Within a week, the British soldiers came back with one hundred armed men. Because it was Eamon McNulty who started the mess, according to them, they burned Paddy's cottage to the ground, took his wife Siobhan, hung her from the same tree and left. We were able to cut her down in time to save her life, but she never spoke again."

Nancy, in almost shock whispered, "They hung Aunt Siobhan?"

"Aye."

Nancy said, "Oh my Lord."

"Afterwards we went to the task of rebuilding Paddy's cottage, but he said to forget it. If the soldiers didn't burn it down his landlord was going to tear it down, so they left for Skibbereen and the workhouse.

"God, it was a miserable place. We buried people everyday, family and friends. Funerals became a part of everyday life. People would've gladly sold their soul to the devil for a bowl of watered down cabbage soup. It was as if God had abandoned Ireland.

"I just couldn't stand it anymore. So I went to Da to tell him I'd saved enough cash and was going to America whether he gave me his blessing or not. I was ready for a fight, instead, to my surprise, he gave me his blessing and I knew that I was heading for Syracuse, New York, in the United States of America. And here I sit."

Nancy said, "You mean to tell me that you were coming all this way to find us and see if we were all right?"

He squirmed in his chair, blushing pink and said, "It was you I dreamed about at night. It was you I was coming to find, but, aye, I was concerned about all of you."

As John finished, all the pain she had suffered in the last five years coupled with the pain everyone back home had suffered, came to the surface. All she wanted at that moment was a hug from her ma or da. For that one moment, she was a nine-year-old child in Upperchurch who had just skinned her knee and needed a parent to take away her pain. The tears ran hot and she wept uncontrollably. Her friends, her co-workers, her boss and some patrons looked on and they all sighed.

John held her hand while she cried. Tears not only for the injustices suffered by her family back home, but the tears she didn't have time to cry for Molly Rose and Moria.

Nancy, tears exhausted, took one last sip from her glass and then laid her head back against the wall. She felt the liquid burn its way down her throat as it continued to warm her insides.

Both lost in their thoughts and wanting it all to go away, not even be a distant memory. Nancy broke the silence and said, "How much sorrow are we going to be asked to suffer? I've lost me home, me parents and me sisters. If it weren't for Pat and Billy I don't know what I'd do.

"Thanks to the good Lord for John O'Hanlon, he's been a father to the boys and me. He and his lovely wife Bridget have us to dinner on Sunday regularly to get us out of that orphanage.

"Also, Sister Mary Therese. You'd have thought that the good Lord took away one mother and replaced her with another. We probably wouldn't be alive if it weren't for her. We certainly wouldn't be together."

John said, "Aye, Nancy, some of us have had guardian angels and others ocean hearses. While still others didn't make it that far, lying dead on the side of the road with green stains around their mouths."

Nancy said, "Aye, of all the memories of that awful journey *that* was the worst. Nay, the worst was coming upon a family on the road just waiting to die."

John said, "Aye, I've nightmares and still see those wee ones staring blankly at me until I wake in a sweat. At least Aidan and Maureen had enough foresight to get you the hell out of there."

Nancy said, "'Twas no foresight as much as necessity."

John said, "The whole of Ireland reeked of death for five years as people starved and died throughout the countryside.

There was no decent burial for any one of them, mass graves for the lot. All the while those English bastards were transporting food out of Ireland. Then they evicted us from our homes. We were too damn dependent on the potato and when it went bad we couldn't pay the rent and were left to starve in the countryside. Then they had the nerve to blame us for what they called a famine. How in the hell can their damned parliament call what happened to us a famine when the bastards were exporting food out of the country, through villages full of starving people?

"Treyvalian, may he roast in hell, said the so-called famine was God's way of punishing the Gael. While our people were dying everywhere, on the road, in the ditches and open fields, he retired and wrote his memoirs about the famine. The Royal bastards knighted him."

Power got so worked up thinking about it, he screamed, "There was no damn famine with so much food. It was murder!"

The bar went dead silent and every Irishman in the place turned and stared with a nod. They had all been there, seen it and felt the hunger. They understood the demons that Power was exorcising because it was an exercise in which they had each participated.

When people started getting back to their own business, Nancy stood and said, "The place is getting full, I need to get back to work."

As she walked back to the kitchen John O'Hanlon walked back to the table where John Power now sat alone.

He sat down and said, "I trust you two got on well?"

John said, "Aye."

"Well I hope you don't think me too big an ass. It's just that Nancy means the world to Bridget and me and it's not everyday a stranger comes in asking for her."

"Aye, I understand. And, Mr. O'Hanlon, I hope you don't think of me as a scoundrel anymore."

"The jury is still out on that one, Mr. Power."

He looked over at John O'Hanlon who was now smiling.

John said, "Nancy has had a rough go of it."

O'Hanlon said, "Aye, she has. I never knew her parents, but after working here a while she told us what happened. When Molly Rose died, she was distraught, but didn't have time to think of herself. She had to keep an eye on her brothers and was so upset when Moria quit talking. As hard as Nancy tried, that child said not one word after Molly died and then she was dead in six months.

"We didn't know what to think, so we stayed close to Nancy and those two hoodlums she calls brothers. Those two have the fight in them and never leave each other's side. They trust no one but Nancy, Sister Mary Therese and maybe me and the wife, that's it.

"When they first got here, they were six and eight and had to use their dukes daily. One day after a few weeks of harassment, they double-teamed a twelve-year-old bully in the schoolyard and gave him a beating. The word spread and now very few kids bother the O'Conlan brothers.

"They're now eleven and thirteen, big for their age and take no guff from anyone, including some of these ruffians that work the canal.

"When Nancy walked over and first saw you this afternoon, it was the first I've seen her smile since before they found Moria a good year and half ago."

Power said, "Well, it was grand to see her smile. When I left Ireland I didn't know if I'd even be able to find them. I'm sorry for all her sorrow, but I'm glad that I've found her."

John O'Hanlon raised his glass and said, "I am too."

Dishes clanked in the kitchen and the din of small talk rose as the pub began to fill in the late afternoon. And the two, heads down, thinking, heard none of it. Finally John Power said, "Mr. O'Hanlon, I have enough money to get by for a few days, but I'm going to need work. Do you have any ideas?"

He sat for a thoughtful moment and then said, "Aye, Seamus Gallagher's a personal friend of mine, a good man. He runs a cooper shop making barrels for the salt industry. A lot of salt in these parts, some call it white gold. Syracuse's nickname is Salt City. Anyway, Seamus is always looking for good men. In the mean time I'm short of help and if you'd like to trade room and board for an eight-hour shift behind the bar, I could use the help. You keep all your tips."

John nodded appreciatively; they both stood and shook on it.

It was getting on in the afternoon when the two O'Conlan boys made their way into the pub with their books strapped across their shoulders. When they walked in, the first one they saw was a tall stranger standing in the midst of the crowd, at the bar with his arm around Nancy. No one noticed the boys' arrival as John Power began to sing:

"Were you ever in sweet Tipperary, where the fields are so sunny and green,
And the heath-brown Slieve-bloom and the galtees look down with so proud a mien?
'Tis there you would see more beauty that is on all Irish ground
God bless you, my sweet Tipperary! For where could your like be found?!

They say that your hand is fearful, that darkness is in your eye.
But I'll not let them talk so black and bitter a lie.
O, no! Mchusla stoirin, bright, bright, and warm are you,
With hearts as bold as the men of old, to yourself and your country true.

And when there is gloom upon you, bid them think who brought it there
Sure a frown or a word of hatred was not made for your face so fair;
You've a hand for the grasp of friendship - another to make them quake,

And they're welcome to whichsoever it pleases them to take.

Shall our homes like the huts of Connaught, be crumbled before our eyes?
Shall we fly, like a flock of wild geese, from all that we love and prize?
No! by those that were here before us, no churl shall our tyrant be.
Our land is theirs by plunder-but, by Brigit, ourselves are free.

No! we do not forget the greatness did once sweet Eire belong;
No treason or craven spirit was ever our race among ;
And no frown or word of hatred we give- save to pay them back;
In evil we only follow our enemies' darksome track.

O, come for a while among us and give us the friendly hand!
And you'll see that old Tipperary is a loving and gladsome land;
From Upper to Lower Ormond, bright welcomes and smiles will spring-
On the plains of Tipperary, the stranger is like a king.'"

What John Power lacked in range, he somewhat made up for in heart and earnestness. When done, the pub sat quiet for a moment uncomfortable at the nasally delivery of Power's song. A small voice in the back shouted, "Erin Go Bragh," to which the crowd cheered, relieved that it was over.

Frank said, "I think Power is a great guy, but someone needs to talk to him about that singing – especially in public."

Liam laughed and said, "I don't think he had any plans to make a living at it."

John turned and was startled out of his thoughts. He was looking at Billy O'Conlan for the first time since he had seen him last as a six-year-old holding his da's hand leaving Ireland. Billy was a grown boy, almost a man. Power smiled but Billy only stared defiantly, not knowing who this man was with his arm around his sister.

Nancy introduced the boys to Power and then said, "Lads, it's getting late. Sister Mary Therese will worry until she sees us in the lane. We need to be getting on."

The boys, who both loved hearing stories of Ireland and Tipperary, complained.

Pat said, "Nancy, the lads are just getting their Irish up and telling some stories; can't we please stay a while?"

"Aye," Billy joined.

"You both know the rules. You have homework and you're probably half-starved after all that schooling."

"What schooling?" Pat replied. "All they talk about is the English, the Protestants and the Mayflower. Who cares about some English ship? Then they say Christopher Columbus discovered America, when the Seanachie back home told us it was St. Brendan who first saw America a hundred years before him. And he didn't need any big ship, he and a couple of monks made the trip in a wooden dinghy they'd built. I tried to tell our Yankee school mistress and I thought she was going to slap me."

With a look of severity, Nancy said, "Don't start lads. We'll be going now," silently pleased with Pat's reply. These boys were Irish to the core and nothing was going to change that. They walked toward the door. John Power followed them and said, "It's been a long time since I've spent any time with people from me own village."

Pat, used to fighting for everything, shot back and said with disdain in his voice, "Since when was Upperchurch *your* village?"

Nancy backhanded him so quick and hard that tears welled in his eyes from the sting and embarrassment. Pat stood his ground, though, still proud and defiant, never to raise his hand or voice against his older sister.

"You apologize now before I backhand you again," she said with eyes so fierce he took a step back.

Pat looked to the ground and said, "I'm sorry, Mr. Power."

John Power smiled slightly, trying to control himself. Billy, seeing this, stepped in front of his brother, ever the iconoclast, staring at Power as if challenging him. O'Hanlon had told him these two lads had the fight in them and he was now convinced that they would have taken him to task if they'd had the opportunity.

"Apology accepted, Patrick. I didn't mean me own village literally, I..."

"Of course you didn't!" Nancy interrupted, "That smart mouth of yours will be the death of if you don't watch it, Patrick O'Conlan."

Power said, "All I meant was that it's grand to be around folks from Upperchurch. I'm homesick and just to hear your brogue makes me feel better."

Both Pat and Billy looked at each other. They thought only children got homesick. It was this kind of simple honesty that attracted them to Power.

Frank looked at Liam and said, "Power's twice their size and those two didn't think twice about taking him on."

Liam said, "They were tough kids and they were used to fighting for everything they believed in. Hell Frank, you heard O'Hanlon, they weren't even afraid of the toughs that worked the barges."

Frank smiled the way a seventeen-year-old boy brimming with testosterone smiled at the thought of a good fight.

Power said, "Mr. O'Hanlon offered me temporary work and lodging until I can find something more permanent. And I would like to spend some time with all of you."

Nancy said, "I think that would be grand. Tomorrow's a busy day at the pub, being Friday and payday. But maybe we could have a picnic this weekend; we could ask Sister Mary Therese to join us. She must be sick and tired of that orphanage."

"That's it then. Nancy, I'll see you tomorrow at work and lads I'll see you tomorrow after school." He reached out and shook both boys' hands, as if they were men.

Power walked back into O'Hanlon's public house, homesickness vanished, at least for a while, and he drank a few more pints and met a few more patrons until O'Hanlon showed him to his room above the tavern. He had a nice bed with plenty of covers and a big pillow that he had to get used to, having never slept on one.

In the corner was a small table with a candle lamp upon it, flickering a slight illumination. Above the lamp hung a crucifix. He noticed a small stack of parchment paper and full ink well with a pen in it. He pulled off his vest and shirt, kept his under shirt on, sat down and began to write.

Dear Ma, Da, Seamus, Pat, Clem and Tom:

By receiving this letter you will all know that I've made it to America safe and sound. And no, the streets are not paved with gold, but there is plenty of work for a man to do. I have made my way to Syracuse, New York. As Nancy O'Conlan wrote, there are plenty of Irish already established here; many of them fare from grand old Tipperary. And like all of you, they didn't seem to appreciate my singing talents either. You would think I would learn my lesson.

I have found temporary work as a bartender in a pub owned by a man named John O'Hanlon. He's going to talk to a man named Gallagher who makes barrels for the salt business here in Syracuse. He thinks I'll have work by this time next week. I will then find a cheap boarding house and start sending money home. In the meantime he is trading me room and board to work behind the bar for him

I have good news and bad news. The good news is that I met Nancy O'Conlan today. She is now an eighteen-year-old woman and doing very well as a waitress in the very pub where I have found temporary work. I also met her two younger brothers Pat and Billy, both with the fight in them if I have ever seen it.

The bad news and why Nancy has not written Paddy and Siobhan McNulty in the last couple of years is that she couldn't bear to tell them Molly Rose died two years ago from smallpox and Moria died sixth months later, they say from a broken heart. After her parents died and then Molly Rose, God rest their souls, Moria seemed to have given up.

Break it to the McNultys and O'Conlans gently. Nancy will be upset when she finds out I've told you, but I think they have a right to know.

I will continue to write and when the money starts coming in, it will be heading to Tipperary.

Sincerely, your son and brother
John Kevin Power

CHAPTER 17

THE QUESTION, THE YANK, AND THE SURPRISE

Out in front of John O'Hanlon's pub was a board walk with two rocking chairs where Liam and Frank now sat and rested from all the excitement. Liam lit his pipe and the familiar smell of the pipeweed drifted pass Frank's nose and he took a deep breath, closed his eyes and smiled. He began to love the smell of the pipe tobacco smoke, a smell for which he would come to long.

Liam said, "I think you're starting to get it."

Frank said, "Get what?

Liam said, "The fact that you got it made, that your life isn't nearly as hard as you thought it was."

Frank said, "I'm getting there."

Liam said, "Frank, John Power and Nancy O'Conlan worked at O'Hanlon's together for two weeks before Power was hired on at Gallagher's Cooper works. He was adept at working with his hands and quickly caught on. Within a couple of weeks he was sending money back to Upperchurch, to help his parents and get one or two of his brothers to America. But as the months passed Power became increasingly more restless. He had heard about all these people going west and homesteading. Getting land for free was incomprehensible to a man who grew up on an island where land was at a premium. He also knew that the only way he was going to get a piece of land, or an opportunity for land, was to get out there and find it.

"Power had heard that the railroad was building west and needed as many hands as they could muster. Many of the Irish, looking for opportunities, were signing up. The wages weren't bad and he wasn't afraid of a long day of hard work.

"The next day he had made arrangements for Billy and Pat to go straight home after school and he met Nancy at O'Hanlon's for a drink."

He said, "Nancy, I've been thinking about our future."

She said, "And?"

He said, "What do you want to do?"

She said, "What do you mean?"

"If you could do anything or go anywhere, what would you do? Where would you go?"

"You haven't been thinking, you've been dreaming, John Power."

He laughed and said, "Is that so bad? This is a land of dreams and loads of opportunity."

She said, "It's also a land of responsibility. You can't just pack up and go anywhere you want."

He said, "Why not?"

She said, "Well, for one thing."

He cut her off and said, "Marry me, Nancy. Let's make it official and then get the hell out of here with the boys. Let's go see America. What do you say? We'll find a place out west that we like and settle down to farm, raise a family, make a life together. People are doing it everyday. This city is choking the life out of me."

She said, "Was that a proposal?"

He said, "No, but this is."

He got out of his chair, bent down on one knee, took her

hand in his, looked her square in the eye and said, "Nancy O'Conlan, would you marry me, lass?" The tears welled in his eyes and he said, "I'll work hard everyday of me life to provide for whatever you need. Just say yes."

All she could do was nod her head yes and they fell together in a lifelong embrace.

Frank smiled wide and said, "Just when you think you're getting to know a guy and then he goes and does something so decent."

Liam laughed and watched, only he was the one with tears in his eyes this time.

There was a large gathering of men milling around trying to hire on to work at the railroad when John Power walked up.

Power said, "Me name's John Power and I've come to answer the ad for work."

Joe Smithson, an engineer for the railroad crew said, "You must be mistaken me for someone who gives a damn. Get in line with the rest of the potato eaters begging for work."

Without even looking up from his plans, Smithson pointed south to the long line of mostly Irishmen looking for an opportunity.

Power had a long fuse, but when the spark was hot enough to touch it off, it burned like lightning and the explosion was like a fireworks display adorning a hot and dark July evening sky.

Smithson's condescension was that spark and Power's temper ignited. Before he knew it Power had Smithson by the shirt collar and lifted him off his chair. John had powerful arms from long days of hard labor and was never afraid to use them. When he stood erect he was six foot four inches tall, a man to be reckoned with.

People stopped what they were doing as if hearing the first percussive wave of the fireworks display and were now waiting for the sparkles of green, red and blue to light up the horizon.

Power said, "I've never begged for anything in me life and I don't plan to start now. You were, however, correct about two things. I am Irish and I do hold the spud in high regard. Do you have a problem with that?"

Smithson said, "N-no."

"As soon as you apologize, I'll be getting in line."

"For telling the truth?"

"So you're telling me that we Irish are beggars. It seems clear to me that we're laying your goddamn rail, and I wouldn't call that begging."

"N-nor would I."

"So you'll apologize for mis-speaking the truth and for being a rude bastard."

"Okay, Okay, I'm sorry for chrissake."

Power held Smithson there a few seconds, staring at him. His nostrils were flaring and his eyes flamed red. He looked like a wounded bull facing a heartless matador. He then came to his senses and set the man down.

Power walked over to get in line, secretly pondering whether he just ruined his chances for railroad work, inwardly cursing himself and his lousy temper.

Meanwhile the crew foreman had come out of the manager's tent when he heard the commotion outside. He looked on with amazement and a bit of amusement.

Frank said, "Granddad, who's that?"

Liam said, "Raymond James, Yankee to the first degree."

Frank said, "Huh?"

Liam said, "His people came off the Mayflower; he was a direct descendant of the Puritans who were of both English and Protestant stock and whom hated Catholics, especially Irish Catholics. But he needed, what he considered, these Paddy bastards to do his hard labor.

"James worked for one of the ten short lines in New York, called the Rochester and Syracuse line. He figured to have a bright future in the railroad business. He was presently a construction foreman, which was a big job with much responsibility. It was his job to see that the track was laid properly and followed the route set out by the engineering group.

"In doing so he needed laborers like the Irish, Chinese, Germans and American Indians who could actually work sixteen hours a day at hard labor and not complain too much.

"James loathed all of these inferior races. In his mind, they were all uneducated, ill mannered and simply beneath him. However, if James were to be successful as a construction route foreman, he needed each of them.

"Of all these groups, he disliked, what he called 'these Irish papists' the most. He was convinced that all we ever thought about was Ireland and the Pope. And of course he wasn't all wrong. However, as much as he disliked the Paddy bastards, he thought, they could work hard and they could lay track faster and more efficiently than any group of people he'd ever seen.

"Frank, at the time, the Irish started coming to America in swarms. In the last few years, they had filled a lot of backbreaking jobs that James couldn't fill previously because others weren't willing to work so hard. If it hadn't been for the shortage of good labor, he would've never dreamed of hiring a good for nothing, drunken Mick. But he had to admit, if only to himself, that the Irish would work long hard hours. He'd actually watched them work other people into exhaustion and death.

"Frank, another lesson he would learn the hard way was that while the Micks worked hard, they also expected their pay on a timely basis. If they didn't get paid what and when they were promised, they could make life miserable for everyone. This would prove to be a difficult lesson for the likes of Raymond James.

"Nonetheless, New York had been caught behind

Pennsylvania and Ohio in the railroad race. They had spent too much time and effort in building the Erie Canal while the rail car became the transportation mode of the future.

"Ray James knew that there were ten short lines in New York that worked with each other from Buffalo across the state to Albany and then south to New York City. He met an iron and hard metals tycoon named Erastus Cornell and heard rumors that he planned to consolidate all ten lines into one.

"Cornell's plan was to make his second fortune in the railroad business by supplying the railroads with all the iron rails and spikes they needed to lay track from ocean to ocean.

"When the irascible old tycoon met Ray James, James made enough of an impression that he figured Cornell may let him run his railroad business while he ran the iron business."

Frank McGrath, enraptured by the story he watched and heard as his grandfather narrated, was deeply moved and thrilled to his core at the same time. He said nothing and looked on as Ray James laughed out loud at the astonished look on his engineer's face, while Power had lifted him off the ground.

Liam interrupted Frank's thoughts and said, "As entertained as Ray James had been with this small episode he had rarely seen the kind of strength Power held in his arms, even in this business of hard labor. He also saw a light in Power's eyes that he had seldom seen before. His initial feeling was that these Paddy's were a dime a dozen and to get rid of this troublemaker. But he had seen something there. This guy could come in handy. Trusting his instincts, he let it pass, but he'd keep an eye on this one. He needed as many men as he could get, especially the big strong ones. He had no idea what he was getting into with John Power, none."

Frank said, "I don't doubt it a bit," and watched as everyone went back to minding his own business, acting as if nothing had happened. The Irishmen waiting in line began to snicker and talk.

Liam said, "The Irish were a proud lot, especially when one of their own took a stand. They looked at Power and rightly guessed that they'd be working for him one day."

Detesting calling attention to himself, John quietly took his place at the end of the line. When he got to the front the man looked up and said, "Can you read and write?"

John said, "Aye."

The man said, "Good, read the form, sign it and date it."

When he was done, John said, "What're the wages?"

"All depends on what you do?"

"What's available?"

"We need track layers, spikers, gaugers, graders, cooks, butchers, and bakers."

"You forgot candlestick makers."

Without a trace of humor he went on, "You look like you'd be a spiker if I had to guess."

"So I'd swing a sledge all day?"

"Yep."

"How much?"

"Three dollars a day."

"The wife's a good cook."

"Have her come down and sign up, head cook's always looking for help. Pays a dollar a day plus meals."

"I've got two boys who..."

"How old are they?"

"Eleven and thirteen."

"They're not old enough to swing a sledge hammer, run iron rails or drop ties, but we can hire them on as runners. They'll run for water, tools or whatever the crew needs. Pays .50 a day per kid. We don't advertise that."

"Understood."

Power figured five dollars per day wages was good money. They could sock a lot of money away and still send what amounted to 50 cents a day back home.

John said, "What about room and board?"

"We offer a three story railcar to sleep in and three squares a day, cost you $5.00 a week taken out of your wages."

Power nodded.

"Be here Thursday morning 6 a.m. ready to work."

"Thank you," Power said as he walked away smiling.

The man at the table interrupted him and said, "Oh, and by the way, it probably isn't such a good idea to lift the head engineer up by the shirt. That is, if you'd like a job."

Power went straight to the cooper mill to give Mr. Gallagher his notice. He then went to O'Hanlon's pub; it was time to do a little celebrating before they left.

He walked in and looked around the pub for Nancy. When he saw her she looked upset and pale. John's mood changed.

"Nancy, what's wrong?"

"Oh, I went to talk to Sr. Mary Therese this morning to tell her we were leaving. She knew the day was coming, but she didn't think it'd be so soon. She tried to be strong, but couldn't. It was awful, John, she's been a mother to us."

Frank and Liam watched as the crowd was gathering larger and larger around them, but they heard none of it. The two newlyweds stood staring at one another.

Liam said, "Power knew there was nothing he could say to ease the pain of yet another loss for his new bride. This was no death but it felt like it to Nancy, another American wake."

Frank watched from what seemed like a distance, as if he were a peeping Tom watching neighbors through field glasses as John and Nancy began packing for their journey and making sure they had everything they needed. Sister Mary Therese, Pat, Billy, Nancy and John all sat down to dinner at O'Hanlon's Pub. John Power insisted that he take them all out to dinner to try to avoid any overly emotional scenes.

Sr. Mary Therese complained at first. “John Power, I can make a fine meal right here and besides what’ll the Reverend Mother say if she found out I went to a pub.”

John replied, “First of all Sister, you know as well as I do that Irish women can’t cook.”

He smiled brightly at her making sure she knew he was kidding. But as brightly as he smiled, he got nothing but looks of disgust from Sr. Mary Therese and his lovely bride. The boys, however, burst out laughing.

“Secondly Sister, John O’Hanlon’s Public House is a well respected establishment. It’s far more a restaurant than a pub before 8:00 p.m.”

Nancy said, “John Power, I’ve never heard so much hogwash.”

“Woman, you’re doing little to help. Sister, I’ll not be taking no for an answer. I want to take you out for a nice dinner before we leave tomorrow.”

With that Sister Mary Therese broke down and cried, then Nancy started to cry, saying, “You really can be an insensitive oaf.”

John and the boys walked outside and sat on the bench.

Pat said, “John, don’t feel too bad, ‘tis a hard time for Sr. Mary Therese.”

“Aye, I know, lad. That’s why I was trying to do something nice.”

Sr. Mary Therese walked out with Nancy and said, “John I’m sorry, I’m a mess. The last time I had a pit in me stomach like this was when I left home some twenty-five years ago. Let’s go tonight, but let’s make it 5:00p.m. It’d make me feel much more comfortable.”

“Fine,” he said with a smile.

Liam said, “Francis, as you now know John began to work at O’Hanlon’s pub and then went to work for the Gallagher cooperage. But what you wouldn’t know was that during all that time he never forgot to send at least a dollar a week back home to Upperchurch. He'd been in America just over a year now and knew his Dad was making good use of the money on the farm back home. He never once spoke of it, but he longed to see a member of his family, and thought it would be a long time coming, if ever.

"In his last letter home he wrote of the railroad and his desire to hire on there. If one of his brothers were to come they would have a hard time finding him on the road."

Frank watched as they were at dinner that night at O'Hanlon's and the conversation was mostly the boys talking nonsense, Nancy correcting them, and Sr. Mary Therese laughing at them all.

It seemed to Frank that John had been lost in his thoughts. Maybe he was thinking of his mother, father and brothers on the farm back home. Or maybe he was worried about what lay ahead for them on the railroad. Nevertheless, Frank could feel for him, he knew where his mind would have been in a similar situation and was glad he wasn't John Power.

When Frank took his attention from Power and the O'Conlans he looked around the bar. He noticed that the crowd up front in the pub was mostly subdued. He walked up there and found that they were talking local politics as well as the latest news from Ireland, when a loud roar went up. The lads were cheering and carrying on as if they'd just heard that Ireland had won her independence and was now controlling Dublin castle under "Home Rule."

Power found himself looking toward the door and saw John O'Hanlon walking in. Behind him trailed a tall, lanky man wearing an Irish hugger cap and smiling. Someone handed him a pint and the crowd cheered again.

Suddenly Power recognized him and jumped out of his chair and ran the length of the pub.

He shouted "James Clemence Power! My God, it's you man!"

He responded, "Sure'n who'd you think it would be, baby brother? Cuchulain."

They hugged so hard that Clem felt the breath being squeezed out of him. There wasn't a dry eye in the place. John finally let go and laughed so hard tears streaked his face.

Liam laughed as the two men hugged and said, "Frank, I think almost every Irishman from Tipperary Hill in Syracuse, New York, to the town of Upperchurch in Tipperary knew that Clem was on his way, save John Power. His dad, Kevin, sent word to John O'Hanlon that they finally had enough for passage and that Clem was coming. He also gave him an idea what date he'd be there. Travel from Ireland in 1852 wasn't easy, but better than during the height of the famine. So they were confident that there would be no problems.

"Nonetheless, he gave O'Hanlon strict instructions not to tell John. He was famous for his gags and surprises back in Ireland and he'd be delighted to pull off such a surprise in America."

All Frank could do was smile. He watched as things settled down and the Power brothers went back to the table for introductions.

Clem said, "John, lad, I've been here for a day and a half and it was the hardest thing not to come straight away to see you. But I knew you were already on and wanted to make sure I got on with the railroad with you. I needed the insurance that I'd be leaving with you rather than having to say hello and then goodbye right away."

Sister Mary Therese, Nancy and the boys all took an immediate liking to their newfound friend. He was four years older than his brother John and the family resemblance was striking. They talked and laughed until dinner was finished, then Nancy took Sr. Mary Therese and the boys home. John and Clem sat in the pub to catch up.

"John, lad, the money you've been sending home to Da has been nothing short of miraculous. It's helped so much. When you left, there were times when we didn't know if we were going to make it. Then money arrived here and there. It put food on the table, helped with the farm, helped get the family business rolling slowly again and it helped get me here. I am indebted to you."

"Nay, you'd've done the same for me. You sitting across the table from me now is plenty payment enough."

"Aye, I'd begun to get a wee bit homesick, but you being here remedied that soon enough. I'm sure it'll come again. I don't think any of us will ever stop longing for the shores of Ireland."

"Clem, don't get me started. When I first got here, there were days on end that I was so homesick I couldn't eat or sleep. Now, every once in a while, when I'm feeling melancholy, it hurts to think of it. But after seeing all the opportunity here and the little that we left, I soon snap out of it."

CHAPTER 18
THE HAMMER COMES DOWN

Liam said, "Frank, the next day when they reported to work, hundreds of men stood around. They were mainly Irish, but there were also some German and Chinese immigrants, and a smattering of Shoshone, Paiute and Washo Indians, all talking nervously waiting to get started.

"Ray James stood beaming in his tent as the New York Central merger had been announced over the weekend. After six months of planning it had finally come to fruition.

"The day before, in front of a large crowd of the industrial elite, Erastus Cornell and his upper management had laid down the first rail on the new line to Rochester. Erastus himself drove the first spike and the picture covered the front page of newspapers the next morning.

"Ray James had his foremen walk through the crew and separate them, appointing graders, gaugers, track layers and, lastly, spikers.

"The graders went out ahead and worked with draught horses to clear the path, clean it up as best they could and ensure that it was level, no more than a 2% incline or decline anywhere. Next came the gaugers who were to set and secure the ties in place at thirty second intervals. Then came the tracklayers who would ultimately set the six hundred pound rails atop the ties. Once the rails were down, the spikers went to work. Throughout the countryside could be heard the scream, "Down!" Every five seconds a helper would put the spike in place, the spiker would scream, "Down!" and down would come the twenty pound sledge, sixteen hours a day, six days a week.

"The crews were set up for speed. Well I should qualify that, by speed I mean by mid-nineteenth century speed. They averaged anywhere from two to five miles of track per day and were set up on a .50 daily bonus for every day they hit 3 miles or more. Mr. James was given a budget and a time schedule. For every day under his target finish date he'd received twenty dollars in bonus pay.

"Payday was set for once a week on Friday night. The workers would line up in front of James' tent and receive a cash settlement. For the most part, this worked out well, but there were a few bumps in the road.

"James posted a memorandum that said they'd be working Sunday from now on, any complaints and they could find work elsewhere, knowing they were working in the middle of no man's land and had no place to go. This didn't settle well with the Irish Catholics who made up the majority of the crew and who meant to keep Holy the Sabbath. John Power was elected their spokesman. He went in and was turned away saying they weren't making good enough time. If they picked up the pace, they wouldn't have to work Sundays. Instead of waging war over this, he understood the man's predicament and Power was a man who knew how to pick his fights."

Frank said, "Granddad, what'd he do?"

Liam pointed and said, "Watch."

The following day was Sunday. Frank looked at his watch

to see that it was a few minutes before 6:00 p.m. when the crew was just coming in from a long day at work. Frank noticed that there was a growing restlessness among the workers, he could feel the intensity. Anticipating trouble, Power called a meeting

After everyone was gathered he said, "I know you're angry about working today. I'm none too pleased about it either, but we're to blame."

With that the men got upset and began to grumble.

"The point is, accept it or not, we're behind schedule. We're not where we should be by now. Everyone to a man knows that we have the opportunity to make bonus. What everyone may not know is the kind of pressure that's coming down from management to make it to Rochester on time. They're not being unreasonable.

"Now, I've figured it out, lads. If we run a minimum of three and half miles of rail a day and don't slack off, we'll make week end bonus, we won't be working anymore Sundays, and we'll get there on schedule.

"I've seen this crew run more than five miles in a day and I know it can be done."

A man stood and said, "I could give a damn how much rail we lay, working on Sunday is wrong."

John said, "Sir, we're in the middle of nowhere and you're welcome to quit. I'm sure Mr. James'll be glad to get you your pay for Saturday and Sunday. Anyone else who feels the same, pack up your gear and get the hell out."

Two men stood and walked away.

Power said, "Laziest louts on the crew, we'll be better off without them."

The one turned and Power turned to face him and said, "You need something?"

Thinking better of it the man shook his head and walked away.

Liam said, "Frank, Monday started their third week of work on the railroad. The beginning of the route they were building to Rochester from Syracuse had started slow, but that had been expected. The men had a learning curve and had to get their system down.

"The first couple of days were bad, running a mile of track, maybe. Then they started to work as a team and, to a man, became more physically fit. They built up to an average of three and a half miles a day and in a few days they pushed past the four and five mile mark.

"However, the plan was to hit Rochester in a four-week stretch. It was eighty-seven miles to Rochester and after two weeks they had only put down 39 miles of track and that included the Sunday they all worked. So at the midpoint in time, they were shy of the distance midpoint by four and a half miles and Ray James was *not* going to miss out on his bonus.

"Before they began work that Monday James came out of his tent and gathered up the entire crew, he was in his typical vile mood, but he was a man who knew how to get what he wanted."

"As you know," James started, "we are behind schedule. As you also know, we are offering a 50 cents a day bonus up and above your regular pay for hitting three miles in any given day. As of today I will offer an additional incentive of .50 a day for every man, up above all other regular and bonus pay, for hitting anything over four miles a day. That means a dollars a day more for every day you run four miles of track or better."

Liam said, "James did some quick math and knew he had to put in at least twelve-four mile days if he was to make his timeline and his bonus. Knowing these Irish papist bastards still didn't want to work Sunday and seeing how much progress they were making working a six-day week, he didn't press the issue. If they didn't get the job done in the next few days he didn't care what they thought, they'd be working Sunday again.

"To James delight, the new bonus structure seemed to be working and the weather also cooperated with James' plan for success. The men on his team had honed their work and skills to precision, slouching off and breaks were not tolerated, eighteen hour days were the norm and breaking the four and then five mile marker per diem became a precedent."

Liam smiled as his grandson watched in utter amazement at the men at work. No machines, no power at all outside muscle and sinew. They glistened with sweat; grunting as they pushed, pulled and lifted and their muscles were as chiseled as any block of Italian marble.

Liam continued, "Now Nancy kept as busy as any of the railroad men. She enjoyed her work and was soon promoted to assistant head cook. They had a herd of cattle that ran along with the men. The butcher provided fresh meat; the baker bread and the cooks did everything else. The plates were piled high with food and everyone ate in silence, too tired to talk.

"Friday night arrived and the men were pleased with the progress they had made during the week. They were lined up to get their pay when an argument broke out. Francis Quinlan was in the tent to receive his pay from Raymond James and his voice was getting louder and louder. It sounded as if fisticuffs were ready to break out when John Power decided to intervene with his brother Clem. The two men walked in while James and Quinlan were in the middle of a heated argument."

Francis Quinlan said, "The way I'm figuring, Mr. James, you owe me $28.00. We put down four miles a day for seven days. That's three dollars for the day and $1.00 bonus."

James said, "So what's your problem?"

"You paid me $24.50 which is $3.50 a day and not $4.00."

"No, Quinlan, you laid just short of four miles every day this week. That comes to $3.50 a day, not $4.00."

Power stepped between the men and told Quinlan to take his pay and leave.

He looked sourly at Power threw his hands up in disgust and left.

As he walked out and began to tell the men what had happened, their moods went south as well and they started to grouse.

Power said, "Is this the game you're going to play, Mr. James?"

Seeing the familiar fire that shown from his eyes, James was disturbed, knowing he had nowhere to run and the back up he had called for had not shown yet.

Trying to show calm confidence, James said, "I don't see our business, Mr. Power, as any kind of a game. You were short each day and your pay is what it is. If you don't like it you can pack your bags tonight."

"I see," Power said. "'Tis a game of inches rather than miles." James said, "As I said, I don't see this as any game, it's..."

"Shut your gob, man." Power said in a low venomous tone. I knew you were a cheat and a swindler the minute I laid eyes on you. But I was thinking what's good for us will certainly be good for you. You're a fool, Mr. James. You could search the world over and not find a harder working crew. When you came out in your piss poor mood on Monday and told us of the bonus, the men were pleased. They worked proud and this is how you repay them?"

"Not repay, Mr. Power, Pay."

"I told you to shut that pie hole of yours or I'm gonna do it for you. Are you daft or deaf, man? Now, what's the pay gonna be?"

"$3.50 and not a penny more," James said, doing his best to keep his courage up.

Just then four large men walked in and surrounded Clem

and John, both smiled, enjoying the challenge.

"Hold your temper, Clem; we want no blood shed here. Let's take our pay and get out."

Feeling a huge sigh of relief, James smiled. He knew there was going to be trouble so he called for some back up. They were late and he wasn't sure if they would make it at all.

"Does this mean you gentlemen are quitting?"

"Oh no, Mr. James," Clem said still smiling, "We know when we're licked. We'll be at it first thing in the morning."

Power looked at James and said, "Give us a minute to talk to the lads, so there won't be anymore trouble. We'll have them all to work first thing in the morning."

After the meeting all the men in the crew came to get their shorted pay and not one of them said anything. James and his henchmen drank brandy and played poker until the wee hours of Saturday morning, laughing at and mocking those dumb potato-eating sons of bitches. Who the hell did they think they were anyway?

James woke late Saturday morning and his boys were gone. Wondering where those louts were off to he walked out of his tent. Blurry-eyed, he poured himself a strong cup of coffee and then he walked to the job site to see how his crew was working out after coming to their senses last night.

As he walked toward the tracks he found his four henchmen lying gagged and tied up, along with a few of the stool pigeons on the crew. He wondered what in the hell was going on. Then he saw an Irishman holding a large pistol over his boys. The Irishman looked up and smiled.

James ran to the fresh-laid track and saw that the crew was tearing it up. They had pulled up a mile and a half of track and didn't look like they were slowing down.

He ran up to John Power in a fury and said, "What in the hell are you men doing?"

Power looked down on him and said, "Did you think you were dealing with fools, man? Get the hell out of me way, I got track to tear up. We decided we're going back to Syracuse and we're taking our track with us."

He shoved James out of the way and as he landed on his backside, Power kept working east.

James jumped up and said, "Okay, okay what the hell do you want? I'll give you anything! Just stop tearing up the damn track."

Power whistled loudly. The men stopped what they were doing and started walking towards James. The Chinese, the Germans, the Indians and the Irish, they all gathered around.

"Lads," Power said with authority, "Mr. James just asked what we wanted. He could've been a reasonable man last night, but some men need a jolt."

They all mumbled.

Then Power looked at Ray James and smiled, knowing he was suffering from a hangover and said, "Mr. James, we had a hunch you might see things our way this morning, so here are our demands.

"A fair agreed upon wage for a hard day's work, paid on time. So we'd like to be paid the $.50 per man that you shorted us last night on last week's pay. And from now on we want our pay in advance weekly and you can settle up bonus on Friday evening.

"You see, Mr. James, we're reasonable men and no reasonable man likes being cheated. If this is unacceptable to you, we'll take this track back to Syracuse and shove it up your arse. I'm wondering what old man Cornell will think of you then?"

James stood in utter amazement, he thought, I can't believe these bastards actually started tearing up my track. He said, "Sorry Power, I'm not paying anyone in advance, what insurance do I have that someone might not just walk off the job. Regular pay hasn't been the issue, bonus has. Come to my tent tonight after work and I'll make up the bonus for last week. But you're still going to have to make up four miles, from where we stopped last night, or no bonus. And if you don't like that then take the track back to Syracuse I can't stop you."

James held his breath wondering. Power measured up the man, knew he made sense and was impressed with his stones.

"Fair enough," Power said.

He then looked at the men and said, "You heard the man. Let's get to work!"

The clank of the sledgehammer and the scream of "Down!" could once again be heard moving west through the countryside of upper New York State.

Frank was shaking with adrenaline and excitement and said, "Man, those guys had some big balls!"

Liam said, "The Irish were actually the first immigrants to do anything like this. This is how the unions evolved. Irish laborers were constantly pushing back on crooked Yankee management. There were all sorts of stories of the Irish on the railroad and the Irish in the coal mines. If pay was ever withheld for any reason, they'd plant dynamite on a newly built railroad bridge, start tearing up track or plant dynamite in a deeply dug coal mine and then ask for their pay or else. And Yankee management found out in a hurry that these threats weren't idle ones. The Irish knew how to fight for their rights, a trait they learned at home and brought with them here."

Frank looked around with pride and a sort of bewilderment that people had the courage to stand up against tyranny and said, "That is so cool."

Liam said, "Not only that, Frank, in the next two weeks they made Rochester and did it on time. After the altercation with Raymond James they didn't know if they still had work once they reached their first destination.

"Their plan was to run track all the way to Buffalo. But now that they were in town, the ball was in James' court. They knew he was an irrational and unreasonable man, but they also knew they had a week off and they weren't going to worry about it until next week."

CHAPTER 19

THE ROBBER BARON, THE INCIDENT AND THE SHARPSHOOTER

Liam sent the now familiar plume of pipe smoke into the air, seeming to Frank that he was immensely content. His eyes suddenly bore down on his grandson, he smiled widely and said, "Frank, I think you're really going to enjoy this next episode. It gets a little hairy."

Frank said, "Yeah? Why?"

Liam said, "Don't want to ruin the surprise. You'll see."

He puffed on his pipe, chuckled with the kind of delight only a wonderful secret can bring and said, "Frank, they tried to enjoy their week off in Rochester."

"You said try as if there was a problem."

"There was. When Clem joined John, Nancy, Pat and Billy that first day in town the plan was to get everyone a bath, haircuts and shaves for the men and to purchase some new clothing.

"Once they got to town, they soon realized that Rochester was not as Irish friendly as Syracuse. However, once they were cleaned up and showed they had money to spend, people warmed somewhat. Nonetheless, they all got the feeling they were not welcome and were glad they weren't staying."

Nancy said, "I'm taking these lads to get new clothing. They've grown out of everything they have."

John said, "Me and Clem are going to get a haircut and a shave. We'll meet you back here in an hour."

John turned and stopped dead in his tracks, which made them all stop and wonder what he was up to now. Power looked at a blacksmith shop. A sign hung in the window that said 'Blacksmith wanted, Inquire within...N.I.N.A.' Nancy looked at the sign and then looked at her husband whose jaw was flinching in anger.

John looked at his brother Clem and said, "No Irish Need Apply, huh? Fuck him. Let's see what he says when *I* apply."

Frank said, "Granddad, N.I.N.A. means no Irish need apply?"

Liam said, "Yes."

Frank said incredulously, "You've got to be shitting me? These guys hung a sign advertising a job and had the stones to make it open to everyone but the Irish."

Liam said, "Don't be naïve, son. If a Black man, a Mexican, an Indian or an orthodox Jew walked in there they'd be laughed out as well. It just so happened that during this time in America the huge influx of immigrants were the Irish because of the blight. The other European immigrants to follow would be treated the same way.

"But now because Caucasians blend in, our ignorance and hatred is targeted against people of color. Anyway you look at it, son, its complete bullshit."

Frank looked at his granddad, shocked at his profanity, understanding his point.

The color rose in Liam's complexion and it seemed to Frank that he choked out his next words. He said, "Frank, like most men of any race, they couldn't stomach that kind of blatant bigotry and the N.I.N.A. sign brought the bile to the back of their throats.

"Clem had a bad feeling about this town and the last thing he wanted was to end up in jail. If his brother went in there, trouble was sure to follow and he couldn't just leave him. He'd have to go after him."

John began to walk to the shop when Clem grabbed his arm, "John, are you sure want to do this?"

"Lad, I *am* sure."

Nancy, who had not left, but hoping that her stubborn husband would make the right decision about all this, but seeing he was incapable under the circumstances, said, "John Power, you're not planning on ruining all of our plans with that lousy temper of yours. What do you hope to accomplish? I've been in America a lot longer than you have and I know that most of these WASPS can trace their ancestors back to the Mayflower. They hated us before they left England and nothings changed. They still hate the Irish and they hate Catholics and their greatest debate over a pint is which one they hate more. You won't change that."

"John, a man like that will always find a reason to hate. If it's not where you come from, he'll hate you for your religion or your skin color. But I guarantee he'll find a reason to hate you. You'll do no good by walking in there. You can't win. Now, if you persist in this tomfoolery I guarantee you'll go to jail and if you do Pat, Billy and I'll be gone. So when you and this brother of yours get out, there won't be a forwarding address."

John grinned at her wisdom and said, "Och woman, you take the fun out of everything." Clem laughed with relief.

Liam said, "They spent the rest of the week in camp, venturing forth for nothing. They felt something bad, maybe the Irish intuition, but they knew it would be best if they stayed clear of town.

"During the day they rested and at night they sang and danced while sitting around the campfire. New hires began to trickle in as the week progressed. The railroad was looking for as many hands as they could get signed."

Liam stopped and lit his pipe as if he were thinking about what he was going to say next. Then he shook his head as if he got his place in the story right and said, "Frank, remember when we talked about Erastus Cornell?"

"Yeah. Wasn't he the rich railroad guy?"

"Exactly. So let's go back a bit."

"Okay, sure."

"Cornell showed great promise. Even as a young man, he was adept at business dealings and had a nose for profitable businesses in which to invest. He trusted his instincts to the point where he would take risks other men wouldn't. As a result he became fabulously wealthy.

"One year while he was building his iron business, his railroad business, and his reputation, he was invited to lecture at Oxford University to a group of business students and businessmen throughout England.

"As crass and outspoken as he was, the business elite in Britain took to him immediately. They realized he was hard driven, smart, funny and had single-handedly built an empire. To them, it was all quite impressive and not to be taken lightly.

"It was at this time in England that Erastus Cornell met Anson Merryweather; both had lost their wives but not their lust for women, drink or song. Both men were wealthy, still driven and found that they had a good deal in common. They became fast friends.

"When Merryweather's business interests would take him

to the United States and Cornell's to England or Ireland, they made sure to get together. Let's go see, shall we?"

Frank found himself in a large billiards room, ornately appointed from Cornell's travels around the world. Anson Merryweather was shooting pool with Erastus Cornell and said, "It's always nice to visit the colonies, but crossing the pond can be rather a pain."

Cornell said, "Yes sir, it is. During my last trip we got caught in a storm and I thought it was going to tear the ship apart, not to mention my insides with that awful seasickness."

They both laughed as the butler brought in two tumblers of ancient scotch.

Merryweather held up his glass and said, "God bless America."

Cornell answered, "God save the queen."

They laughed again and sat puffing on big Cuban cigars.

Cornell broke the silence and said, "Anson, what's on your mind? You seem preoccupied."

"Honestly Erastus, other than the fact that you've taken me three in a row."

"That's what I mean, I don't remember ever beating you before."

"It's my son Miles. I don't know what to do with him. He'll be finishing up his education at Oxford here in June and I don't know what's to become of him."

"Why wouldn't you have the boy go to work for you?"

"Because he couldn't handle it. He's a small effeminate man, has been his whole life. It's been hard watching him grow up because since he went off to school all the bigger boys have tossed him around, humiliated him, really. He's never been able to defend himself and so he's become a bitter little man with a lousy disposition. He treats all the hired help with contempt. Oh hell Erastus, he treats everyone with disdain. I don't even like to be around him myself.

"I thought the service would toughen him up, see the world, lead some men, gain some practical experience but they wouldn't even take him."

Cornell said, "I have an idea."

"Yes?"

"When he's finished with school have him come see me. I'll toughen him up and give him the chance to do everything you said the service would do for him. You know, see the world, lead men, gain the practical experience."

"What did you have in mind?"

"Building a railroad."

Frank said, "No way. This isn't the same spaz that Power and O'Hurley tied to the horse?"

Liam said, "The very same. But you haven't seen anything yet."

Liam said, "The railroad workers reported for work once again early Monday morning after a welcomed two-week layover and Ray James was nowhere to be seen. Rumor had it that old man Cornell gave him an office job, which didn't bother anyone on the crew.

"In his place stood, you guessed it, Miles Merryweather. His hair was well oiled and parted precisely down the middle. He wore a sliver of a mustache just over his upper lip. He was dressed smartly in woolen riding pants, leather riding boots to his knees and a thick cotton turtleneck. He had a riding stick in his hand and was wearing leather gloves. Behind him stood his mount from which he was going to work.

"Frank, you may have noticed already the fact that Merryweather was very self-conscious of his short stature and his Napoleon complex soon manifested itself once again when he came to America and tried to assert himself."

"Listen up," he screamed in a high-pitched voice, causing some snickering among the men. When he noticed this he immediately climbed on to his horse.

"My name is Miles Merryweather, with a "y". You can call me Mr. Merryweather or, better yet, do not address me at all. Our mission is to make Buffalo in twenty-one days. I know the first few days will be slow going until we all begin to work as a crew. But after reviewing your results from Syracuse four miles a day should be attainable."

Liam said, "When he was finished John Power stepped forward and stood there before him, not moving. He stared at Merryweather with venom in his eyes. He would never forget the words, the stinging, malicious words that fell from this vile little man's lips so easily, words that cut him like a knife and left a scar.

"The men noticed Power's change of mood and the hatred that seemed to radiate from him; they became restless.

"Merryweather was going to continue but was disturbed by the large Irishman staring across at him. He stopped and they stared each other down. Power looked familiar to Merryweather but, as hard as he tried, he couldn't place him."

Finally Merryweather said, "All right, what the hell is it man? Speak up."

That irritating voice brought it all back for John Power. Merryweather's high-pitched voice echoed in his mind,

"Clever, you peasants really are rather clever. Let's see, you're clever at making unwanted babies, clever at being unable to feed them, clever at being out-of-work misfits and making an awful mess of things throughout the countryside with all your starving, what. But you always seem to have enough grain to make your tax-free whiskey, don't you?"

He then recalled Merryweather tied to the horse and the

look of shear horror on his face when the horse shot away. The thought brought a bit of relief and laughter, but Power found that he had to force self-control, without it he would have broken the man's neck."

Still trying to figure out where he'd seen this man before, Merryweather said, "Would you like to tell us what's so damn funny?"

Power brought himself under control again and walked to Merryweather's horse and said, "Mr. Merryweather, I can see by the question on your face that you still don't recognize me. Me name's John Power. However, I think you look much better hog tied to your horse rather than sitting upright."

Frank looked on and saw that the recognition was immediate and the horror that filled his face was priceless. As the blood drained there, Frank saw the look of satisfaction on Power's face and knew he had Merryweather right where he wanted him. Frank surmised that the look on Power's face brought the thought of hanging Merryweather from the nearest tree or hog tying him, once again, to his horse. And sending him on his way was a temptation so strong that Power had to consciously take a step back and steal a deep breath.

Gathering himself, Power said, "Are you expecting us to hit four miles a day for three dollars a day?"

Merryweather said with all the courage he could muster, "That's your agreed upon wage, is it not?"

"Aye, that's our agreed upon wage, and that'll get you oh, two, maybe two and half miles of track a day."

Liam said, "Frank, Doing some quick math in his head, Merryweather realized that would put him in Buffalo nine days behind schedule. That would not only mean no bonus, it would mean no job and probably a trip back to England, a failure. But he was damned if he was going to negotiate with a bunch of ignorant shanty Irish and had to exhibit his mettle with a man like John Power.

"Power and the other men, on the other hand, knew the clock was ticking and that Merryweather couldn't replace them without at least two weeks of recruiting. Cornell would have him by the throat."

Merryweather said, "What's your point, Mr. Power?" recognizing that he wasn't in the driver seat anymore and that his negotiating position was weakening by the minute.

Power said, "We have simple demands, Mr. Merryweather. They worked well for the crew and they worked for Mr. James before you. And, if you have your wits about you, *Miles*, they'll work for you as well. Everybody'll gets what they want."

Merryweather said, "Okay, get to the point, man, we have track to lay," trying to convince himself and the crew that he was tougher than he was. He also had in the back of his mind what James had told him about these paddies tearing up track. They did not play games. He could also see himself tied to his horse as it sprinted throughout this wild countryside; it was all very unsettling.

Power said, "We had an agreement with Mr. James. We get three dollars a day base pay for showing up to work. If we put down three miles of track we get an extra .50 per day and anything over four miles we get another .50 a day."

Power walked over to the horse and looked Merryweather damn near in the eye. He leaned forward and said quietly, "Mr. Merryweather, there are a couple of things to consider here. Number one, I know you get a handsome bonus if we arrive in Buffalo on time and even better if we get there early. Number two, we're hard-working and honest men and we don't like being squeezed. Number three, if you don't agree to what we consider reasonable terms, every man here walks, not just the Irish, but everybody. It'll take you a month to replace us with people who have no experience. Mr. Cornell'll gut you for a stupid move like that.

"Lastly, Miles," he said, just to get under the man's skin, "Spread the wealth. You can't get your bonus without us. I know you hate our guts but greed will get you further than hate. Look at us as a good investment in your future, sir. We have an old saying in Ireland."

"Good God," Merryweather said irritated beyond reason, "Pray tell what would that be, Mr. Power?"

"Pigs get fat and hogs get slaughtered. Come to think of it, hogs sometimes get tied to their horses on their way to the slaughter."

With that Power smiled at Merryweather and walked back and stood amidst his peers. Merryweather was so annoyed with this situation that his upper lip began twitching.

Frank said, "Holy crap."

Liam nodded and said, "Frank, when it came to his inbred hatred of the Irish, Ray James had nothing on Miles Merryweather. He sat on his horse and the crew watched as he visibly tried to gain his composure. This went on for a few quiet moments."

Frank watched as the situation grew with intensity, his stomach filled with nervous butterflies. Finally Merryweather, unable to remove the emotion he felt to make a rational business decision said, "You men *will* work for three dollars a day and no more. We *will* lay down four miles of track a day and we *will* be in Buffalo in twenty-one days."

Liam said, "Knowing that he had just blown the biggest

opportunity of his life and feeling one of his moments of severe anxiety and panic coming on, he dismounted and walked into his tent. Not wanting the men to see him hyperventilate, he stayed in the tent for fifteen minutes or so. Once he had gained his composure, he walked back out to give further orders only to find the entire crew — men, women and children — gone.

"Merryweather had no idea where they went or how to get them back and knew that when Erastus Cornell got wind of this, he was finished, whether his father was a Viscount and personal friend of Cornell or not, it was over before it started. How could he have been so stupid? Of course, this wasn't his fault; it was the fault of those barbaric Irish. It was a moment that defined this man's propensity to hate. For as much odium as Miles Merryweather had for the Irish, if possible, his tiny faint heart grew just enough to make room for still more loathing and revulsion.

"The next day Erastus Cornell woke up in his mansion and the Times front page headlines read, "Railroad workers walk out on New York Central in Rochester" with a sub heading that said, 'Drunken Irish to cause riots.'

"Under the subheading the Yankee press printed cartoons portraying Irishmen as apes with their knuckles dragging on the ground holding bottles of whiskey, wearing bowler hats and slurring 'Erin Go Braugh.'

"A day later Cornell's train car pulled into Rochester with all the newspaper reporters there to greet him. He ignored them, got into a horse drawn carriage and went straight to the rail yard."

Cornell walked into the tent, caught Merryweather off guard and said, "You want to tell me what in the hell is going on here? I hired you to get a job done. They haven't put down so much as one damn rail or pounded one damn spike under your watch and you've got the whole crew to quit."

Miles said, "There was an uprising, this man named Power..."

"Power!" Cornell said, cutting him off and then walking outside the tent. His personal assistant, a smart and tough man named Edward "Big Eddie" Gage, was standing there.

Cornell looked at him and said, "Eddie, remember when Ray James was talking about this guy named Power?"

"Yes sir."

"As much as he said he hated the son of a bitch, you could tell there was a respect there. He's the guy who got the crew to start pulling up track. Now this same son of a bitch pulls this on me. He's got to have balls of steel, this guy. He's messing with the wrong man. I want to meet him. Would you do me a favor?"

"Sure boss."

"Go into town and find this guy Power. Don't get tough, be a gentleman and just ask him if he would meet me in my suite , at say, 4:00 today."

"I'm on my way, sir."

Cornell walked back inside, his temper now under control and said, "Miles, I expected more from you than this. You couldn't have had a better opportunity."

He reached inside his suit coat and pulled out his long wallet. He drew out a hundred dollar bill, handed to Merryweather and said, "Son, you're fired. This should get you wherever you want to go. When you see your father tell him I'll be in touch."

Liam said, "Frank, at precisely four p.m. Power knocked on the door of the largest suite in the hotel. Big Eddie answered it and nodded as John walked in. He had never seen luxury like this before; it'd be something he'd tell his grandkids about.

"Cornell sat at a large round oak table with papers strewn all about him. He was drinking single malt scotch whiskey and pulling on the largest cigar Power had ever seen."

Frank and Liam watched as John Power stood at the front of Cornell's desk for a minute too long waiting for the man to recognize him and finally said, "You wanted to see me?"

Cornell looked up from his papers and said, "Yes," and then went back to the papers on his desk.

Power, incensed, said, "I don't have time for this. I didn't ask for this meeting, you did. When you're ready to talk I'll be back in camp," and he turned to walk away.

Cornell looked up in surprise. He was not used to being talked to like this. He had acclimated nicely to a position of power and yet he had done so by the same obstinate impatience used by this young Irishman ready to walk out of his office.

He remembered, with relish, the days of scrapping, not two nickels to rub together, forcing his voice to be heard, his ideas to be discussed, by arrogant, old blue bloods with closed minds. He wondered to himself, "Had I become one of them?" He had always prided himself on listening to men with balls enough to stand up. Now whether they had anything worthwhile to say was a different matter.

He said, "Wait a minute."

Power stopped and turned around. Cornell stared at him and Power stared back unflinchingly. Cornell thought, either this man's too ignorant to know who he's dealing with or he's got balls of steel. He prided himself, as well, on sizing up a man and he surmised the latter.

He said, "Have a seat, young man."

Power sat down and waited.

Cornell said, "You're John Power?"

"Aye."

"And you know who I am?"

"Aye."

"You a drinking man, Mr. Power?"

"Aye."

Big Eddie put a tumbler in front of Power and poured some mature scotch in the glass. Power took a sip and felt the familiar burn in his mouth and throat as the liquid coated them both. The after taste was unfamiliar, though. It had a tobacco leaf finish, typical of scotch whiskey, which he wasn't accustomed to, but thought he could get used to it.

After a few moments Cornell said, "Power, why do you keep causing me problems?"

Power said, "Excuse me?"

Cornell said, "Trouble, Power. You're a troublemaker and I want to know why?"

Power said, "Could you be more specific?"

Cornell said, "I get these reports, see. One says you threatened one of my engineers, held the guy off the ground by his collar. Had I seen it, you wouldn't have been hired.

"Then they tell me you had the crew tearing up track and now you've got the whole damn crew walking off before they even got started. This is costing me money, damn it! Now I want some answers!"

Cornell was red in the face and breathing hard and Power smiled. He hadn't meant to be disrespectful, he just hadn't realized, until now, how much trouble he had caused and what it must look like without an explanation. Cornell was ready to come over the desk at him when Power said, "Sir, I'm not the one causing you trouble and costing you money. It's the idiots you hire to run your crews."

Cornell said, "Get the hell out!"

Power said, "I'm not leaving until you hear me out."

Big Eddie walked over and said, "You want me to take care of him, boss?"

Power stood and said, "You and who else?"

Cornell began to laugh at the matter of fact certitude in Power's voice.

He said, "Eddie, let me take care of this, thanks. Mr. Power, please sit down and explain to me what you mean by idiots running my crews?"

Power went on to explain the altercations he had had with both James and Merryweather and finished by saying, "We weren't asking for any more than what we thought was fair."

Cornell said, "Understood."

Power said, "However, my father used to say, you can't reason with the unreasonable. I've never met a man more unreasonable than Miles Merryweather. After meeting with you I'm surprised you hired him at all."

"It was a risk I was willing to take, one of the few that didn't pay off. Not that it's any of your business, Power, but I was doing a favor for his father, a friend of mine."

Power continued, "Anyway, if Raymond James, Miles Merryweather or any other foreman you may hire want four to five miles of track laid a day, then they're going to have to pay for it. If these foremen are going to get a handsome bonus on the backs of these working men, by coming in ahead of schedule, they should be willing to spread the wealth. Especially when there's no way in hell they're going to get it without us."

Cornell said, "What's your definition of your fair share?"

"Three dollars a day base pay, four bits more for hitting three miles and four bits more a day per man for anything over four miles. I don't think that's an unreasonable request or too much to ask. Everyone from the men building the rail, to the foreman, to you Mr. Cornell, win. You'll sell more iron rails and spikes, sell them faster and you'll get your railroad up and running quicker."

Cornell said to John Power, "Is that your proposal?" "Aye sir. We had to negotiate a little harder than I thought with Mr. James, but he finally agreed and everyone won. We got to Rochester ahead of schedule and it wouldn't have happened otherwise."

"Is this what you proposed to Merryweather?"

"Aye."

"And of course he refused."

"Aye. Pardon me for saying so sir, but the man had his

head in his arse."

"Apparently," Cornell said, spinning the whiskey in his glass and watching it streak down the sides

"Do you get along with Ray James?"

"No sir, but I'm not paid to get along with him. I'm paid to get a job done. Up and above that, I make damn sure we get what was agreed to. My men look to me for help and I'm glad to oblige them."

"Well, Mr. Power," Erastus Cornell said pouring them both more Scotch, "I'm glad we had this time to talk. I think you're being reasonable and I appreciate a man who's not afraid to speak his mind. I agree to your terms. Ray James will not be as pleased because he's coming out of the office and back on the road, but he'll take no cut in pay.

"However, I still expect a twenty-one day arrival into Buffalo. Let your people know what we agreed to and be ready to go to work the day after tomorrow."

Power finished his drink, got up and thanked Cornell for his hospitality. As he walked out, Cornell said, "Power?"

He turned around and Cornell said, "I don't want to be hearing from you again, sir. Next time won't be nearly as pleasant."

Power smiled at him and said, "Keep your end of the bargain. Otherwise I'll look forward to our next meeting."

Cornell let out a short wily laugh while Big Eddie showed Power to the door.

Frank said, "Cornell was right."

Liam said, "About what?"

Frank said, "Power really did have balls of steel."

Liam laughed and said, "He really did, didn't he?"

Liam stared at Frank and Frank said, "What?"

Liam said, "I was just trying to find my place. Let's see, oh yeah. It took two days to get their routine honed once more, but when they did they were like a well-conducted orchestra.

These Irishmen worked like they were possessed.

"It took them only seventeen and a half days, almost three days ahead of schedule, and it would've been sooner had it not been for a twenty-four hour altercation."

Frank said "What altercation?"

Liam said, "You'll see."

"Does this have anything to do with Merryweather?"

"I said you'll see. Now where the hell was I before you interrupted?"

"Sorry."

"No you're not. Let's see, oh yeah, there were six days in a row that they worked twenty-hour days. They would have made it seven, but they weren't interested in spending extra time in purgatory for breaking the third commandment.

"In those seventeen and a half days they had worked two men to death and worked five other men into utter exhaustion. When they reached Batavia they stopped long enough to eat dinner, drop off the dead for a proper burial and the five others to recover. Then, once again, the clang of the mighty sledge against the iron spike could be heard throughout upper New York State."

Frank said, "Hold it right there."

The irritation was plain on Liam's face and he said, "Right where?"

"You said they worked two men to death?"

"Yes, I believe I did."

"And this is the truth? No crap?"

"Have I lied to you once?"

"No."

"Why would I start now?"

"You wouldn't and that's not what I meant. It just seems kind of incredible."

"It was incredible and that's the point."

Liam took a deep breath and tried to relax at the irritation he felt from all the interruptions and finally he said, "Miles Merryweather did very little well in his life, but when it came to revenge and marksmanship he was first rate."

Frank said, "I was going to ask you about him."

Liam sighed and said, "What were you going to ask about him?"

"Whether he went back to Ireland or maybe England after he got fired."

"You're about to find out."

Liam took a few paces and began once more, "Throughout his life, he spent hours on the firing range taking secret revenge, in his mind, on all those who had done him wrong. He became a first rate sharpshooter, able to shoot the wing off a fly at twenty-five yards. Because of the abuse that he suffered at the hands of ignorant people, simply because they didn't understand him, he became a recluse with no friends but his firearms, his targets, and his imagination. He came to hate all people, he misunderstood them and they *all* misunderstood him.

"Had the British army known what kind of shot he was, he would have been sought out and drafted instead of being turned away. After all there was always room for a good sniper. He said nothing, he trusted no one and, if they couldn't accept him for who he was, then screw them, they didn't need to know.

"The wheels, however, came off the fast moving wagon when he had his confrontation with Power. He had taken abuse his whole life and was quite accustomed to it; he even began to accept it as his lot in life. His escape was the firing range, enabling him to blow off steam and control himself. But he finally got the job that *meant*_something. He finally had the power and the position that he craved. He was going to make it after all. He would show his dad and all those naysayers back home that he would make something of himself in the colonies. But to have it all taken away by some lousy Paddy bastard was unconscionable. He lost his reason and became stark raving mad. Miles Merryweather transmogrified into full-blown lunatic, with no reasoning and a great deal of ability as a marksman —a rather dangerous combination.

"He never traveled without his small arsenal. So when he was fired from the railroad, he took the hundred-dollar bill, rode into Rochester and bought provisions, whiskey and ammunition. Since coming to Rochester he had a homemade firing range where he took refuge now.

"He dreamt at night about the opportunity to put a bullet in John Power's brain. In his dreams, he would walk up and urinate all over his bloody skull. He would wake up laughing to himself in a sort of sick orgasmic reverie."

Frank said, "Scary."

Liam said, "Yes, but it gets scarier, watch."

The day after Merryweather had been fired and Cornell's meeting with Power, Big Eddie was about town seeing to some last minute errands before he and his boss headed back to the big city. He came upon Miles Merryweather walking out of a local fire arms store loaded down with ammunition. On a hunch Eddie decided to follow him to see where he went.

He watched as Merryweather went to a local stable, saddled up his horse and began to load down his saddle bags with lead shot and gun powder for the long range musket loaded English made Ensign Rifle he was carrying on his horse.

As luck would have it an earnest young man of no more than fifteen was riding by in an empty buckboard. Eddie said, "Whoa there boy."

The boy stopped and said, "You talking to me?"

Eddie said, "I am. How'd you like to make some money?"

"That all depends, mister." Came the reply.

"On what?"

"My Pa has me running some errands."

"You look familiar. Your Pa owns the hardware store?"

"Yessir."

"Run back and tell him that Eddie Gage, personal manager of Erastus Cornell, wants to use his buckboard for an hour and

I need a driver. Tell him I'll pay five dollars."

The boy's eyes went wide and before he said anything he turned his buckboard around and headed for the hardware store.

Eddie, meanwhile, watched as Miles mounted his steed and headed north out of town. The boy returned, Eddie jumped on pointed and said, "See the fellow with the strange riding boots and funny hat?"

The boy said, "Yeah, I've seen him around town lately. He's different."

"He's English, not American, that's why he's different. Follow him, but stay back a bit I don't want him to become aware of us."

They followed him for three miles or so out of town where they watched as he dismounted and pulled out his long range rifle and ammunition.

Big Eddie had the boy park the buckboard near a grove of trees and without being seen they watched for just over an hour as Miles took target practice then mounted and rode away.

Eddie said, "Boy, pull up where he was, I want to see what he was shooting at."

They rode into a clearing where they saw a large red brick buried in the grass with a white 100M painted on it. They looked up and at the distance of an English rugby field they saw the torso of a mannequin on a pole buried in the ground. Eddie said, as if to himself, "Must mean one hundred meters."

They walked the hundred meters to the mannequin and upon closer inspection there were two circles painted upon the dummy, one around the heart on its chest and one around the forehead. They saw small-bore holes which pockmarked the inside of the circle on the chest as well as the circle on the head and no where else on the frame.

Eddie pulled out his pocket knife and cut into the small holes pulling out lead shot. To his surprise he pulled out several balls from each hole.

He said again as if thinking out loud, "This guy is an

amazing marksman."

He looked at the boy and said, "Let's get you back home, son," handing him five large gold coins.

Eddie Gage walked into the suite that his boss occupied at the hotel where they stayed when they traveled to this part of New York State. Cornell was working at a large table, volumes of papers spread out and clouds of cigar smoke snaked all around him.

Eddie said, "I have something that may be of interest to you."

"What?" Came the typically impatient and gruff reply.

"I saw Miles Merryweather come out of the gun shop this afternoon with a load of ammunition and a rifle on his horse."

"I fired his useless ass yesterday, Eddie. Why in the hell do I care about this?"

"Well boss, I followed him on a hunch just to see where he went and it paid off. I watched him take target practice for an hour or so and this guy is a hell of a shot."

"Is that so?"

"Yes sir. After he left we..."

"Who the hell is we?"

"When I saw him mount up I had to think quick, the hardware store owner's kid was riding by with an empty buckboard and I paid him five dollars to follow the Englishman for me."

"Hmmm."

"Anyway, after he left we went into to see what he had set up for a range and that's when we saw two circles painted on a mannequin, one over the heart and one over the forehead."

"A mannequin? That's actually pretty good thinking."

"Yeah. He had it mounted on a heavy pole which he had buried deep in the ground so it was sturdy. When we got closer we noticed that there were no bullet holes outside the circles and then I pulled out my pocketknife and found several bullets in each hole."

"That good huh?"

"The best I've ever seen."

"Eddie, everybody has their talents. The trick to good management is to find them. Are you thinking what I'm thinking?"

"I think so, sir."

"That's why I like you Eddie. Get Merryweather in here right away."

Miles Merryweather sat in a chair in front of Erastus Corning twitching uncomfortably. Big Eddie had to have some of his muscle literally carry his skinny body in as he had refused to come see Erastus Corning after the disaster yesterday.

Erastus said, "I understand your reluctance to come see me. I'd've done the same in your shoes. Scotch?"

Merryweather said, "I prefer Cognac but Scotch will do."

"It's twenty years old, it better do."

They sat and sipped their highballs and suddenly Miles, showing a bit of his anxiety disorder, said, "What do you want with me? Isn't humiliating me once enough for you?"

"Miles relax; I've got a little proposition for you."

In his spoiled pampered demeanor he said, "And what, pray tell, would that be?"

"Eddie here saw you taking some target practice this morning. Says you're a helluva shot."

"What, he was spying on me?"

"So what if he was?"

He thought it over, shrugged and said, "Yes, I'm actually an excellent marksman."

"And humble too, I like that. How'd you like to do a little job for me?"

"Depends."

"Kill John Power."

The hatred seethed in Merryweather's small beady eyes

and the disdain was palpable. Cornell stared at the small man sitting in front of him and was reminded of a weasel that just happened upon some succulent chickens lost in the woods. But he was also surprised at the control Miles showed over his insatiable loathing of the Irish and in particular John Power when he said, "How much?"

"One thousand American dollars is a damn bargain to be rid of this man. You get caught; you're on your own. You talk and you'll be dead so fast you won't know what happened to you. Do we have an understanding?"

"Mr. Cornell, you've got yourself a deal. How do we do this?"

Cornell pulled out a map of the route to Buffalo and said, "I want you to follow the crew for a week. I want them to be in the middle of nowhere. Then use that little brain of yours to set up the shot. I'll know when I hear from Mr. James. I'll meet you in Buffalo at the railhead to pay you. Here's a hundred to keep you until then."

Frank laughed uncomfortably like he wasn't sure he wanted to hear what he was about to hear and Liam said, "Frank, Merryweather followed the trail of the crew for one week. He wasn't the most stable guy in the first place, but he became less so as the week wore on. He continued to have his sick dreams of Power's death, he drank heavily and hindsight being twenty/twenty, even though he was an excellent marksman, he was too crazy to be effective.

"John Power had been standing in front of Waning Moon, a Shasone Indian on the work crew. They had just filled their bowls with stew and were getting ready to eat. Merryweather was able to creep within twenty-five yards of their camp and was watching and waiting for John Power to walk into his sights. He finally had him; it was Power's turn to pay.

"Power began to feel uneasy, to feel a sort of dread that he couldn't explain. He lost his appetite, poured his stew back and began to walk off.

"Merryweather had Power in his sights for a long moment, relishing it. He was licking his lips insanely and went in to his daydream of seeing Power's bloody skull on the ground; he felt himself grow aroused and lost his concentration. Suddenly Power was no longer in his sights and, forgetting where he was, whispered too loudly, "Damn the luck."

"Power, hearing something, turned and stared intently at the bushes to the north of camp, saw the barrel of the gun sticking out of the bushes, screamed and jumped. Merryweather took several shots trying desperately to hit Power and wasn't sure who he'd hit, but knew from the screaming he'd hit someone. With dishes flying everywhere, the entire camp dove for cover, startled and not knowing what was happening. When the dust settled two Irishmen and an Indian lay dead. Merryweather began taking random pot shots into the camp. No one dared move and it stayed that way all night long.

"Finally, as the sun was coming up, two Shoshone Indians crawled to where Power lay. Painted Horse was Waning Moon's brother and Singing Owl was his cousin."

Painted Horse said, "We think we can sneak up behind this man and take him."

Power said, "You know who it is, don't you?"

Singing Owl said, "We guessed it was the small man with high voice here to kill you, John Power."

"You guessed right, lads."

Liam said, "With great stealth, the two Indians circled around Merryweather, one to the east and the other to the west. When they met up behind him they slipped into his camp only to find Merryweather laying flat on his back. He was snoring loudly and had an empty whiskey bottle in his hand. They tied him up and carried him back to camp.

"When Merryweather woke he found himself tied hand and foot and surrounded by a group of men guarding him.

"John Power and Ray James had come to agree on nothing. Their relationship was one of mutual respect and hatred. They needed each other and were all too aware of each other's capabilities. They stayed out of each other's way, lived within their agreement and worked like hell. When it came to Miles Merryweather they once again didn't see eye-to-eye."

Power walked into James' tent and said, "The men are restless. I'm afraid they're going to lynch this little prick. If we don't make the decision to hang him I'm afraid we might have a mutiny on our hands. "

Liam said, "Frank, James didn't give a damn that Merryweather had killed three of his men. He was even pleased that he tried to take out Power—he thought it was good to bring him down a notch. He was angry only because he needed every hand they had and it would only slow them down. Two of his men were already dead and five were left off because they couldn't keep up, and now this. But he didn't have the stomach to hang a man either.

James said, "Well Power, even though the son of a bitch killed three men, I'm not interested in hanging anyone; we are not the law here. I'll put two men on him and let the sheriff in Buffalo handle this."

"James, he's a rotten son of a bitch and if you don't have the guts to hang him, I can't guarantee his safety."

"It's just the way it has to be then, because we're bringing him to Buffalo."

"He's your responsibility."

Power called the crew together and told them about James' plan for Merryweather.

Liam said, "Frank, the next morning, Merryweather was nowhere to be found. Some thought he escaped while others suspected foul play.

"The crew started back to work and began the pace in which they had become accustomed. Men with guns were posted along the workers in case there was trouble. Just after noon they rounded a bend on their path and there Miles Merryweather was hanging from a large oak tree.

"There was plenty of talk as they worked past the corpse swinging in the wind. Had he escaped and hung himself? Had someone on the crew taken him last night and hung him? No one was sure and it really didn't matter. To the crew, justice had been served; to Ray James, it was one less thing he had to deal with.

"Billy was bringing a bucket of water to the men as they stood and stared at Merryweather hanging from the tree. Out of the corner of his eye he caught Clem looking at his brother John, eyes smiling. Miles Merryweather was never discussed again."

Frank said, "Did they do it?"

Liam said, "Did who do what?"

"Did John and Clem Power take Miles Merryweather out and hang him?"

Liam said, "We'll never know."

Frank said, "That's crap. You know the answer."

Liam shrugged and walked away."

CHAPTER 20
THE RIVER AND THE LOST LAUGHTER FOUND

After they had time to cool off Liam said, "Francis, do you still think I lied to you about Miles?"

Frank said, "Yes, I do."

"That's your prerogative and I do appreciate your honesty and candor. But I really don't know whether they hung him or not."

Frank said, "Well, let me put it to you this way. Whether you know or not, which I think you do, you're just pulling the old Irish trick of circling the wagons and covering for your own. I think they did."

With a smugness that irritated Frank, Liam said, "We're all entitled to our opinions, aren't we? Anyway, where was I? Oh yeah, every morning after reading his financial reports and The New York newspapers, Erastus Cornell reviewed the telegraphed reports coming in on his team working toward Buffalo.

"Cornell's was a tight rope act with the Irish that worked for him. They were hardly an idyllic bunch, constantly pushing on his management team. Gone were the days of holding payroll for a few days to garner a few extra interest points. But in a way he respected them for their gumption. Hell, he thought, he hadn't made his wealth by letting people push him around. But they continued to amaze him with their balls; they took guff from no one.

"Not only that, but their precision, skill and stamina were becoming legendary. People were lining the way to watch. "

Cornell continued to read the telegraphs waiting to hear about the death of John Power when one morning he screamed, "Damn that stupid son of a bitch!"

Big Eddie looked over at his boss and said, "What is it, boss?"

"That son of a bitch, Miles Merryweather, got himself hung."

"What?"

"Apparently he got drunk, went crazy, shot three of the crew and missed Power altogether. This says he spent the night taking pot shots on the camp until a couple of Indians snuck around and found him passed out drunk. They had him tied up and James was going to bring him into Buffalo and it looks like some of those Paddies took him off and hung him. Well, it's just as well, we didn't get Power but at least now Merryweather can't talk."

Cornell stared out his office window for a moment and then said, "I'll tell you what else is amazing?"

"What?"

"These Irish bastards are coming into Buffalo ahead of schedule and people are lined up to watch." He turned and said, "Eddie, let's go."

"Where we going, boss?"

"Buffalo. We're going to meet them when they come in. I've got to see this for myself."

Eddie looked at his calendar and said, "They're not scheduled into Buffalo for six days?"

"I got news. James says they'll be there the day after tomorrow."

Liam said, "Are you still brooding over the hanging or am I capturing your attention with new ground?"

Frank said, "I don't brood."

Liam said, "Then you can hardly call yourself an Irishman. We're world renowned brooders."

"Granddad, can we get on with it. I'll get over it in a year or two."

"That's my boy. Anyway, it was an unusually hot summer that year that they were coming in to Buffalo. The sun beat down mercilessly in the heat of the late afternoon. Cornell mounted a horse and rode out to meet the crew as they worked their way in.

"As far as the eye could see, railroad ties lay in immaculate rows, twelve inches apart, on top of neat, smooth, palm-sized rocks. Every thirty seconds a team of two men pulled a six hundred-pound rail off the bulk head wagon and laid it precisely in place.

"Four-two men sledge teams worked, two on each side of the large, gleaming iron rails. The first man held the iron spike in place, the second man screamed, "Down!" And after two perfectly placed blows the spike was secured and the first man reached for a new spike.

"Cornell looked at these men, glistening with sweat. Their once columbine skin now tanned and leathery, muscles ripped from use and then he heard something so out of place that it stopped him in wonder.

"One man who was swinging a sledgehammer was singing in a baritone voice, beautiful and resonant, ringing in perfect pitch and rhythm with the blows of his hammer. He sang a verse of a song unfamiliar to Cornell's ear and then the group rang out with the chorus and sounded as if they belonged in a Cathedral of a European capital.

"Cornell was astounded, thinking that most people working this hard would not be able to catch their breath, let alone sing like they were standing in front of an audience. But an audience they had, as hundreds of people watched while the men worked their way down the rail."

James pulled up on horseback next to Cornell and said, "I didn't expect to see you here, sir."

Cornell replied, "After your telegraphed reports, I had to see this for myself."

"You have to get used to the singing, sir, it goes all day long."

"As hard as they're working I'm surprised they can catch their breath at all, let alone sing. It really is quite impressive."

James looked at him lugubriously.

Cornell said, "When you finish up, meet at my suite. I want a full report.

Cornell poured them both a couple of fingers of scotch and said, "James, first tell me what happened with Merryweather?"

"He must have gone crazy, sir. I only heard bits and pieces of the run-in he originally had with Power but I can imagine what John Power did to the likes of Merryweather. After that I'm guessing he followed us from Rochester and was looking for the right opportunity to take out Power."

"So it was Power he was after?"

"That's my guess, yes sir. We stopped in Batavia because these Paddies actually worked two guys to death and five others into exhaustion. When we camped the next night, the shooting started. I was in my tent and when it was all done three men were dead, two Paddies and an Indian. Just before dawn two Indians slipped in behind Merryweather and found him passed out drunk. They tied him up and brought him to camp.

"I did everything I could to keep the men from hanging his ass right there. I told Power we were bringing him to Buffalo because we weren't the law. The next morning he was gone, no one saying anything. After noon we found him hanging dead in a tree along the route we were working. Now, whether he escaped and hung himself or someone kidnapped him and hung him, is anyone's guess. All I know is the guy's dead and no one on our crew was too upset about it."

Cornell said, "Well, I don't make too many hiring mistakes, but Miles was a big one. I was blinded, I guess, by trying to help his father, a personal friend of mine.

"So the reports I've been reading on these Micks working twenty hour days and working people to death are true?"

James said, "You have no idea, Mr. Cornell. You know me well enough and you know my feelings about these Irish bastards. But I'm also smart enough to know what's going to line my pockets. These men don't work for me – I simply manage budgets and time. They work for John Power.

"But I can honestly say that I've never seen the likes of it. I didn't have to tell them when to start or when to quit, Mr. Cornell. There were six days straight that these sons of bitches started at four o'clock in the morning and worked until midnight. The only reason they didn't make it seven is because they're a bunch of Catholic bastards and they wouldn't work on Sunday.

"I've never seen men work as hard and long in my life. They're working at backbreaking labor all day long, singing and telling stories as if they were sitting around a damn campfire."

James stopped like he was thinking about something and Cornell said, "What is it?"

James said, "I would watch them while they worked and when one of them would glance my way I noticed something they all had in common."

"What was that?"

"They had a fire burning in their eyes, like they were

possessed. It was eerie."

Cornell chuckled and said, "Well, now that I have it first hand, I'm glad they're working for me. Give them two weeks off. It'll give us a chance to plan."

"What's in store?"

"Well, first of all, I've got to get Merryweather's remains back to Ireland. His father is my friend and the least I can do is send the body back.

"Then I'll also be working with the Pennsylvania boys the next two weeks. We'll be tying Buffalo to Erie along the lower side of the lake."

Cornell showed Raymond James the door and said, "Be back here a week from today, tell your team two weeks off and nice job."

James did his best to hide his jubilation. He was planning a week of drinking, gambling and fornication.

Liam said, "Frank, the year that followed were twelve months from hell. Cornell said eight months work to get to a town called Clinton, Iowa, but he hadn't figured on blizzards, floods and tornadoes. Not to mention influenza, smallpox and other illnesses too many to mention.

"Raymond James had agreed to let John Power use a horse to scout out ahead. They had run into so many problems that he had taken to running out ten miles or so to see the lay of the land. This would take several days, while his brother Clem ran the daily crews. This way they were able to anticipate any obstacle that may lie out there in the future.

"He had developed a particular fondness for his young brother in law, Billy, my father. As young as he was, he was tough, never complained, and put in as long a day working as any man on the crew. He never touched a rail or a sledgehammer, but running buckets of water to thirsty men and heavy tools all day was tough enough for any young man. Occasionally, he would invite Billy to ride on the back of his horse with him while he scouted out ahead.

"It was on one of these scouting trips that they had run into the Mississippi River for the first time. It just so happened that young Billy O'Conlan was riding shotgun with his brother-in-law on this ride when they saw it together.

"They could hear the water running from a distance and heard the clang of steel against steel. Power knew before he got there that it was the Mississippi and the clanging steel was the men building the bridge that the railroad was to use to run track across the river into Iowa.

"They rode the horse up to the edge of the bluff. Below, the largest waterway in North America, the Mississippi River made its hegira south. Neither had ever seen a river this large and all they could do was stare in awe. They jumped off the horse and stood listening to the silence of the prairie being broken by the rhythm of the water and the steady clang of the sledgehammer.

"But it wasn't the water or the enormity of the river that they stared at, or the crew working above the water. It was the rolling green hills of home that awaited them on the other side. John Power felt as if he had just walked through a door that led back to Ireland. The grass was taller than back home but every bit as green.

"He knew then and there that his railroad days were coming to an end. He, all of the sudden, wanted nothing more in this world than to kneel down and run the rich, dark, land through his fingers. Land was the true standard of a man; to these Irishmen it's what *made* a man. The dreams were endless and, Frank, all the hard work on the railroad was about to pay off.

"Billy had been away from Ireland for seven years now. But not a day went by when he didn't daydream about the green rolling hills, the small running brooks and the stone hedgerows of Northern Tipperary. He would never forget the land of his ancestors, no matter how long it had been. How could he?

"As he stood on this bluff in western Illinois overlooking

the green rolling hills of eastern Iowa, he felt like his daydreams of Tipperary just became reality.

"He knew somehow that he was staring at his new home. He stared, lost and dazed, and a feeling of overwhelming joy passed through his veins, causing him to laugh out loud."

John Power looked at Billy, who by now was laughing so hard he was doubled over and trying to catch his breath. The laughter was infectious. It had been so long that any of them had anything to laugh about that Power couldn't help but to join him.

Soon, like a couple of kids in church, they were beside themselves with laughter and couldn't stop if they wanted to.

Power, in between breaths said, "Billy, what in the hell are we laughing at, lad?"

Billy catching his breath said, "We're home, John Power. We're home."

Frank, who had been so caught up in everything that had been happening, sat down in the tall prairie grass of western Illinois and began to laugh as well. When Liam looked over at him he had a tall piece of grass in his mouth and he beamed with delight at the boy's laughter.

CHAPTER 21

THE PAINTING OF THE PAST, THE BEER AND THE LAND

When Frank had settled down and was no longer laughing but paying rapt attention once more to his granddad, Liam said, "They finally finished the Illinois leg and came into the town of Clinton, Iowa. The railroad was finishing up the Mississippi Bridge project for the railroad track to come across and so the crew had a longer hiatus than usual.

"It was during this time that John Power began to explore the Mississippi valley in eastern Iowa. He and Nancy would take long walks and roam the countryside, having picnics with Billy and Pat and enjoying themselves.

"They all felt at home here amongst the green grass, the beautiful streams, brooks and rolling hills. They felt as if they were living in a painted picture of their past in Tipperary. Not only that but Power was astounded at how rich and dark the soil was. Both John and Nancy agreed that it was time to settle down and this was the place to do it.

"Frank, the next day John Power informed the railroad of

his intentions to quit and collected his last pay. Some of the workers were upset at the news. They had grown very fond of him and had gotten used to him taking care of them."

Frank said, "What about Clem?"

Liam answered. "Clem was way too restless for farming. He said goodbye to his brother, promised to visit and took over as the "go to guy" that his brother had been on the rail crew and worked his way to Council Bluffs, Iowa where the east met the west and the railroads were connected from ocean to ocean. He then took a job as an engineer driving trains for the Union Pacific and was on the rail for the rest of his life, stopping whenever he could in eastern Iowa to check in on his brother and family."

Liam looked off over the town of Clinton and then back at the Mississippi River. The wind blew his white wispy hair about a bit and he smiled as the wind caressed his face and made him feel good.

Liam said, "John Power wanted land and he wanted it in Clinton County. He trusted his instincts and knowledge; he loved this soil.

"Power, enjoying one of the only furloughs in his entire life, was in the town of Clinton inquiring about the purchase of land with some of the local businessmen.

"He happened to be in the general store when a farmer named James Fitzpatrick walked in. Fitzpatrick was a big, burly man who was in the store to buy his monthly supplies. He had come from his farm outside a small settlement in north central Clinton County called Delmar.

"He was dusty, dirty and out of sorts as he had just spent the last day and a half in his buckboard, driving the twenty-eight miles in from Delmar.

"Fitzpatrick purchased one hundred acres of land in 1841 with money he had made while working on the Erie Canal. In the fourteen years since he had purchased his property, he had fifty acres plowed and farmed. He was independent and making more money than he ever thought possible. But he was frustrated, because the remaining fifty acres were still covered with the tall, Savannah grass that was native to the area. There weren't enough men to do all the work that needed to be done.

"The storeowner, a colorful man named Karl Hoffman, was a German immigrant who came to America because he wanted to, not because he had to. He came from a long line of merchants in Munich, but he had too many older brothers to get a fair piece of the family business. He learned as much as he needed to from his father's business, saved as much money as was necessary and then immigrated to the land of plenty to ply his trade.

"He made it to Clinton five years earlier and built his store, literally, from the ground up. He didn't know it at the time, but he was in luck because the railroad was coming straight through town, which meant good business for a retailer in Clinton.

"James Fitzpatrick and Karl Hoffman developed a friendship over the last five years for two reasons. The first was that Fitzpatrick needed supplies and Hoffman developed a reputation as a reputable store operator. He was fair, honest, and delivered what he said he would, when he said he would.

"Secondly, Hoffman, the proud German, made marvelous beer. This was a well-kept secret, as he didn't sell the brew. He brewed it and made it available to family and close friends only.

"John Power had been coming to Hoffman's store for several weeks now and was slowly developing a relationship with him. Power was looking for the right opportunity to buy some land and Hoffman had told him he would help any way he could. John Power had walked into Karl Hoffman's general store with Billy and Pat and they were talking to Hoffman when Fitzpatrick walked in."

Karl looked at Fitzpatrick and said, "Well, if it isn't my favorite customer."

Fitzpatrick answered, "Karl, cut the crap. I feel like I've swallowed a pound of dust, I'm thirsty, sore and hungry. Needless to say, I'm glad to finally be here."

Looking at the pocket watch in his vest, Hoffman said, "Well, it's four-thirty, let's place your order. Hopefully, I've got everything you need. We'll turn the store over to my assistant for any latecomers and go upstairs. I can't do anything about your sore muscles but I think we can take care of the hunger and thirst."

Fitzpatrick smiled and said, "Aye, a man builds up a powerful thirst running a buckboard up and down these dusty roads."

While these two talked Power and the boys stood quietly and listened.

Then Hoffman turned and said, "James Fitzpatrick, I'd like you to meet John Power and his two young brothers-in-law, Pat and Billy O'Conlan. I believe you all have something in common."

Fitzpatrick put his hand out to shake Power's hand and the two boys and said, "The pleasure's mine."

The two men shook hands and Power said, "Where are you from?"

Hoffman raised an eyebrow and said, "What do you mean by that? He's from Ireland, same as you."

Power and Fitzpatrick smiled at each other and Hoffman said, "Did I say something wrong?"

Fitzpatrick said, "Not at all, Karl. John Power knew sure that I was from Ireland. What he was asking was what county; we're all proud of Ireland, but amongst the natives, even more proud of our county."

Hoffman said, "Ahh."

Fitzpatrick said, "Galway. A small fishing village in west Galway called Ballinaboy. And you, lad?"

"Tipperary. A small farming village in north Tipperary called Upperchurch. I came for the opportunity, for there was little back home."

Fitzpatrick said, "Aye, we all have our reasons. And the lads?"

"Same place, Upperchurch."

As the immigrants were wont to do, they stood lost in their thoughts. Both were secretly wishing they were back home.

Hoffman said, "Well, let's get to your order, James. Mr. Power, if you'd like to stay, we'll be having a drink when we're done here."

Power said, "Well, that would be grand."

Fitzpatrick looked at Pat and Billy and said, "You lads don't look like you're afraid of a little hard work. Sturdy, the both of you."

They smiled at the man and simply nodded.

Power said, "Neither of them is. We ran rail for damn near a thousand miles and these two pulled their own weight with no complaining. I'd put them up against any man I know."

Fitzpatrick said, "They'll come in handing when you start busting sod, if that's your plan."

"'Tis."

Power looked at the boys and said, "Would you two run and tell Nancy that I have a meeting? Tell her I'm after finding out about some land with Mr. Hoffman, the general store owner and another gentlemen and that I won't be late. Now be off to the flat to let her know."

The boys took off at a run as Power turned his attention toward Hoffman and Fitzpatrick while they were finishing up their business. Hoffman gave final instructions to his assistant and they all walked upstairs to his home above the store.

Fitzpatrick said, "Karl, I've been looking forward to that home brew of yours since I left Delmar yesterday afternoon. I laid in that buckboard last night under the covers and could almost taste it and knew for sure I could smell it."

Hoffmann laughed out loud and said, "You're in luck my friend. A fresh batch is ready to drink; it's a fine lager. There's an old saying where I come from in Germany, 'Beer is like bread, the fresher the better.'

"You see, beer isn't like whiskey or wine, like some people might think. It takes around ninety days for a good beer to brew and be ready to drink. You want to store it in a cool, dark place like a cellar or a cave, where no light or heat can get at it, and then you want to have it consumed in less than three months. Otherwise, it begins to lose its flavor, natural carbonation and rich color. I keep strict records to ensure the finest and freshest brews."

Fitzpatrick said, "Well now, you'd be preaching to the choir and selling to a couple of lads who're already buying."

Hoffmann, who by now had a strong grasp of the English language, laughed out loud. He never tired of listening to the Irish description of things.

He said, "In that case we'll have to have a stein or two."

Hoffmann then looked at Power and said, "Most of the time when I bring a new friend home I have to give them fair warning; my brews are powerful, sending some stout men stumbling. But for some reason, that has never been much of a problem for my friend Fitzpatrick."

It was John Power's turn to laugh and he said, "Well now, Mr. Hoffmann, the bottom of the glass has never been an Irishman's friend. We're known for our whiskey and the Irish make some fine brew as well. You might say it runs in our veins."

Hoffmann laughed again as he poured three steins to the brim, running over with a rich foamy head and said, "I'm finding, Mr. Power, that the Irish constitution is much like the Germans. It's good to have friends who don't readily stumble."

Hoffmann lifted his stein and said, "Zum Wohlsein!"

They lifted their steins and drank and then Power said, "What would that mean?"

Hoffmann said, "Cheers!"

Power lifted his glass and said, "Slainte Var!"

They again lifted mugs of brew and drank deeply. Hoffmann said, "What does that mean?"

This time Fitzpatrick answered, "Health to you and your family!"

Hoffmann said, "Well, thank you very much."

They drank in silence for a few minutes. John Power broke the silence and said, "This is the best beer I've ever tasted."

Hoffmann smiled widely; he loved making beer and loved it more when people enjoyed it.

Power said, "It has a smooth, almost creamy texture."

Fitzpatrick said, "Aye, mother's milk. Why do you think I was dreaming about it last night?"

Hoffmann said, "Okay, enough about the beer. Let's talk business. James, you have one hundred acres, do you not?"

Fitzpatrick said, "Aye."

Hoffmann said, "You've mentioned to me on several occasions how frustrated you are that you've only been able to cultivate, what, fifty of those acres?"

Fitzpatrick agreed one more time and said, "Aye, so what are you getting at, Karl?"

"What I'm getting at is that Mr. Power has the money and the desire to buy some of those acres from you and break sod. All the land around Clinton and north of here, along the Mississippi is already settled. Mr. Power is looking for the opportunity to buy land and you, James Fitzpatrick, can help him and yourself at the same time."

Hoffmann was a shrewd businessman. He knew that the more sod that was busted, the more goods he would sell and the more prosperous he would be.

Fitzpatrick said, "Well, I *have* been frustrated, looking at those wild acres sitting out there and costing me money."

Power looked at Fitzpatrick and said, "Is the soil as dark and rich in the north central part of the county as it here?"

Fitzpatrick said, "Richer. When you see what you can do with that land, you'll be stunned."

"Would you be willing to sell me those fifty acres you haven't farmed yet?"

Fitzpatrick thought about it for a while and then said, "Aye, under one condition."

Power said, "What's that?"

"That one of those big strong lads that I met earlier comes to work for me on my farm."

"Well now, I can't make a decision like that without discussing it with me wife and the boys."

Fitzpatrick said, "Fair enough. But know a couple of things before you mention it. First of all, I'm a fair man and I'll take good care of the boy. He'll work for room and board until he turns eighteen. At that time, if he works out, I'll give him an acre of his own to start his own farm."

Power said, "All right, let's talk price. How much is this going to cost me?"

Fitzpatrick said, "Because the Savannah grass still grows on the land and I know personally the work that goes in to busting that kind of sod. I'll sell it to you for market price which is running at $1.50 an acre."

Liam smiled at Frank who was engrossed in the conversation among the three men and said, "After doing some quick math in his head Power figured $75.00 for all fifty acres. He could cover that, plus supplies, equipment, and horses. Even with the money he planned on sending home, he would still have enough left over to keep the family fed for that first year, until that first harvest. He even started thinking about building a home and livestock."

Power stood and put his hand out and as he shook hands with Fitzpatrick, said, "Back home a handshake meant an iron clad deal. But I'll say that I do have to talk to me wife about one of the boys. I don't think it'll be a problem, just so the wife can see her brother every once in a while. She lost both parents and two sisters since coming from Ireland. It'll go sorely with her not to be able to see her brother regularly."

Fitzpatrick said, "If anyone understands that, I do. Tell her I'll have the boy home on the weekends."

They were finishing up their fourth stein of Hoffmann's delicious brew when his wife, Louise, brought out a plate of some strange foods that these two Irishmen had never seen. It was a large plate heaped with German bratwurst sausage and sauerkraut, with a side of dumplings and gravy.

Power said, "Whoa, 'tis a strong smelling dish. What is it?"

Hoffmann made an explanation and Power said, "You mean to tell me that your people make this sauerkraut out of cabbage?"

Hoffmann said, "Ja."

Liam smiled and said, "They all dug in and enjoyed good food, good beer and good company. An hour after dinner Power decided it was time to leave. He stood, thanked his host, and left. As he was walking home, he stared up at the twinkling stars realizing that his dreams were about to come true. Land, more important to him than money, was about to be his.

Frank said, "So is this the farm you were born on?"

Liam said, "No. But you're about to find out."

CHAPTER 22
HOME AT LAST

Liam said, "Frank, the long hard days on the railroad were paying off. John Power had purchased fifty acres from James Fitzpatrick and then spent two weeks buying supplies they would need to get started. A buckboard, drawn by two fresh draught horses, contained everything they needed to start their new lives.

"By noon on the second day out of Clinton, John Power, his wife Nancy and his two young hellion brothers-in-law, Pat and Billy O'Conlan, were nearing the small outpost of Petersville, Iowa, just southeast of Delmar. Fitzpatrick, his wife and two small sons met them as they drove into town."

Frank said, "Hey, Gramps, we were there!"

Liam said, "Yes we were. It was, however, a little busier then than when we visited."

Before they got to where Fitzpatrick and his family waited, Nancy began to cry.

John Power stopped his wagon and said, "Look darling,

this isn't the end of the world. You're not losing your brother; we're simply splitting up the workload to get the most out of the land. Think of it like this Nancy — It's an investment in his future. In five years, if this works out, Billy will get an acre of his own to start his farm. What more could a man want? Anyway, if he were working for us, he'd be out on the land sixteen hours a day. So you wouldn't see him much anyway."

"Well, at least I'd see him at breakfast and dinner."

"Aye, that you would and aye, this is a sacrifice. But seeing him weekends is better than never seeing him again."

"That doesn't make me feel any better, John Power."

Liam said, "Frank, when they first got to the land, my dad Billy had it better than his own family. He slept in the loft in the barn on the Fitzpatrick farm. He had a roof over his head with blankets and hay to keep him warm.

"Nancy, John and Pat slept in tents while they broke sod and began to build housing and barns.

"It was a slow process. Billy worked the Fitzpatrick farm during the week and went to spend weekends with his own family. The weekends were spent building the Power home and the barns for the farm, while the week was dedicated to farming. Billy looked forward to the weekends because he did get homesick during the week for his family. He especially missed his brother, Pat, and to work with him at week's end was something to look forward to. The carpentry and building was a nice change of pace on the weekends.

"To turn his raw land into a working farm took Power five years of hard labor. During that time other immigrants settled on the land around them and Petersville became the center of all their community activity."

Liam lit his pipe and looking thoughtfully as he inhaled and exhaled a large cloud of white smoke and said, "The year now was 1860, Abraham Lincoln was just elected the president of the United States and the war was breaking out between the North and the South. Billy O'Conlan was to turn eighteen years old in two days and his brother Patrick was twenty. Nancy and John Power had begun their family and had two boys.

"It was a Friday evening in April and Billy O'Conlan was just finishing up his chores. He was getting ready, as had become his custom, to walk to the Power farm for the weekend, when James Fitzpatrick approached him in the barn."

Fitzpatrick said, "Billy, have you finished your chores yet?"

Billy said, "Aye, just finished. I was going to wash up and go."

"Well, before you leave come inside, lad. The wife and I would like to talk to you."

"All right, then."

Billy O'Conlan finished washing up and walked into the big farmhouse that sat on a hill over looking the farm. Marian Fitzpatrick sat at the kitchen table with her two growing boys.

She smiled at Billy and said, "Sit down, lad. James will be out in a minute."

He felt a bit queer and was wondering if he had done something wrong or maybe they were about to let him go, when Fitzpatrick lumbered into the kitchen and sat down.

He looked at Billy and said, "Lad, your eighteenth birthday is coming up, is it not?"

"Aye, I'll celebrate it with John, Nancy, Pat and the kids on Sunday."

"That means on Sunday you become a man. You've served us well, put in long days of labor on this farm and have always done what we've asked without complaint. This farm wouldn't be where it is today without your help. Marian and I are grateful to you and wanted to do something special for you."

Fitzpatrick handed him a handwritten piece of paper naming Billy O'Conlan the owner of one acre, any acre he chose, to begin his farm. Billy O'Conlan sat there speechless, as the grandest gift he had ever received lay on the table in front of him.

Fitzpatrick said, "It means that you're no longer in my service. It's time for you to start your own farm. You're as able as any man I've ever known and we're grateful for all you've done for us."

With that he handed him an envelope with one hundred dollars cash and said, "You've worked for me for five years for nothing more than room and board. You've never asked for anything more. This cash is nothing more than payment for services rendered. Also, the land will do you no good unless you have some start up funds; the cash will help with that. I'll help you build your house and barns and clear any piece you want.

"You can continue to stay on here as long as you like. It'll take time to get started. Happy Birthday Billie, now go enjoy your weekend."

Billy stood and tried to speak but the words were caught on the lump in his throat as he thought of the land, the precious land, and the dark rich soil that he so coveted. He felt unworthy of such a fine gift. He tried unsuccessfully one last time to speak but was incapable of a single sound; not a syllable would pass his lips. The tears welled at the corner of his eyes and he turned and walked out.

The Fitzpatricks knew the reverence he held for the land and they recognized his failed attempts as unspeakable gratitude. They knew that there was nothing he could say that would so eloquently tell them how he felt as the reaction he had so humbly portrayed. The screen door slammed behind him as Billie O'Conlan's lifelong dream had just materialized and he walked away down the lane into his new life.

Liam looked at Frank and said, "Nothing I've said since we've been together could come even close to that in understanding how my dad felt about the land, the soil, the earth beneath his feet. It was a precious gift and not to be taken lightly, nor taken for granted. Other than his wife and children, it was his love, his life."

Frank nodded and understood.

The next morning at breakfast, Pat O'Conlan said, "I have an announcement."

Nancy said, "What's on your mind, lad?"

"The Civil War is on and they're looking for volunteers. The pay is good and I'm going to fight with the Irish brigade."

John Power said, "This isn't our war. Have you thought this through, lad?"

"Aye, John, I have. However, this *is* our war and this *is* our country now. We'll never see the shores of Ireland again."

Power said, "Aye, said like that, I guess it's true. A sad thought, but true. What side are you going to fight on?"

"I'll be fighting for the North and was hoping to take Billy with me. The Irish brigade is looking for volunteers."

Before he could answer, Nancy, unable to contain herself any longer, interrupted, "Patrick Joseph O'Conlan, you'll never persuade me that this is our war. We're Irish and that's all we'll ever be. If you have to go off and fight some war, I'll not be part of it. But you won't be taking Billy. I've lost enough clan and won't be losing any more."

Billy smiled and patted Nancy's hand and said, "Aye, we are Irish, but your children are American."

This statement hit Nancy so hard it took her breath away. Her wee ones were born Americans. She had never thought of them as anything but Irish.

Pat said, "If we don't fight to preserve the Union what'll happen to these wee ones?"

Billy said, "Pat, you do what you have to do, but I won't be joining in this battle unless I'm called."

He laid the hundred dollars on the table and told them what had happened.

He said, "In the last few months I'd begun to wonder what I was going to do. I couldn't work for James Fitzpatrick for room and board forever. I certainly didn't want to appear ungrateful, but I've yearned for a piece of land to call me own. So now it's settled and I'm going nowhere."

Pat said, "All the more reason for me to go. Honestly,

farming is great, but it isn't for me. I want to go see some more of this new country of ours."

John said, "Why don't you get on with the railroad like Clem. You can see the country that way too."

Pat said, "Agreed, that would be a way, but not the way I want. I believe in this country, I believe it's worth fighting for, they're asking for volunteers and I'm going come hell or high-water."

Liam said, "Frank, my dad, Billy O'Conlan was now a man, a landowner and secretly in love. Now that he had the land he could pursue his love.

"There was a small pond high on a hill that overlooked the valley where the Fitzpatricks lived. The pond had four or five large pine trees that surrounded it. Billy discovered this place quite by accident one day and it became *his* place."

Frank said, "Was this the place he went when you and he were going at it?"

"Exactly, for him it was a place of great peace and serenity when life got hard, as it so often did. He would think back to Ireland, sometimes reliving his short time with his father. He remembered with clarity the poem he read he and Nancy on the boat. He swore at times that he heard his father's voice on the wind as it wrapped itself around the trees. He spent time thinking about his burial at sea and as hard as he tried he couldn't get the sight of his father's corpse, which was slowly swallowed up by the ocean, out of his mind's eye. Then the memory of his Mother dying in the dirt of New York harbor would take hold of him like a banshee screaming in the night. He would recall his three older sisters holding each other in quiet desperation on the ground as their mother lay waxen and cold next to them.

"How he missed Molly Rose and Moria. Their memory cut him so deep that the wound would never heal. He loved those two with every fiber in his body. When he allowed himself to think of his sisters he would collapse in grief. He desperately missed them all and here he could cry his heart out and not worry about being seen or heard. He could spend quiet time with them alone.

"It was here that he began to appreciate his sister Nancy. She was thirteen years old and had taken care of four siblings; she had no childhood because she gave it up for them. He would be eighteen in a day and was not sure even *now* that he could have done what she did then, at thirteen.

"It was here, as he matured, that he began to realize just how desperate their situation was when his parents died. Five orphaned, immigrant children, lost in a strange country. He wondered how much more desolate five kids could have been? He was only seven then, how could he have known? He was grateful that he was even alive. Why his sisters, his mom and dad and not him? Why?

"It made him appreciate the land all the more and it was here where he would choose his first acre. It was from here that he would build his farm, because it was here that his family rested in his heart and they would help him to prosper. It was here, now, that he would always come back to when life got too hard.

"Billy O'Conlan was an intense boy who grew to be an intense man. The intensity came from working for everything he had. It came from working eighteen-hour days starting when he was only twelve years old. No one had ever given him anything. It also came from the great loss that he'd experienced with his parents and his sisters at such a young age. This intensity was his shelter from it all and it never let up. There were times when he'd walk the thirteen miles to Mass on Sunday. He'd get up early, wash up, get something to eat and go. Nancy would worry about him and try to get him to stay and ride with them. But when his mind was made up there would be no changing it.

"As he began to mature into a man, he began to notice a young woman named Katherine McGowan at Mass on Sunday.

It got to the point where he was thinking about her all week long and, truth be known, the long trek to town was motivated by more than celebrating the Holy Eucharist.

"It had been three weeks since he had received the news of his new inheritance and two weeks since Pat left for the war. He and John Power were mending fence on the farm and doing odd jobs late on a Saturday afternoon."

Frank turned his attention from his Granddad without a word and began to watch his great granddad and great uncle as they worked and talked.

Billy said, "Son of a bitch!"

Power said, "Billy O'Conlan, where's your head today, lad? That's the second time I've seen you pound your thumb with the hammer in thirty minutes."

Liam said, "Frank, as you're aware, John Power and Billy O'Conlan were far more than brothers-in-law. They were far more than brothers. They were like war veterans who had been through hell, who'd stared death in the eye and lived to talk about it, but only to each other.

"They knew and trusted each other with a proven confidence. Billy considered John a father and John knew the kind of guts Billy had by the punishing work he had done at an early age with no complaint."

"Damn it John that hurts like hell." Billy said as the hammer came down on the same thumbnail again.

Knowing Billy to be a competent man with his tools Power said, "What's on your mind?"

"Nothing," he answered too quickly sucking on his thumb.

"Come on, I've never seen you pound your thumb once let alone twice in less than a half hour. Your mind's not on your work."

"I'm telling you it was just a stupid mistake, I've got nothing on my mind," he lied.

"Well, let's call it day."

Later that evening when Billy was in his room asleep, John and Nancy Power lay in bed chatting.

Power said, "Billy's in love."

Nancy, more an overprotective mother than a sister, said, "What gave you such a crazy idea as that?"

"Because he's acting the same way I did when I was eighteen. I was crazy in love with you and could do nothing about it. The control came and went, but by the time I had worked up the courage to tell Da that I was leaving I couldn't concentrate on a damn thing."

"What does this have to do with anything?"

"I'm working with him this afternoon around the farm and he was in a daze. I've worked with him for seven or eight years now. I know what he's capable of and I've never seen him so scatter-brained. I asked him what was on his mind and he said nothing. I'm telling you the boy's in love."

Liam said, "My dad was on his way to church the next morning, walking an eight-minute mile, adrenaline and testosterone pumping through his eighteen-year-old veins. He was debating with himself as to how he was going approach mom's father, my Granddad Jimmy McGowan.

"He couldn't keep his mind off the woman and he was trying to cope with all these strange emotions and feelings that he'd never before experienced. He couldn't concentrate on his work and as was typical of any eighteen year-old in love, he'd daydream about mom constantly. Trying to cover up his love and total infatuation with her, he would whack his thumb with his hammer or say something stupid. Then, John Power, according to Billie, asking questions that didn't need to be asked. A man he'd trust with his life, though, and he lied to him. As he walked with fury he then questioned whether she'd even want to see him if my maternal grandfather did say yes.

"It was typical during these long treks that Billy would work himself into a lather with inner debates."

Frank smiled as he watched Billy O'Conlan, walking fast, all worked up as he did so.

Billy, knowing he was alone and talking out loud to himself as he went, said, "Even if I did work up the guts to talk to her old man, would she even want to see me? How the hell am I going to convince the old goat? I don't think I can do it."

His alter ego fired back,"Sure you can, just walk right up and ask him."

"That's easy for you to say, even if the old man does say yes, she probably couldn't care less."

"My arse! You've seen the way see looks at you. Quit being a coward and do it!"

"Well then, you tell me how I'm supposed to convince the old man that I'm worth a darn?"

"Why all the questions? Whatever happened to all that self-confidence? You're off the boat from Ireland, you're Catholic, you've got money, a nice piece of land and you've proven yourself to be a reliable, hard working man. What more do you think the old goat expects, canonization?"

"Well, I'm not from Mayo."

"Stop it now. Go ask the man. All he can do is say no. You don't have horns growing out of your skull!"

Frank, walking hard now to keep up with his great granddad, looked on as the internal debate raged while he kept up his eight-minute mile. By the time he got to Immaculate Conception church in Petersville Frank noticed that Billy had sweat running down his brow and his shirt was wet from the armpits to the waste.

Billy stood at the foot of the stairs leading to the church and said out loud, "I can't talk to her da sweating and smelling like an ox. Oh, Lord have mercy on me ever loving soul, how is this ever going to work out?"

As he began to walk up the stairs John and Nancy Power and their two boys pulled up in their buckboard.

Power saw Billy standing there sweating and knew he had practically trotted the thirteen miles blowing off steam. Not being able to help himself, he laughed aloud.

Nancy, seeing her brother in a physical struggle with himself and recognized now why Power was laughing, elbowed him in the ribs so hard that his laughter became a wince. Billy's Irish pride was building a thick wall of brick and mortar. He was *her* brother and now she knew that Power spoke the truth last night. Smiling to herself, she found his behavior adorable. This big, tough lad who stood up to the likes of canal workers as well as the toughs on the railroad; now stood almost trembling before the stairs of the church because of a five foot two inch Irish lovely sitting with her parents inside.

They followed close on the heels of Billy up the stairs into the five-year-old church. They walked in to a full house, people nodding and smiling at them and they reciprocating.

Frank wanted to laugh out loud watching while Billy who had stopped dead in his tracks in the middle aisle and John Power running dead smack into the back of his head, with everyone staring. Billy trying to keep his cool had casually looked to his right to where Katherine sat. She smiled at him and gave him a little wave as if she could read his thoughts. He didn't even notice Power slam into him.

Frank standing next to the commotion they were causing in the isle of the big brick church noticed Billy's heart racing, his chest heaving and seemingly unable to move. This went on for a few seconds, but it seemed like an eternity when the church organ started and the priest and altar boys began to walk toward the altar.

Frank smiled at Liam as they watched John grab Billy under one arm and Nancy under the other and they scrambled to find a seat. Once seated, Billy buried his chin in his chest as he tried to steady his shaking hands. His chest heaved and his heart would not stop racing and the sweat was worse now than before.

He finally settled down, his breathing became regular once more and his heart stopped racing. But for the life of him, he couldn't concentrate on the Mass. All he could think of was that it wouldn't wait another week. He was determined to talk to her father today and see this thing through.

After Mass they congregated outside and chatted about the weather, this year's crop, the latest stir in Irish politics and the upcoming church social.

Billy stood aside speaking politely to several parishioners waiting for the right opportunity. When the McGowans started for their buggy, he made his move.

John Power whispered to Nancy, "Watch this. You're about to find out who Billy is in love with."

"I already know. You were too busy running into the back of Billy's head to notice the smile and wave of young Katherine McGowan. He could do worse."

Billy walked up behind Jimmy McGowan and said, "Excuse me, sir."

McGowan, a short and stout man, turned around to see this tall, lanky young man trying to get his attention.

"What can I do for you, lad?"

Billy stood awkwardly staring at the man with his wife and two youngest daughters standing there, staring back at him.

He thought, no backing out now.

"Sir, I would like to request permission to see your daughter socially."

McGowan said, "Which one, lad? I have an eighteen-year-old daughter as well as a fourteen-year-old daughter here."

"Katherine, sir."

Again, purposely making this as awkward as possible he said, "Have you asked her about this?"

At that the two McGowan sisters smiled at their mother, trying not to make it too obvious, knowing what their father was up to.

He said, "Without your permission sir, I thought it a waste of time."

He smiled, knowing that the lad had had enough and said, "Well, you thought correctly. But I'm afraid the answer is emphatically no, now off with you lad."

Billy's heart sank and, as he turned to walk away, he saw John and Nancy. John began to laugh again, hearing the sarcasm in McGowan's tone. Billy was too heartsick to pick it up. This time there were too many people around for Nancy to slug her husband and still remain respectable, but her glare was sharp enough to slice skin.

At her father's response Katherine protested and said, "Daddy, no."

Jimmy was the one to laugh this time and said, "Well, lad, you now know what my say is worth in all of this. If you don't have any plans you can join us for Sunday supper."

Frank, off balance, as if someone had just shoved him into a room, looked around at the only familiar surrounding he had seen all night long.

Liam sat at the foot of Frank's bed and said, "Within six months they were engaged and within a year they were married. Nine months after that their first son, William Jr., known as Will O'Conlan, was born. He, of course, was my oldest brother and a story all by himself."

With that Liam slapped the palms of his hands on his lap and stood, eyes sparkling with temerity and mischief as if he knew something no one else did and he laughed saying, "Quite a story, huh?"

Frank, purposely avoiding eye contact with the old man, stared long and hard at the window resting in the eastern wall of his dormer and watched as the sun began to move higher and shine brighter through it.

He was fighting with every emotion that existed within him and was losing the battle. His lips quivered and he began to quietly cry. He sat on the side of his bed, pulled the pillow between his arms and could taste the salt in his tears as they streaked past his lips.

Liam smiled at him and said, "Lad, now is not a time for sorrow. Now is a time of great joy and happiness. You're now as well versed on your clan history as any Seanachie ever was and it's your turn to live the legacy that you'll pass on to your grandson. *Now* you know that the Irish are far more than the quarrelsome louts you thought we were. Far more. We've suffered and overcome great odds, like all immigrants into this country; it's what makes America great. But like the great melting pot that it is, it's important for all of us to know from whence we came. So that we never forget and never fail as a nation."

Frank whispered in a scratchy voice, "Oh, Granddad."

"Francis, like all good things, there's a beginning and an end. This is my end and your beginning. Know that I'm happier than I've ever been and that you'll always have me with you."

"But I won't see you."

"No, no you won't. But when you least expect it you'll feel me and know it's me and I'll be there to help. Just close your eyes tight and call out and I'll be there."

Frank shut his eyes tight, called his granddad's name and opened his eyes. Liam John O'Conlan was nowhere to be seen but Frank heard in his mind, "Just like that, lad, just like that."

PROLOGUE
EIGHT WEEKS LATER

Frank's older brother Sean said, "Happy St. Patrick's Day, dude."

Frank opened his eyes, yawned and said, "Holy shit."

He had forgotten. This was the day he had so looked forward to since Liam left. He had so missed him and thought that somehow today he might see him or hear him. He got dressed and headed to the kitchen. His Mother no longer pinned shamrocks on them, but she did have an array of different sizes and colors of green laid out on the table and insisted they pin one on themselves. No one resisted.

Frank said, "Mom, what time are people coming over?"

"They'll start showing up around noon. Should be a good crowd by the time you get home from school."

"Why do we even have to go to school on St. Patrick's Day? It's sacrilegious."

She said, "Don't even start with me duckle butt, just get your fanny in gear."

As he arrived home from school, Frank made his way through the crowd of St. Paddy's Day revelers. He spent some time saying hello to old acquaintances, hugging aunts, shaking hands with uncles and giving cousins the old, 'I'll see you in the backyard for a smoke and beer' wink, sincerely glad they were all here.

He walked up to the dormer, which was dark with all the shades drawn, set his backpack on his bed, used the toilet and was set to head to the gala downstairs, when a feeling came over him that he couldn't explain. He reached for his backpack, pulled out a pad of paper and a pen, sat down at his desk and closed his eyes. The wind outside the window began to blow and somewhere in the back of his mind he began to hear the tight rudiments of a marching snare drum. He felt himself begin to sway to its rhythm when he suddenly heard soft fiddles playing to the same rhythm, then came the uennean pipes and flutes. Tears unexpectedly began to run down his face and, as if in a trance, he began to write. He wrote with the intensity of one possessed, like a writer trying to find that last sentence for a novel well done. Sweat began to bead on his forehead and upper lip and mingled with his fresh tears. Upon finishing, he felt exhausted, as if he'd been in some time warp. He looked at his alarm clock, it had only been twenty minutes and the din downstairs was rising in pitch. He looked down at what he had written and almost screamed, it read:

Cloisim do ghlor ar an feothan
Thar thuairt na n-uisce salainn
Cloisim macalla do ghlor
Gach aon do bron
Chomh an mhuir uasal rollaim
Taim sui agus eistim conas ta deanann am
t-uisce an cladach
an dtabharfaidh me feart saile
duinn teanga
filiocht scriobhaim ar gcroi amhail

da caoi eile orainn go h-oibrionn saol seo
da dheireofai an eachtar bais
an gceadfa do shalann go siorai
fagaim small ar an bruth ata ann
feartlaoi ar ghear goirt
an bhfagofa in ar an Seanchai saol seo
sceal gan insint tine dhoin cluas fhuirim
ta amhras moran agus do rhollach amhain
fuaruisce a leaba a chomhlionaim me leirim
mear thar mho feithe go fhaighim tu
fhuil an Ghael arsa
an Files, an Brehon, an Caollam agus an Seanchai.

He had no idea what he had written or what it said, all he knew is that it was the Irish language he had seen while traveling with his granddad. He was suddenly filled with fear when he saw something out of the corner of his eye disappear down the stairs. He ran to the top of the stairs and looked down and saw it turn the corner at the bottom of the flight. He thought, “Granddad.” He unintentionally grabbed his pad and sprinted down the stairs and ran to the kitchen. He looked around frantically and then caught the illusion descending the basement stairs.

He gave chase to the boiler room and once inside he pulled the chain that hung from the light in the ceiling. The old forty-watt bulb gave off an antique light that lit up the old room accordingly and he looked around for his Granddad who was nowhere to be seen. As his eyes searched the room, they landed behind an old wood-burning stove on a small corner shelf. It was then that he realized in all the years he’d lived in this house, he’d never noticed that shelf before. The shelf itself was dusty with cobwebs and there sat an old wooden jewelry box. He was inextricably drawn to it. On its front was a small hook that held it shut; it looked as if this box had been here undisturbed for many years.

At first all he could do was to stare at it with question.

Frank then reached for it and opened it. The box contained a shiny brass key; he pulled it out and engraved on the key in small letters it said: Upperchurch, County Tipperary, Ireland, 1846.

Frank said, "Holy shit."

He looked around the room again and on the floor next to the wood-burning stove were four or five old tarpaulins folded neatly on top of a wooden chest that he'd never noticed before either. He pulled them off and on top of the chest were the words, "O'Conlan, Upperchurch, Tipperary 1846."

He looked at the chest and, with goose flesh, said, "Why should I even be surprised?"

He trembled as he placed the key into its long forgotten home; it fit snuggly and turned with ease to open the antiquated trunk. He lifted open the lid. Inside was the old beautiful oiled wool throw that had been around Aidan's shoulders the night before he left. He wrapped it around his shoulders and inhaled deeply of the wonderful old, musty blanket and smiled. Feeling a deep sense of comfort in the old throw, as it warmed him all over he peeked once again into the chest and this time he caught his breath. He slowly lifted a parcel from its berth and cradled a beautiful old shelaighly, the very one that Aidan had gripped in his agony that rainy night so long ago.

He stared at the beautiful staff and shiny polished lion's face at the tip that he had not noticed before because Aidan's large hands. There were no words to describe how he felt at that moment, but humility and gratitude would have been at the top of the list. He heard a distinctly familiar voice that had a spiritual lilt to it. He felt Liam.

He was suddenly drawn back to the trunk. He looked inside and saw laying there on the bottom a piece of antiquated, yellow parchment. Then he heard the same music that had haunted him in his room just minutes ago and he began to read:

I hear your voice on the breeze,

Over the crash of the salty waters.
I hear your voice echo
Each one of your sorrows
As the waves gently, gently roll.
As I sit and listen how the water laps the shore,
Will you, salt water tomb,
Bring me to our language,
Poetry inscribed, our hearts like sand?
If we had another way to operate this world,
If the experience told of death,
Would you let your salt
Continually stain the existing surf
An epitaph for salted tears?
Would you, our Seanachie, leave this world:
Stories untold, fires burning, ears waiting?
I have many questions and only your rolling,
Watery grave, which keeps me tracing
A finger over my veins, finding you,
The blood of the ancient Gaels:
Files, Brehon, Collam and Seanachie

When he had finished he looked around the room. The music stopped. In his mind, like the moment he had closed his eyes eight weeks before as Liam had left him for the last time, he had heard Liam's voice say, "Poetry, an indelible part of our past is now inscribed on your heart. This, as well as the rocking chair, is my parting gift to you." Frank felt peace and contentment that he had never felt before and knew intuitively that it wouldn't last, but with gratitude he looked up and whispered, "Thank you."

After a while he opened the trunk, laid the shelaighly, neatly folded in the throw, at the bottom and then gently set the poem on top of it. He pulled the shiny key from his pocket, carefully locked the trunk and put the key back in its tiny wooden crypt.

Then he said to himself as if just hearing what was said,

"Rocking chair. What the hell?"

He shrugged, reached up and turned off the yellowing forty watt bulb that scarcely illuminated the room. In the sudden darkness he turned to leave the room when he tripped over a piece of furniture and said, "Son of a bitch." He reached back up and scrambled to find the pull down switch to light the room once more. He turned to the object of his newly sore knee that blocked his passage from the room and a shudder ran down his spine as his eyes rested on the rocking chair, Aidan's rocking chair, the one thing that was left uncompleted. He felt something missing and couldn't put his finger on it until now. He looked closer to make sure there was no mistake and there was not.

He sat down very slowly in this most precious of gifts, afraid that it might fall apart, but it held as solidly as if it had been built that week. He rocked ever so gently; his hands laid carefully on the armrests. He looked around wanting more than anything to see Liam but didn't and before he got up said simply, "Thanks, Granddad. Oh yeah, and I love you."

With a happiness he had not known for weeks, Frank walked upstairs and joined the ever-growing mob, but found himself suddenly all alone in the crowd. He looked around and smiled. His first thought was to sneak a brew from the fridge and go to the back yard to meet his cousins for a smoke. Then a feeling came over him as if his next actions weren't his own. He grabbed a Coke from the fridge and poured it over ice. He then walked into the living room where he found an empty plate, fork and wineglass on the mantle above the fireplace. He stood up on the stone hearth a foot above the crowd and rang the wineglass with the fork. When the boisterous crowd became silent, they all looked up at Frank as he said, "I'd like to make a toast."

They all said, "Cheers!"

Frank waited for them to quiet down once more and they stared at him questioningly. A tear ran down his face and the growing lump in his throat fought back all the words resting painfully there. And the company seeing the emotion there became deathly silent

Frank's father, Emmet, squeezed through the crowd to his son and, in a rare gesture of public affection, put his hands upon Frank's shoulders. Emmet looked at his son and in his eyes lived a truce. He knew the pain Frank had suffered since the accident and Liam's death. It was, in the only way he knew how, his way of showing his love for his son and Frank now understood.

Emmet said, "Son, I'm sorry and I miss him too."

Frank said, "Thanks dad."

Frank then looked back at the crowd after gathering himself and said, "Like I said, I'd like to make a toast. A couple of months ago I got the chance of a lifetime to spend a weekend with my grandfather, Liam O'Conlan. I got to know this wonderful man that I really never knew before. He told me his story, the whole story and, at times, it was hard to hear and hard for him to tell. It almost felt like he was going to confession or something. Anyway, I learned a lot of things from him during those two days. When he was taken from us suddenly it hurt and still does. I'm not sure I understand everything that happened that weekend, but he told me that he sought forgiveness and on the way back to Omaha he said he had received it. I know, just by being with him, that he was much happier on the way home than he was on the way there. So whatever it was that bothered him—and I've got a pretty good idea what it was and maybe I'll tell you sometime—it was gone and his pain eased. That helps me when I think about him not being around anymore. So, please raise a glass in honor of Granddad O'Conlan. He was proud of his Irish heritage and proud of his family and friends. He was my good friend and he was a master storyteller. To Liam John O'Conlan, The Seanachie."

Printed in the United States
54513LVS00003BA/85-138

9 781598 005547